Shadow of the Cataclysm

S.D. Baldwin

ISBN-13: 979-8-2185-8184-8

Shadow of the Cataclysm

Copyright © 2025 by S.D. Baldwin

All rights reserved.

No portion of this book may be used or reproduced in any form without written permission from the publisher or author, except in the case of brief quotations embodied in critical articles and reviews.

This is a work of fiction. All names, characters, locations, and events are either products of the author's imagination or are used fictitiously. Any similarities to real persons, living or dead, locations, or events are entirely coincidental.

Cover design by James T. Egan, www.bookflydesign.com

Editing by Sarah Reilley

To Sarajean,
Who means more to me than
all the words on all the pages.

In a world marked by despair, the skies have fallen and the land is barren. Darkness has consumed all hope, and the world is at war with itself. The land is broken, and light is the scarcest resource. But legend tells of a hero, worthy of the light. One for whom the darkness breaks, who will bring hope to the people. A hero with the power to restore life to a broken world. But the darkness will not relinquish control of the world so easily...

Chapter 1

The Darkness

Is this a dream? It feels so real, as if the pain of the world is emanating from the very core of my being. The darkness engulfs—no, suffocates me, as I feel all hope draining from my fractured heart. Death would be welcome, a relief from the suffering of the world, if only it were within my grasp. I can't help but wonder—what have I done to bring myself to this point? What sins have I committed that bear upon me such a heavy burden? For now, my penance is solitude; my punishment, life.

Elucido awoke abruptly, feeling the cold, damp air upon his flushed cheeks. He had grown accustomed to the feeling of the cold, as had all who survived the Dark Cataclysm on Terrus. The absence of daylight made it difficult to know precisely how much time had passed since the darkness had taken over. All Elucido knew was that it seemed like years since he enjoyed the warmth of the sun. Darkness had enveloped the land when the mighty Aether Orbs shattered during the battle at the Great Tower. The battle was a clash for the very soul of the world—a conflict in which, despite humanity's best efforts, darkness triumphed.

As Elucido sat up and stretched his back, he reflected on the memories of the way the world had once been—the way his heart hoped the world could become once more. He longed to feel the warm sun upon his face in the early morning, to smell the freshness of dewy grass, and hear the songs of young sparrows as they fluttered about, searching for an early meal. His hometown of Spiti was once the embodiment of a beautiful country town, littered with thatch-roofed bungalows, beautiful peonies, and the echoes of laughter along the meandering roadways. He had lived there all the days of his youth, and he could not recall a more joyful period of his life. He wished, now more than ever, for a return to those simpler times.

His thoughts, meandering as they were, ultimately converged upon the objects that imbued the essence of life into the world and made his memories possible, the Aether Orbs; the very things that allowed humanity to prosper as they had for thousands of years. The Aether Orbs were sacred objects guarded by the Protectors of Light. Even those who spent their lives dedicated to the study of the orbs could only speculate on how they came to be. One thing was certain, however; the orbs existed long before humanity came to power. In fact, many believed that the orbs originated at the very moment the world came into existence. Regardless of the debate surrounding their origin, there was one thing that none contested—these orbs were sacred objects to which humanity owed its very existence. One orb resided on each continent of the sky-world, five in total. The energy of each of the orbs formed a sort-of conduit to the Palace of Sheut on the continent of Umbra, the largest of the continents on Terrus. This conduit of energy flowed into the orb in the inner sanctum of the central tower of Sheut, which then spread the great light across the vast open sky between the continents of the world, giving abundant life everywhere it touched. Day and night ebbed and flowed, the passage of time marked by the waxing and waning energy of the orbs, which moved with synchronicity and elegance in an unending cycle of power, life, and light.

Though the Aether Orbs had survived for eons, and possessed a power strong enough to provide life-breathing light to the world, their existence was fragile. The powers of darkness constantly sought to destroy them—how they had survived before the formation of the Protectors of Light was a mystery. Stories of their origin and longevity were merely fables. The orbs' survival was as delicate as the balance between light and darkness itself. After all, something that existed with such opposition could only survive while there was something—or someone—whose purpose was to protect and defend it, for even the slightest push could send that balance sharply from the edge of the blade on which it rested. Humanity assumed the mantle of that protection, fighting to keep the orbs in harmony and balance, defending against the darkness that sought to consume its share of life from the world. That balance was counteracted by those who sought to gain power and control through the darkness—they used the suffering and hopelessness of others to manipulate and destroy, taking whatever spoils they desired.

The Protectors of Light were an elite group of humans who dedicated their lives to the protection of the Aether Orbs. They were chosen at birth for their innate connection to the light energy and trained specifically for the task of guardianship. Often, the Protectors of Light took on apprentices, as it took nearly a lifetime to gain true mastery of the skills required to defend the Palaces of Light against the onslaught of darkness that existed in the world. Some palaces were governed by a young Protector due to the untimely passing of their mentors. The fight against the darkness, after all, could be a costly one—but it was a price that the Protectors of Light were willing to pay.

Elucido had served as an apprentice Protector in the Palace of Ren on the continent of Nomen from the days of his adolescence. He had the responsibility of researching and archiving records related to the growing darkness in the land. His purpose was as critical as it was singular—identify what drove the darkness forward and determine how to push back with greater force. This did not represent the first time that the Aether Orbs had been in jeopardy. The Palace of Ka on the continent of Vita nearly lost its orb thirteen years ago, when a spy infiltrated the ranks of the palace guards and attempted to destroy the orb under the cover of night. From that moment forward, the Protectors of Light not only bolstered the process by which they vetted their guardians, they also created a new branch of research to thwart the plans of those who would seek to extinguish the light from the land.

Protectors of Light and their apprentices lived by a singular motto, Lux Superesse Est—light must survive. This phrase was enshrined in an engraving above the arched entryway into the research center at the Palace of Ren. It was a mantra used daily by those in the Palaces of Light, a greeting of sorts, that fortified the reason for the Light Protectors' existence.

That existence, however, was not free from opposition. There were creatures whose very purpose was to push against the light with the full force of darkness. One such creature was known as a Nullblight, a being that existed exclusively as a weapon of the Shadow Garrison, used to seek out and extinguish any remaining light seekers in order to advance their power and control. They moved with a swiftness that was unmatched by any human, as they did not rely on the light for their movement. They were slender, hairless, dark, and their physiology had adapted over time to become nearly invisible in the darkness. Even their disproportionately large fangs were covered in a matte black film—an adaptation that prevented any light from reflecting from their mouths as they thrashed their enemies in battle. These creatures often stayed close to their primary base of operations on the continent of Umbra to protect the Shadow Garrison from any who would challenge their power and the reign of the darkness.

As Elucido stood up from his cold, damp bed of rock, he instinctively reminded himself of his purpose.

"Lux Superesse Est," he said to himself as he gathered his belongings and stretched his weary legs. He had no memory of what events had led to the catastrophe known throughout the land as the Dark Cataclysm, in which darkness surged into power, upsetting the balance between light and shadow. In fact, when it came to his life in the years leading up to the destruction of the Aether Orbs, his memories were as difficult to see as the world itself. But it ultimately did not matter to Elucido what events had led to this moment in time. His job remained the same—find what was driving the darkness forward and, by any means, push back with greater force. Light must survive, at all cost.

It had been some time since Elucido had spoken with another sentient being. The shadow that covered the land made life challenging. Those who survived struggled daily to meet even the most basic of needs. Light was the primary means by which life could survive on Terrus, and without it, hope of survival seemed to fade. Rumors circulated about light-producing shards that scattered when the Aether Orbs were shattered during the Dark Cataclysm, but Elucido had never seen one with his own eyes. If one were to be lucky enough to obtain such a shard, they could use the residual light energy to find their way more clearly in a lost and nearly lifeless world.

Food was scarce, and often consisted of plant life that could survive and grow in dark, humid environments. As such, Elucido's satchel often contained a modest supply of dried moss and bulbous honey fungus. It not only grew well in the darkness, but had a bioluminescent property that, despite emitting only a small amount of light, produced a spark of hope every time he retrieved one. It was a hope that the light could in fact be restored to the land and life could thrive once again. After all, there can be no death without life, no despair without hope, and no darkness without light.

As difficult as survival was for most, many creatures in this realm thrived in the darkness. The Shadow Garrison weaponized those creatures, seeking to destroy the light. They had achieved that goal in their victory during the Dark Cataclysm years ago. Those who served the light found themselves in hiding, fleeing from the beings that were governed by darkness. Chance encounters with any of the expansive array of beasts could prove quite costly if one was not fully prepared. Unbeknownst to Elucido, he was about to have such an encounter.

While traversing the path leading toward the Great Chasm, Elucido saw a faint glow over his left shoulder. His experience told him it was a bioluminescent mushroom, based on the hue of the faint light it emitted. He unhooked the clasp on his satchel in preparation to add the rare food to his collection, but as he turned to home in on its precise location, his foot caught the rough edge of a rock. He stumbled sideways, unable to catch his footing. As his feet moved upward toward the darkened sky, his collection of mushrooms scattered in the air, illuminating his surroundings in a constellation of misfortune. This is where his misfortune ended, however. The faint glow of light produced by the mushrooms revealed the shadow of a figure rapidly approaching his position with a silent fervor that moved his heart even farther from his upended feet. He knew, almost instinctively, that this shadow was that of a Nullblight. If not for his most fortunate misstep, Elucido would have never seen the danger he now faced.

As he fell, Elucido grabbed the dagger he kept sheathed on his hip. His reflexes surprised even himself, as he had the dagger drawn before his back hit the ground. He reached out to cover his face, anticipating the impending attack, and in what can only be described as sheer dumb luck, his dagger stuck deep into the enemy's throat before its teeth had the opportunity to tear his flesh. It writhed for only a brief moment before it no longer possessed enough blood or breath to continue its fight. Elucido was surprised to learn that, despite the beast's flawless adaptation to stealth in darkness, its blood reflected the light from his scattered mushrooms in a shimmering pool that simultaneously turned his stomach and brought an anxious half-smile to his face. He had felled the beast as quickly as the encounter had started.

Elucido's hands quivered, unable to maintain their grasp on his blood-soaked dagger. He was not used to such battles, and many of his fellow Protectors of Light had fallen to such beasts as quickly as this encounter had ended in his favor. He was not a warrior—he had served his job at a table, knee deep in the archives. His foundation was knowledge and reasoning, which rarely lent themselves to swiftness of foot and sharpness of sword when engaging in combat.

"How did this beast find me?" he wondered, as he gathered himself from the ground. "More importantly, what was a creature this powerful doing this far from the Palace of Darkness?" The fact that they were this far into Elucido's home territory concerned him greatly.

After a brief search of the archives that he carried in his memory, he arrived at a strikingly sound conclusion. The sole purpose of these beings making such a rapid move of aggression this far from their home base could only be finding and extinguishing any remaining shards of light and those who aimed to employ their power in the fight against the darkness. Elucido's legs, already weary from the rush of adrenaline from his encounter, gave way as he realized how much danger he was now facing. The realization that the darkness was growing more powerful meant that the light had limited time left before the Shadow Garrison could no longer be overtaken and the darkness consuming the world became permanent. But there was hope, yet.

"If the beings were searching for shards of light this far out, there must be one nearby," he spoke aloud, as if there was another person nearby to hear his words of encouragement.

Shaking the dirt from his cloak, Elucido swept his head from side to side. He moved as quickly as his legs could respond to his thoughts, toward the rocky outcropping to the north. As he rounded the corner, it was not difficult to find the shard, whose light provided a sharp contrast to the bleak darkness surrounding the area. He ran toward the light. Approaching the illuminated ground, Elucido felt an unsteadiness that surpassed what he had felt during his brief encounter with the Nullblight. He had only heard whispers of the existence of the shards of the great Aether Orbs. The shards were rumored to have been scattered across the land when the Aether Orbs were destroyed during the Dark Cataclysm. The idea of these fragments was as foreign to him as the memories of how the darkness came into existence. As he picked up the light shard, he gazed upon it with utter bewilderment. Hope was alive.

Chapter 2

The Cloaked Enigma

"At the ready!" A mysterious cloaked man called his troops to attention. He sat upon the throne of the Palace of Darkness; a throne made from the bones and dried flesh of the Shadow Garrison's deceased. His demeanor was menacing; despair the emotion projected by his very being.

"Caligo, are your troops prepared?"

"Yes sir, the Tenebrae are ready for action, at your command."

"Excellent. Send them out! I want the Protector of Light found and brought to me at all cost."

"Consider it done, my King," Caligo responded as swiftly as the mysterious, dark beings left the palace.

The Tenebrae, a terrifying race of creatures, were composed entirely of darkness. In fact, the only means by which a human could see them was from the vague whirlpool of light that surrounded their core; the result of any light nearby being sucked into their bodies for destruction. Everything they touched turned cold and lifeless, and they fought with a vigor unparalleled by any other soldiers in the Garrison. The Tenebrae's sole purpose was to consume all the remaining light left in the world. They were the physical embodiment of hopelessness.

The Palace of Darkness sat across the sky-world, in the heart of the continent of Umbra. Its foundation laid where the Palace of Sheut once stood. In fact, the central tower of the Palace of Darkness was the very tower that once spread light across the land. Those who built the palace intended for those who were loyal to the light to see the constant reminder of how their way of life now lay under the control of their enemy.

Caligo, commander of the Shadow Garrison, was as menacing as he was mysterious. He reached the fullness of his power during the Great Battle that extinguished much of the light from the land. His strategic prowess and cold-hearted ruthlessness made his place of power in the Palace of Darkness inevitable. He possessed an intuition for battle that was advanced far beyond his years.

Prior to the Great Battle, Caligo, a former Protector of Light, had aspirations of becoming the greatest general in the land. His pride and defiant arrogance fueled his belief that he would achieve such a lofty goal. He spent his free time around the Palaces of Light, studying the tactics, strategies, and methodologies of the battalions that defended the light towers. His analytical nature, ingenious mind, and resourcefulness gave him the tools he needed to learn everything he could about how the Army of Light operated. This proved to be incredibly useful as he unscrupulously pilfered the most sensitive secrets that he would ultimately use against the palaces in his meteoric rise to power.

Intelligent as he was tactically, Caligo's truest strength lay in his ability to read and manipulate others. His quick wit, unfaltering charm, and emotional intelligence allowed him to rise as a shadow in the darkness, unseen, unheard, and altogether unexpected. No problem existed that Caligo could not find a solution for, not a person he couldn't bend to his will. None had suspected him to challenge the world order and rise to power, let alone in such a magnificent manner. Caligo's conversion from light to darkness had been absolute, and his malicious intent without question.

The formation of the Shadow Garrison and the creatures of darkness that amassed such a threat to the light was one of the best kept secrets of the age. Their creation was unseen, despite the efforts by the Light Protectors to find those seeking to destroy their way of life. Yet Caligo, despite never holding a generalship in the army in the light palaces, was responsible for the Shadow Garrison's creation. His deceit was commanding and unbounded. He built the largest force the Protectors of Light had encountered right under their noses, with not even a whisper of the impending destruction they faced. His creations, the Tenebrae, were his pièce de résistance, the pride of his faithful efforts. Their elite fighting abilities and physical power resulted from years of research and development, trial and error, and many encounters that nearly ended his life as a fearless insurrectionist.

As with many successful commanders before him, Caligo timed the formation of his garrison with patience and precision. He spent eight years of his life researching, building, and preparing for the day that he would claim his place as the Bringer of Darkness and rise to a level of power he had dreamed of attaining since the rebellious days of his youth. When the time came, he exercised no restraint. His victory was as swift and authoritative as any commander had ever seen.

When his army was ready, and Caligo was prepared to strike, he had started the campaign against the light in an instant. Ironically, his assault on the Tower of Sheut had taken place at midday, in broad daylight. He moved in the light to demonstrate the power of his creation and their mastery of darkness.

As the Regent of Light took his afternoon tea from the observation platform in the Central Tower in the Palace of Sheut, he felt a rumbling in the ground. Before he had the chance to ask his counsel if it was a terrestrial tremor, he saw pockets of light beginning to swirl around the palace. Tens, hundreds, then thousands of whirlpools of light were visible from his elevated position in a matter of seconds. He had seen nothing like this—it was no tremor; it was something altogether foreign and unspeakably terrifying.

It took only three minutes for darkness to consume the palace. The Tenebrae had done their job flawlessly, completely absorbing the surrounding light and replacing it with confusion, chaos, and terror. The regent crawled on all fours; his lack of vision in the darkness prevented him from finding his way to the command room and calling his generals to action. As he moved frantically around the pitch-black room, he reached forward, grabbed hold of a cloak, and followed it to a pair of boots covered in armor plating as cold as the presence he now felt.

"Regent, we now control the Palace of Light. It is futile to fight my army. Giving into hopelessness and accepting the darkness is your only choice. Ah yes, forgive my rudeness. I am Caligo, the commander of this new army, the Shadow Garrison. You most certainly don't recognize me—the darkness has changed me from the person you think you once knew."

The regent had looked up in disbelief. Could this indeed be someone he knew? He had not recognized Caligo's shadowed face, but his confidence and gait seemed somehow familiar. He acted as if he belonged in his position of authority and made no apology for anyone who found themselves in his way. Taking a deep breath and trying to discern more, the regent noticed something out of the corner of his eye, as a flicker of residual light reflected upon the surface of a small object. Caligo wore a broach on the side of his cape that appeared to be more functional than decorative. Despite its rust, tarnish, and age, he recognized the emblem as the crest of the elite Protectors of Light. Could Caligo have been one of the regent's men?

"By the light, it cannot be!" said the regent in disbelief. "How could you do such a thing? You have betrayed your sworn oath to protect the light at all cost!"

"I have found, dearest Regent, that there is far more power, control, and superiority in harnessing hopelessness and fear. And darkness provides the world with ample quantities of both."

"You will never prevail, Caligo. Where there is darkness, there will always be light. Even in the depths of hopelessness and desperation, humans have always been able to find hope. Your actions will fail. *Lux Superesse Est*—no, *Lux Superstes Erit*, light will survive."

"Unfortunately, you will not live to see the last light in the land extinguished. Your reign ends here, in darkness, at the hand of the enemy you failed to see rising. Hubris will be your downfall; your blindness the predecessor to the blindness the world now faces."

Caligo's dagger had entered the regent's back without resistance, missing his ribs and plunging directly into his heart. Swift as the regent's death had been, Caligo took a few moments to remain in the silent, still darkness. He took a deep breath, removed his dagger from the regent's lifeless body, moved to the far edge of the observation tower, and shouted for those who remained in the palace to hear, "Thus ends the reign of light!"

In the distance, from his vantage point in the Central Tower, Caligo saw a faint light on the horizon. Though powerful, the Tenebrae only consumed the light within a limited radius, and they had not yet reached all corners of the land. But the limited range of the Tenebrae in their consumption of light was of no concern to Caligo. His plans to stamp out the remaining light from the land had only just begun. He entered the inner sanctum of the Central Tower, eyeing the glow of the Aether Orb that sat upon its pedestal. The Tenebrae approached the illuminated orb in a circular pattern, with Caligo at the center of their approach. They absorbed the light that emanated from the orb as quickly as the orbs produced it, in an endless pattern of swirling light, like tentacles grasping the darkness in a hopeless attempt to overpower their despair.

As masterful as Caligo's ascension to the tower and assassination of the Regent had been, they were inconsequential compared to what transpired next. Out of the darkness emerged Caligo's commander, the mysterious cloaked enigma known as the King of Darkness. His nameless, emotionless presence created a void where hope was meant to live. Underneath the cloak, the figure of a man appeared, faintly silhouetted by the glow of the passing light. His movement toward the orb was fluid and smooth, as if he took no steps in his approach, merely gliding. With his hood still covering his face, he wrapped his arms in a cradle-like position around the pedestal, taking care not to touch the orb. He spoke an incantation in a language even Caligo did not understand. The faster he spoke the incantation, the brighter the core of the orb glowed until, in an event of cataclysmic proportion, the orb shattered. As it shattered, pulses of energy shot forward toward each of the other four sky-continents on Terrus. The pulse headed toward the Aether Orbs that fed the energy to the central tower in a reversal of flow too powerful for the orbs to contain. The profusion of energy shattered the Aether Orbs in the towers on the other four continents. A flash of bright light illuminated the entire world, and then darkness.

A Great Battle had followed, between the Defenders of the Light and the Shadow Garrison; though the lack of light turned the battle into a slaughter. Warriors engaged the Tenebrae on every continent with all of their might, but the darkness overtook them. Some survived and scattered into hiding, holding faith that they would, at some point, regain enough light to launch a counterassault. Hundreds of thousands died in a matter of hours as the Tenebrae gorged themselves, devouring all remaining hope from the land.

In order to cement a definitive victory, the cloaked man ordered Caligo to set up an outpost at each of the locations of the remaining Light Palaces. He wanted to ensure that the light would never be restored through the towers, and to make a clear statement to those that fled into hiding that he was in control of the darkness. As the Shadow Garrison troops conquered the final tower, the war ended as quickly as it had begun, and hopelessness became the new rule of the land.

Despite the swift victory at the Central Tower, much time had passed since Caligo's ascension to power. The time had now come, however, for the next phase of the war. Survivors from the palaces of light still lived scattered among the continents, known as the Defenders of the Light. Though they were few in numbers, their purpose remained resolute; *Lux Superesse Est* continued to be their mantra, despite the strength and hopelessness of the emergent darkness. Yet rumors circulated of a hero amongst the Defenders of the Light, known as the Luxcreare—the Creator of Light. Legends described the Luxcreare as one who would drive out the darkness, restore light to the land, and usher in the next Age of Illumination. The emergence of such a hero threatened the way of life that the King of Darkness had fought so hard to create. Caligo knew that the only way to secure his position of power was to seek and destroy the remaining Defenders of the Light in hopes of finding and extinguishing the life of the Luxcreare. After all, as the cloaked enigma, the King of Darkness, unrelentingly reminded him, *Nox Praevalet*—night must prevail. With his objective in mind, and at the command of the one who sat on the throne of darkness, Caligo set off on his search.

Chapter 3

The Journey Begins

Elucido reached into his satchel, retrieving the light shard he had found only moments earlier. The shard glowed with a pulsing rhythm, ebbing and flowing in time like the beating of a heart. It felt as if the very rhythmic pulse of the world itself was at his fingertips. He clutched it tightly, wondering how many pieces of light were still active. He thought to himself—"Is this the only hope of the world? Is it possible to restore the light of the Aether Orbs and bring life back to the continents? There must be a way to undo the damage done in the Dark Cataclysm."

As he gripped the light shard more tightly, his knuckles whitening, he sensed an energy building in the core of his soul. As quickly as the energy flowed into his body, he was struck with a sharp pain. He collapsed to the ground, writhing on the hard rock he had once been standing on. Unable to release his grip on the light shard, he saw what he could only describe as a vision.

"The power is all mine now." A cloaked figure moved effortlessly across the room, his unfaltering confidence bringing a faint smile to

his shadowed face. A dark orb sat next to the cloaked figure, resting upon an altar of stone, cold and lifeless. The orb was cracked and worn, black as night, yet somehow its presence commanded the unrelenting attention of everyone in the room. "With the orbs drained of power, my supremacy is inevitable—none can stand in the way of my dominion, and the coming Age of Darkness. Let them come if they may; their efforts to usurp me will be futile. I will drain all remaining hope from their meaningless lives and replace it with the darkest despair—a despair that will fuel my power and bring me an unending reign." The figures standing in the shadows nodded in agreement, their faces hidden by the lightless room. The cloaked figure led his team from the room without a word, as if they knew the part they were to play in this game of dark dominion. As they left the room, a faint glow emanated from the orb...

Elucido had never experienced such a pain, especially not while such an expanding hopefulness and energy surged through his body. "What was this vision?" he wondered. "Could it be that these are things that will come to pass? What did the glowing orb represent? Is there hope for the future to restore light to the land?"

Elucido's shoulders sank as the pit in his stomach grew deeper, filling with nothing but emptiness. He needed to know if the future could be redeemed from the all-consuming darkness that covered Terrus. Taking a deep breath, he centered his focus on finding answers. As studious as he had been at his post in the archives, he understood he did not have the knowledge needed to unravel the enigma surrounding his vision. Wiping the sweat from his palms, he rose to his feet, his legs quivering from the surge of adrenaline that passed through them only moments ago.

As had been the case so often in his past, Elucido hoped he would find answers in the depths of the archives. He had not been to the facility since before the Great Battle shattered the soul of the world. As much comfort as the archives had provided him in the past, his encounter with the Nullblight convinced him that safety and peace on his next visit was unlikely. He grasped the light shard, rotating and inspecting it as he passed it between his trembling hands. He understood the shard represented so much more than a small light-bearing stone. The shard represented the growing hope that, despite the dangers ahead, he would be able to find a way to push back against the darkness. Doing nothing was not an option; inaction would only allow the hopelessness of the world to consume all remaining light, life, and hope from those who still lived for the light, including himself. Kneeling on the cold, damp ground, Elucido closed his eyes, the weight upon his shoulders growing heavier at the realization that the choices he now had to make would invariably shape the future of Terrus.

The archives were kept in the basement of a structure next to the main tower of the Palace of Ren. Since the darkness had conquered the towers, Elucido was unsure what he would find when he arrived. If he was lucky, he could enter the basement through the ruins with no need to gain access to the main tower, which would certainly be fortified by the enemy. Elucido checked his belongings to ensure he was leaving nothing behind, tightened the strap on his worn leather satchel by two notches, then began the dangerous trek to his forgotten second home at the palace. He was now aware of the dangers that awaited him, and he would not be as lucky the next time he encountered a member of the elite Shadow Garrison. He had to step up his awareness, increase the speed at which he moved, and find a new ability to fight—something he never envisioned or desired in his establishment as an archivist. His life and the very survival of the light required nothing less than the oath he swore when he took his post as a Protector of Light. *Lux Superesse Est*.

With the light emanating from the Aether Orb shard, Elucido began his trek along the main path toward the Palace. Before he reached the tower, he would pass a treacherous route along the Great Chasm. The chasm was a gaping hole in the center of the continent, a location of immense beauty in the days of his past, and a point of abrupt danger should his footing fail in the darkness. Carelessness carried a price too great to pay. Precision and swiftness of foot were the skills he now needed to master.

The path was slow-moving, rough, and lined with sharp rocks, dangerous outcroppings, and areas of sliding, craggy footholds. Elucido shuffled his feet, nearly tripping many times as he traversed the uneven ground. A journey that he had typically made in a day would take him at least three days under the darkened sky. While his light shard increased visibility in his immediate vicinity, it did little to help his navigation around the dangerous chasm. Not only did the light not extend for a long distance, the cliffs and hills absorbed the light before it reached any familiar points of interest. The muscles in his legs burned, growing more tired with every step;

he had not remembered the journey being this exhausting. Despite the many trips he had made along this very path, Elucido felt lost, uncertain if his next step would bring him closer to his destination. Elucido was navigating by intuition, instinct, and memory.

Memory was an interesting, often funny, thing. The strength of his memory was the only force guiding him forward. In its absence, he would be lost. Elucido focused on those memories as the long hours of his journey grew more wearisome. He and his friends used to follow this path on their pilgrimages from their village in the valley to the Palace of Light to see the various ceremonies and celebrations that the palace offered. Elucido was only 14 years old when he first attended the Illuminating of the newest Light Protector, a ceremony that held the highest respect and admiration of those whose lives existed outside the palace. This ceremony did not happen very often, as new apprentices only replaced those who had retired, died of old age, or suffered an unfortunate passing. He remembered this ceremony as one of specific significance to him, as his older brother Frater was sworn in as an apprentice in the Light Guard, a unit dedicated to the protection and defense of the palaces. Frater was tall, strong, and had a much more physically commanding presence than Elucido. He had trained his entire youth for the day that he was called to the guard.

Elucido recalled with exquisite specificity every detail of the ceremony, from the illumination of the guardsmen's shields to the trumpeting of the bugle regiment as the new inductees entered the palace. His most vivid memory was watching as a broach was pinned on Frater's uniform—the hallowed Broach of the Defenders of Light. It represented their commitment to protecting the light against any who would seek to extinguish it. The pinning of the broach to his brother's uniform was a memory that brought a rare smile to Elucido's face. The smile, refreshing as it may have been, was short-lived. The memories that flowed next were as piercing as the moment itself. It was believed that Frater had perished in the Great Battle at the hand of Caligo's dark forces, as had his entire regiment. On the day of the Great Battle, Frater was on the frontline protecting the tower of Ren, when a legion of Tenebrae descended upon his battalion, leaving nothing but a field of blood-soaked grass behind as they marched toward the tower. No bodies were found, only empty memories of those left behind. This thought, coupled with the bitter-cold breeze, reminded Elucido of how alone he was in this dark world. No happy memories rejuvenated his soul—not, at least, while knowing what had come to pass, and what may yet lie ahead.

A noise shook Elucido from the distraction of his memories. He heard a faint whirring in the distance. It was the sound of a generator used to power the machinery for the Shadow Garrison at the Palace of Light. Since the Aether Orbs' light had been stamped out, it was longer used as the unbounded source of power that the Protectors of Light had once harnessed. After the Shadow Garrison took control of the tower, a more rudimentary, much less efficient, coal generator replaced the systems that powered the Palace. The burning coal produced a faint, ruddy glow that shone from underground near the base of the tower. The furnace provided a rare warmth and illumination to an otherwise cold and barren land.

As he leaned around a large boulder, getting a closer look at the generator, Elucido recognized the danger he now faced on his journey. He froze, the large, ridged back of the Nullblight patrolling the facility only a few feet from him. How the guard had not heard him was lost on Elucido. Perhaps the loud droning of the generator had drowned out his heavy footsteps. Or perhaps the Nullblight was not expecting a surprise visitor. Elucido slowed his movement, though his heart continued accelerating beyond his control. He retreated, first behind the boulder, then carefully toward the tower's entrance. He was safe, for now.

As he moved closer to the tower, he recognized the archway leading to the archives nestled underground. The stone arch was not as grand or ornate as those found within the palace itself, standing only a few centimeters taller than Elucido. It appeared as little more than a wind-worn limestone entrance to a man-made cavern, covered in a light moss. Despite the destruction that had befallen the palace, the archives were in reasonable shape. The condition of the archway itself inspired him, as he could still make out the engraving on the top of the stone—*Lux Superesse Est*. Not only was the engraving on the top of the entryway visible, but the faint glow from the coal furnace provided just enough light for Elucido to descend the stone staircase with ease. The steps were dusty, and worn from many years of foot traffic, now containing small divots where the archivists' feet had routinely stepped. The concave depressions in the stone held Elucido's feet securely in place, their embrace bringing a comforting familiarity to him. He entered the chamber below, the ambient light from the furnace above filtering through, allowing Elucido to consume the information from the pages contained inside the library with relative ease. He searched with expediency, knowing that a patrol of the Garrison might crash upon his location at any moment. The problem he now faced was that he didn't know specifically what he was searching for. There had to be something in the archives that would tell him more about the Aether Orbs, and whether it was possible to piece them together, reactivate their power, and restore light to the land. But he had no clue where to begin his hunt.

He removed the shard of the orb from his satchel to investigate it for any markings or other indications of how he might use it to restore the orb in its entirety. It was smooth and heavy, resembling a piece of obsidian, with beautiful radiance from the light it produced. It fit comfortably in his hand, filling his palm while still allowing him to curl his fingers around it, securing it in his grasp. He saw no marks, no indications that it held any answers about its constitution. As he manipulated it further, an almost gravitational force pulled him toward the back of the room. Elucido responded to the shard's prompt, advancing across the floor. In the room's corner was a small opening in the wall that he had not noticed during his tenure in the archives. Something had damaged the wall during the Great Battle, revealing a hidden chamber that Elucido had never seen. Holding his breath and tightening his stomach, he squeezed his small frame through the opening in the wall, moved to the corner of the secret chamber, and held the shard above his head. The shard's light revealed shelves containing what appeared to be ancient texts. Uncertain of what he had discovered, he approached the closest shelf and pulled a tattered parchment from underneath a stack of dusty scrolls. The top of the parchment displayed the words "Elementum Potentia—Rubrim". "Elemental Powers—Red. What does that mean?" Elucido had never heard of Elementals, and the notion of a set of ancient powers intrigued him in a way he had not been for a long time. His eyes quickly parsed as much information as he was able. The text described an ancient form of power that could be used to harness different colored Light Elementals and create new abilities for those who mastered that power. In this case, the Red Elemental harnessed the energy of red light to summon an orb that contained a burst of fire that the wielder could control at will. If this was a power that Elucido mastered, it would undoubtedly aid his journey to find any remaining light shards. But how would he be able to manifest this ancient power? Was he even capable of such an ability?

He rolled the parchment up and placed it in his satchel so he could study its contents later. He continued his search for any additional information that would show how to restore the Aether Orbs, if it was even possible. Not too far from his current position, a large, well-maintained tome stood balanced on the edge of the table, barely holding its position above the floor. He read the spine of the tome easily in the muted, radiating glow of the burning coal. It read 'On the Constitution of Aether Orbs'. Fortuitous as this discovery was, it would take some time for Elucido to understand what he needed to do with the information it held. As he opened the text to investigate its contents, he heard a noise.

Crash!

Elucido's attention shifted to the sound of pewter stemware hitting the barren stone floor as a pair of Nullblights carelessly entered the hallway leading to the central room of the archives. He retreated to the far corner of his hidden chamber, hoping that he would remain unseen as the enemy passed through the larger adjacent room. He positioned the tome under his left arm, wrapped the shard of the Aether Orb in his handkerchief, and tucked it deep inside his satchel to keep its light hidden.

These Nullblights were louder than the one he first encountered; they had no need for stealth in their stronghold at the palace. Moving slowly, one creature picked up the pewter goblet he had knocked off the table, tilting its head as it examined the pattern engraved on its side. The other Nullblight approached, trying to take the goblet from his counterpart's hands. Snarling, the first beast showed its displeasure that his possession interested the other. The aggression sent the empty-handed creature into a rage. It swung its sharp claws at the other Nullblight, drawing blood. The two beasts engaged one another in a brawl. Elucido heard the creatures moving closer to him as their duel escalated. He slowed his breathing as much as possible, squatted in the corner in as tight a ball as he was able, and anxiously hoped the two Nullblights would not stumble upon his hiding place.

At that moment, one beast kicked the other, sending it hurtling into the wall where the small opening to the hidden chamber was. The force of the beast hitting the wall opened the gap as chunks of stone broke free. The chamber was now clearly visible. Elucido silently gasped, the air involuntarily drawn into his lungs. It was only a matter of time before the beasts would find him. Finding his courage and wit, he grabbed a small bronze bowl from the table nearby. He threw the bowl past the Nullblights and into the larger chamber, resulting in a loud clang. The sound drew the beasts' attention, distracting them from their feisty duel. They ran toward the noise, ready to defend their stronghold against whatever danger it presented. This was his chance. Elucido tiptoed from the chamber as fast as he was able, behind the Nullblights, and toward the opposite end of the room. He hoped that the back exit to the archives was intact. If not, his journey would be over before he discovered how to restore the orbs.

As he exited the main chamber, now out of the Nullblights' line of sight, he stepped quickly and effortlessly through the hallway toward the back of the archives. While he could still see some of the stone tiles on the floor from the furnace's glow, his vision was not needed. He knew the archives nearly as well as he knew himself. His years of service researching in these hallways proved to be the very thing that saved him from an encounter in which he had no intention of participating. He reached the rear exit quickly and sprinted toward the rocky outcropping at the far edge of the palace boundary. Kneeling and catching his breath, he listened, waited, and hoped that the beasts had not seen him.

After a few anxious moments that seemed much more like a lifetime, Elucido's chest relaxed as he breathed a sigh of relief.

Nullblights moved so quickly that, had they seen him, he would have been dead already. His hiding place was safe, for now. Thinking about what came next, however, brought a new set of fears to Elucido's mind. He pulled the scroll from his satchel and read the ancient text under the light of the shard. His eyes flickered back and forth as he reached the end of each line, opening wider at each new revelation. The text spoke of the makeup of the Aether Orbs that brought light to Terrus, and the fragility of their constitution. It revealed a theory, yet untested by humankind; the proposition that the orbs, should they be broken, could be mended by the power of the Luxcreare, if all their pieces were brought together.

Elucido understood that in order to have any hope of restoring light to the land, he needed to find the remaining shards of the orb, learn how they were constructed, and find the way to piece them back together. In order to do that, he would first need to find a way to fight the Shadow Garrison's relentless troops upon their next encounter. He would need to study the Elementum Potentia on his journey and try to harness the power of the Red Elemental to aid in his fight, if it were even possible. While his mind and will were strong, they alone would not be sufficient to survive.

Elucido wondered where the other shards were. He needed to find their location. He pulled the solitary shard from his bag and clenched it in his grasp. With the same gravitational pull the shard exuded in the archives, it now registered in him the direction he needed to travel. Trusting the orb, he set out on the path toward the Misty Marshes.

Chapter 4

A New Enemy is Named

"Let him go. He will be back soon enough. That is, if my handsome nocturnal pets don't kill him first." A singular, concussive chuckle resonated in the empty chamber. Onymos, a general in the Shadow Garrison and one of Caligo's most trusted men, laughed as he observed Elucido leave the palace grounds and head for the Misty Marshes. Onymos was small in stature, but what he lacked in physical constitution he more than made up for in intellectual prowess. His presence had a chill about it, as if the very core of his body lacked any ability to produce warmth. Even his army of dark creatures distanced themselves due to his unforgiving nature. He paced calmly through his throne room atop the tower of Ren, his every step leaving the floor icier than it was prior to his arrival.

"The boy will never defeat me; I have fought too hard to earn my place in the Shadow Garrison." Onymos was as bitter as he was ruthless. His desire to destroy everything in his path motivated his rise to power in the Shadow Garrison. Onymos had spent most of the days leading up to his assimilation into the Shadow

Garrison hiding in the shadows, secretly researching the creatures of darkness, the Aether Orbs, and a variety of dark powers. The more he learned, the deeper the obsession rooted in his core. The darkness took hold of him and led him down a path of destruction that would ultimately place him in his position of authority in the Army of Darkness.

He walked the palace halls, waiting for Elucido's return, wanting nothing more than to destroy the young man and extend his favor with the King of Darkness. Onymos was not only focused on victory over those who celebrated the light, but he was filled with a deep-seated desire to extinguish their bloodlines and erase their names from history itself. Anyone who crossed Onymos paid in the most permanent manner—when he was finished with them, in the eyes of the world, they no longer existed, neither in flesh nor memory. He cemented his post as Caligo's trusted servant by annihilating an entire battalion of light defenders in an instant by crushing them beneath an avalanche, their bodies never found, their memories left to fade with time. Elucido, he expected, would suffer a similar fate.

The Great Tower on the continent of Ren became Onymos' home following Caligo's victory over the Defenders of Light in the Great Battle. Caligo assigned him the post to secure the tower as a fortification of darkness. He was charged with defense of the tower, as well as maintaining research and developing new technology that could help search for and stamp out any light seekers that challenged their rule. It was he who sent the Nullblights in search of the Aether Orb shards and, subsequently, in pursuit of Elucido.

While Onymos's post placed him far from the central tower on the continent of Umbra, where the King of Darkness sat on his throne, he was pleased to have autonomy in how he carried out his barbarous tasks. Solitude was his ally, and he embraced the power of being the only general of the Shadow Garrison in the entirety of the continent.

Accelerating the pace at which he paced through the hallways, Onymos twirled his hands in a circular motion, a wisp of frost following his movements through the air. A faint light surrounded his ice-cold hands in an alluring azure glow. Onymos wielded this glacial power with ease, as if it was embedded within his core, obeying his every command. It appeared as though his research into the dark arts had proven to be fruitful, as he had acquired the ability to manipulate the cold with extreme precision.

Onymos, secure in his palace, had been tracking Elucido for months before he approached the tower in search of information about the Aether Orbs, aware of what the young man could one day become. For now, he did not see Elucido as a threat—in fact, it amused him to see Elucido struggle to survive in the unrelenting darkness. If the time ever came that Elucido posed any credible threat to his post, he would crush him, taking the utmost pleasure in erasing Elucido's name from existence. In fact, he hoped Elucido would rise to confront him someday and give him something new to look forward to destroying.

For now, Onymos watched Elucido through the large glassless windows that adorned the throne room. With the openness of his palace halls came an icy wind that brought Onymos an atypical measure of comfort. His plan for now was simple—observe Elucido from his tower, report any interesting findings back to Caligo at the tower of Umbra, and wait for the opportunity to challenge the Luxcreare.

Chapter 5

Rouge

As he approached the base of the valley leading up to the mist-covered marshland, Elucido stopped to find shelter and catch his breath. The marshlands were harsh and unforgiving, so he would need to recover as much energy as he could before delving deeper into the terrain. He found a small cavern on the edge of the marshes to get some rest. Confident that he was out of danger for now, he laid his head on a moss-covered rock and entered a deep slumber.

A ruddy swirl of light surrounded Elucido as he felt the power of the Red Elemental grow within him. He focused his energy, and almost instinctively cycled the power of the Red Elemental into a hue shift toward blue. Before long, the red light became fully blue, and he felt a cold, ice-like energy surrounding him. He continued in this manner—from blue to yellow, then to purple, and finally green, as the light contained within the Elemental transformed its nature at his behest. He observed five colors of Elementals, each with a distinct power. Elucido could feel the control of those powers manifesting in the core of his being, as if they were becoming an extension of himself. Swirling in a dance of colored light, Elucido moved his arms smoothly, controlling the Elementals with utter mastery. He was completely in control; the lights obeying his every command.

Elucido jolted awake, his nerves on edge after a dream that felt more real than he could have imagined. He knew deep down that these were the powers that could give him the edge in the fight to restore the luminosity of the Aether Orbs and bring light back into the hopeless world. All he had to do was figure out how to master them. Standing, he took a deep breath, closed his eyes, and shifted his focus to the red light he saw in his vision. As he opened his eyes, he reached into his satchel and grabbed the parchment "Elementum Potentia—Rubrim".

As Elucido dissected the information in the scroll more thoroughly, he came to realize that the parchment was written more like a manifesto than an instruction manual. It contained strange incantations in a language that he could not decipher. *Congrega lucem. Uniendis lux. Lucem propagationem.* Elucido's brow furrowed, uncertain what to make of the words. He continued reading. The text described the Elemental powers and their importance as the most powerful means of controlling light and manipulating the world to the wielder's advantage. The Elementals were fueled by emotion, controlled by extreme focus, and used to whatever ends suited the one who could control them. They were not, however, limited to a single user. It was clear from the exposition contained within the parchment that there might be others who were capable of controlling the Light Elementals. An encounter with someone who had mastery of the Elemental powers could prove disastrous—that is, unless Elucido could surpass their level of skill.

Elucido was not accustomed to harnessing his emotions. He was a logician, a researcher whose existence relied more on reasoning than emotion. He had developed an innate ability to dismiss emotions and focus on rationality over reaction. Elucido would have to tap into a part of himself that he made a habit of ignoring. He started sifting through the emotions he felt, searching for something to hold on to while trying to summon the Elemental. He had no idea if it would work, or if he was even capable of such powers. He landed, perhaps superficially, on loneliness as the dominant emotion of his current state of mind. Embracing the loneliness and allowing it to surround him, Elucido breathed heavily. The heartache of his solitude swelled as he succumbed to the realization that he may never see another Defender of Light, especially if the Shadow Garrison's growing power should overcome him. Exhaling sharply, he wrenched his hands into tight fists, pushed his arms forward, all the while attempting to shift the power of his loneliness into the bright Red Elemental power from his dream.

Nothing. No light was created, no power manifested, no help presented; only loneliness remained. Hours passed, the pain of isolation bubbling within his soul, yet still nothing came of his efforts to summon the power of the Elemental. He tried everything he could think of to harness the power of his loneliness and invoke the fiery orb, to no avail. Maybe this was not his destiny, after all, he wondered. Perhaps his usefulness had been exhausted doing his research before the Great Battle. Maybe he was meant for nothing more than to be a gatherer of information. It was at this moment that Elucido felt more alone and hopeless than ever. Trying to regain his composure, he shifted his thoughts of the growing loneliness toward his memories of his brother. He longed for another moment with Frater, another opportunity to laugh, smile, and share a warm meal. Elucido would give anything to not feel the invasive loneliness any longer. He wished with all remaining hope in his heart that he was not alone.

His wish was quickly granted, though not at all in the manner he intended. In an instant, he heard the crunching of leaves underfoot as a pair of Nullblights approached the entrance of his shelter. They moved slowly, searching for any signs of life. Elucido understood it would only be a matter of moments before they smelled him, entered the cavern, closed in on his location, and killed him. "Would death be so bad at this point?" he wondered. The hopelessness of his current predicament, coupled with his overwhelming loneliness, made the prospect of death seem almost a relief. All he had to do was wait a few moments, and it would all be over.

The memory of his brother persisted, however, and conquered his resignation to the inevitability of his death. "Frater would have fought with all of his might. He would never allow the darkness to extinguish his hope." Elucido knew in an instant that death was not the answer—at least not for him. As he turned toward the entrance of the cavern, filled with a renewed sense of hope, focusing on the bravery and light of his brother's memory, Elucido felt a newfound warmth come over him. The Nullblights entered the cavern, and with a swiftness that was new to Elucido, he charged them fervently.

He threw his right arm in a large circle, focusing on the memories of Frater and him playing in the yard as young children. A small flash illuminated the cavern as a series of red sparks flew from his fist, none of which bared any significance in the impending fight with the Nullblights. Again, he swung, throwing both fists horizontally toward his center, focusing on his memories of the ceremony that inducted Frater into the Defenders of Light. This time, a small burst of flame carried itself forward, fizzling only moments after its formation. Elucido was only a few steps from the Nullblights' position; he would have to act quickly if he wanted to overtake them. His focus now shifted to the battle that took his brother's life. Channeling the bravery he had seen Frater demonstrate so often, he raised his hands once again. The Nullblights turned to meet Elucido, but it was too late. His hands formed a cradle from which a bright, swirling red light emanated. Before the Nullblights could defend themselves, a burst of fire spewed from the Red Light Elemental, incinerating the dark beings with a burning red illumination brighter than any fire Elucido had ever built. As Elucido came to a stop, the beings' smoldering bodies warmed him and ignited a new fire within his soul.

He had done it. The Red Elemental Orb floated around his body as if it were a shield, ready for his use whenever he needed it. As it orbited, it illuminated his surroundings, increasing his visibility of the obstacles he now faced in the marshland. He had gained an added advantage—not only in his ability to navigate, but in his ability to defend himself against foes far greater than he expected he would ever be capable of vanquishing. The feelings of loneliness and despair melted with the warmth of the light he now possessed and were quickly replaced with hope. He was not alone, after all.

Elucido emerged from the cavern and entered the marshland with cautious optimism, for the first time feeling like he may be capable of learning to use the Elemental powers and fight for his survival, despite the fear the Shadow Garrison still brought upon him. His search for the next Aether Orb shard would be easier by the light of the Red Elemental. But that illumination did not come without a price. The increase in his ability to see in the darkness would attract unwanted attention from the Shadow Garrison. If he could see the world more clearly, they undoubtedly could find him more easily. He would have to keep his alertness with unfaltering diligence. At present, however, none of that mattered compared to the inspiration he felt.

He continued along the pathway leading into the marshes. Not only was the ground soft and full of sunken voids, there was an overgrowth of thorny shrubs that made traversal difficult. Elucido meandered slowly due to the harsh obstacles, but continued to progress, nonetheless. Any time he reached a point in the pathway blocked by the thorns, he placed his hands into a cradle shape, focused on hope, and incinerated the blockage. The ashy remains left a trail that he could use to track his progress and make sure he was not getting lost or wandering in circles. This allowed him to navigate expertly—but the path was still treacherous, full of unknown dangers.

As he rounded a sharp bend in the pathway, Elucido's footing gave way on a soft patch of earth. He tumbled down a long, steep hill in a dizzying spiral. With both his tunic and pride covered in mud, he brought himself to an upright position and regained his orientation. Before him stood an old building, dilapidated and covered in moss. It had not been inhabited in some time. Despite its emptiness, the building held a gravitas that Elucido could not ignore. There was something about this location that bore significance. "Why would someone go to all the trouble of setting up a home in the middle of a soggy, godforsaken bog like this?" Elucido understood the allure of introversion, but this seemed extreme. He figured that someone must have been hiding something of value here.

Two torches marked the entrance to the building, covered in dust, but presumably still functional. Using his new powers with increasing ease, Elucido summoned a bolt of fire upon each of the torches, lighting the entrance to the building. Inside, he found modest furnishings, but very little in the way of other possessions. The floorboards creaked as he walked, whimpering with every step he took. He completed his inspection in no time, as there was not much to check. The single room was large, but the most prominent feature he could identify was the thick layer of dust that had been gathering for quite some time.

Elucido pulled the Aether Orb shard from the leather pouch resting on his hip to see if its resonance would offer more information as to the whereabouts of the next shard. It was not leading him in any direction, but vibrated with a slow, rhythmic pulse. "Perhaps the shard is nearer than I thought." Elucido swept the room once again, paying closer attention to see if there was something he missed. He had traveled this deep into the bog and was unwilling to let the next light shard elude him.

He felt the creak of every step he took as he walked through the room in a sequence of lines parallel to the floorboards. Once, twice, three times he walked the floor, hoping to see something he had missed. He saw nothing new on each passing traversal, frustration and weariness growing with every step he took. That is, until it hit him—he was not seeing anything new, but he was focusing on the wrong sense. Near the southwest corner of the room, on his fifth lap, there was a single floorboard that sounded different when he stepped on it. He hadn't heard it before, but there was no doubt—this floorboard did not echo the creak when tread upon. There was something below it that warranted further investigation.

Kneeling on the hard floor and taking a sharp tool from his satchel, Elucido removed the floorboard with modest effort. As he lifted the floorboard, a light shone through the new opening. In disbelief, Elucido lifted another shard of the Aether Orb from the floor and placed it in his collection. The two shards resonated in harmony, issuing a gentle tug on Elucido's bag, presumably in the direction of the next shard. Who had found and hidden this shard was a mystery to Elucido. For now, he was simply grateful to them for keeping it safe and hidden from the powers of darkness.

After reversing his steps back out of the marshland, Elucido gathered his composure, brushed what dirt he could from his clothing, and pulled the shards from his pouch. The shards tugged him upward and to the north, indicating an extreme change in elevation that urged his thoughts in a singular direction. "There must be a light shard near the impassable mountains of the north". The passage to the mountains would not be brief. Though the trail was easy to walk, it amassed a great distance he would have to navigate in near-total darkness.

The sharp peaks of the northern mountains, known as the "Glacies Mons," were foreboding, even for the most seasoned mountaineers. In the light, they created a serrated ridge across the skyline, covered in glaciers of white and blue. Even the valleys between mountain tops were treacherous, covered in icy sinkholes that were created by the constant freezing and melting of the streams that flowed through the glacial range into the cold, clear lakes below. Many people had died over the years while trying to traverse the range to reach the beautiful golden coastline north of the mountains. Elucido had never considered an attempt to pass over the mountain range. It was too daunting and not worth the risk—until now.

As he made the five-day trek toward the mountains, Elucido tried to plan another way through the treacherous range. He had no experience mountaineering and was filled with trepidation at the thought of falling into a glacial sinkhole. His stubborn unwillingness to risk his life crossing over the mountains pushed his mind to wonder if the glaciers that had carved the mountains over time, and created the labyrinth of crevasses and sinkholes, may have carved a way for him to navigate under the glacier to reach the other side of the range. Perhaps, if he didn't want to hike over the mountain range, he could move underneath it.

Elucido spent three days wandering the base of the foothills in search of crevasses or caverns that could lead to a way through the mountains. He stretched his mind, exploring the depths of his research as aggressively as he explored the terrain before him. There had to be something that he had read about that could offer some insight into how to pass through the mountains. Try as he might, no memory formed of anyone finding a safe passage underneath the icy range. The only thing he was sure of was that the cold described in the texts was wholly insufficient in preparing him for the immeasurable iciness that had seeped through to the marrow of his bones. The weariness his muscles felt from the constant shivering grew increasingly heavy.

Survival was Elucido's first goal; if he froze to death, his search for the Aether Orb shards will have been in vain. He stopped to set up camp, though he had no experience sheltering in such an icy environment. Using a large boulder to block the wind, he draped his cloak over a branch, creating a tent-like structure that secured him from the wind chill. Some nearby kindling, coupled with the fire of the Red Elemental, served as a good fire starter, and he was able to warm his hands as he cooked some mushrooms over the open flame. His stomach filled with a warm meal, and the red coals of the fire heating his shelter, he finally slept.

On the third day, exhausted and out of ideas, Elucido sat on a large boulder to gather his thoughts. He closed his eyes and held his face as he breathed in the fresh, albeit frigid, mountain air. Returning his focus to the base of the hills, he scanned as much of the terrain as he could. It was hard to see the hills, and even harder to see if there was a way through. Elucido crafted several small Red Elemental Orbs and fired them like flares toward the hillside. The first three orbs struck the side of the hill, leaving a residual amber glow on the snowy ground. The fourth orb, however, disappeared into a large crevice at the base of one of the rolling mounds of snow. This, he thought, might be his way to the other side of the icy mountains.

Entering the small crack with cautious optimism, Elucido cinched the strap of his satchel tighter, to ensure he did not lose its contents in the depths of the glacial shaft. The only comfort afforded to Elucido in this dangerous crevasse was the illumination of his surroundings—a luxury afforded him by the vibrant light emitted from the Aether Orb shards. One advantage of such a small space was that the light from his shards reflected broadly across the icy surfaces, giving him full visibility of his surroundings. He had not experienced this level of brightness and exposure since before the darkness took hold. As his eyes took a few moments to adjust to the illumination, his fear was slowly replaced with wonder and awe at the sheer beauty of the blue ice that now surrounded him.

Minutes of frigid navigation turned to hours as Elucido delved deeper into the maze of caverns and crevasses that lay beneath the mountain peaks. He wondered now if the labyrinth would ever end, or if he would become lost in an icy tomb forever. His eyes grew weary from the constant illumination within the caverns, and he was tired. Elucido needed to rest but was afraid that he would be unable to find his bearings if he stopped for too long.

Almost instinctively, Elucido shifted his focus away from the blinding reflections of the icy walls. He hoped to extend the endurance of his vision by finding pockets of dull, rocky surfaces within what he feared was now his glacial prison. The increasing tightness of the cavern seemed to suffocate Elucido, fear of entrapment growing within him. A cold sweat dampened his shirt as his heart raced. The space felt as if it was closing in, trapping him in an ever-shrinking tomb of ice. He had never felt this type of panic before; his body screaming at him to run, but his mind was powerless to tell it where to go. Unable to calm himself, Elucido ran, directionless. Speed, however, was not Elucido's friend in such a slippery place. He struggled to keep his footing, especially while shifting his gaze toward the shadows and away from his direction of travel. He had to calm himself and stay warm. In that moment, Elucido realized he had an ally far more powerful than icy fear—he could control the Red Elemental, and its warm, fiery powers.

Elucido stopped, took a deep breath, relaxed his shoulders, and focused his energy on controlling the red orb that now formed around him. As the orb grew, he felt the warmth it provided. Along with that warmth, Elucido felt a renewed sense of hope and energy.

The orb's powers were far more than a physical manifestation of light and fire. They were the embodiment of faith, optimism, and hope. In its warmth, he truly believed that he would find a way to the other side of the mountains.

None of this optimism helped reduce the strain of the light on his eyes, however. He had lived in the darkness following the Great Cataclysm for so long that the physiology of his eyes had adapted almost completely to the absence of light. The fullness of the illumination in the caverns was becoming nearly as challenging to his weary eyes as the slippery cavern floor was to his frozen feet. Focusing on the dim parts of his surroundings, Elucido noticed something that made his heart flutter. There was a patch of total darkness in the far reaches of the cavern in which he stood. Total darkness could only mean one thing—the light was not being reflected back into the opening of the cave at that location.

"If the light can escape the cavern, then perhaps so can I!" he thought. As he approached the darkness in the cavern wall, he stepped through an opening that was not much bigger than the opening he used to enter the glacial maze hours ago. Squeezing through, he found himself in a place he never imagined he would ever step foot. He had reached the Golden Shores of the north.

The utter beauty of the shores struck Elucido, despite the limited light from the Red Elemental Orb and the shards of the Aether Orb he carried. Rocky foothills gave way to the delicate golden sands of the beach. The shoreline extended as far as he could see, the light from his shards fading before the beach ended. He smelled the salt of the ocean as the mist from the waves hit his face. The water, much to his surprise, was warm and soothing. The sand, however, is what he found the most inspiring. He had never felt such a soft, comforting footing in his life. He took a moment to lie on the comfortable sandy ground, stretch his back, and relax with a smile so big his frozen cheeks hurt.

This sanctuary gave Elucido a much-needed break. He was so comfortable here that, for a moment, he wondered if he could just make this his permanent hiding place and live out the rest of his days in peaceful isolation. He knew that this would not be possible. If darkness were to fully extinguish light from the land, not even these luscious golden shores would be safe from the roaming creatures of darkness.

Elucido refocused on his goal. He had to find the next shard of the Aether Orb. Grasping the two shards he possessed, he navigated to the western part of the shore. There were no obstacles in his path, though he found walking on the soft sand to be difficult and tiring. As he approached the edge of the beach, he could see a faint glow from underneath the sand. He dug a shallow trench with his bare hands and found it—the next shard was now in his possession. This confirmed his suspicions that the shards of the great Aether Orbs had dispersed quite widely when they shattered in the Great Cataclysm, reaching even the most remote regions of the world.

The three shards in his possession now resonated with one another with a powerful energy that drove him toward the deepest valley in the land. The Valley of Shadows in the southernmost part of Ren would be his next destination. But first, he had to say goodbye to his safe, sandy haven, backtrack through the glacial labyrinth, and find his way back across the continent to the south. It took him nearly ten days to complete his reversal through the caverns and arrive near the continent's southernmost point.

Skeletons lined the pathway into the Valley of Shadows in what he could only describe as a descent of death, decay, and darkness. The darkness in this place was stronger than that on the other parts of the continent. It was as if the valley accelerated the siphoning of hope because of the evil that lived within. Elucido's confidence faded as rapidly as the light of his shards, whose brilliance could not overcome the entropy of the valley. Even with three light shards in hand, his visibility had returned to nearly nothing. He had never heard of anyone who returned from their exploration of the Valley of Darkness, and now he feared he would join those who came before him.

Chapter 6

Fire and Sulfur

The ground had a distinct, pungent odor that Elucido identified as a cross between rotting leaves, burning sulfur, and an iron-like musk that almost certainly came from the stains of dried blood on the surrounding rocks. Death certainly knew its place here, and Elucido hoped with all that was within him that he would not become acquainted with death while on this journey. Loneliness was a far better companion, even in these dark times.

As he trudged through the murky path, Elucido could hear large bursts of air pushing through the rocks in a forceful eruption of sulfuric gas that reached far into the sky above him. Uncertain of the harm they might cause, he took care to avoid areas where he heard these high-pressure bursts. These hazards only slowed his progress toward his undefined waypoint. Elucido did not think that these bursts of sulfur caused the many deaths in the area, however. Based on the grisly scattering of bones and dried blood, he suspected something far worse had wreaked this havoc.

Moving deeper into the darkness, Elucido had to rely more and more on his other senses. Despite his experience navigating the darkness, it was a feeling he was still not comfortable with, especially in this extreme environment. Listening carefully for the sounds of the brimstone bursts, he inched forward, following the slow pull of the light shards in his satchel. Burst. Pause. Repeat. The rhythmic expulsions had a cadence to them that Elucido learned to anticipate. The next burst, however, did not sound quite the same as the last.

With a whooshing sound, Elucido heard the air moving in a swirling, almost dive-like pattern through the sky. This was not a burst of air—it was a creature, moving through the sky with precision, unaffected by the all-consuming darkness. Elucido ducked as he heard the sound coming closer to him. As the whooshing passed, his senses told him that this creature was large—at least two meters across in wingspan. It passed again, this time grazing his shoulder with what he assumed was a large claw. Crying out in pain, Elucido grabbed his wounded shoulder, falling to his knees. He had to think quickly if he wanted to survive the next pass.

Burst. Pause. Burst. Pause. Elucido's ears registered the timing and locations of the sulfur bursts as he listened for the contrast of the distinctive whooshing sound of his dangerous dark foe. Taking two steps to his right and one step backward, Elucido followed the whooshing sound of the winged creature as it approached again. As it neared his location, he heard the beginnings of the sulfur burst, opening up for another forceful barrage of air. He fired a burst from the Red Elemental at the sulfur, trying to catch the beast in a pillar of flame. The fire spewed upward, missing the beast and nearly igniting Elucido's cloak. As the beast turned to avoid the flames, it struck him with its wing, sending him rolling backwards.

Elucido stood, shifting his gaze in all directions, searching for the creature and listening for another sulfur vent that he could use to continue his assault. He heard the whooshing of the wind as the creature flew past him again; this time too late to react. The beast picked him up with its massive talons, throwing him across the path and into a stone wall. Elucido fought to catch his breath, uncertain where the beast had retreated. He rose from the dirt, captured a deep breath, and listened to the sound of the sulfur pillar that he was now standing beside.

With expert timing, Elucido swung his arms in a circular motion, summoned the Red Elemental, and sent a small burst of fire toward the sulfur spring. The gas ignited in an incredible pillar of flame that illuminated the area brightly. Just as the pillar of flame rose, Elucido saw the winged creature on its descent toward him. It was gargantuan, its wingspan reaching nearly three times Elucido's height, bright red-orange feathers fluttering in the sharp wind created by the blazing ignition. The creature did not expect Elucido's powerful spell, nor the flames it would produce. It recognized the danger too late. The pillar of flames shot upwards violently, shaking the ground and engulfing the beast.

As quickly as the pillar of fire shot upwards, the sulfur burst stopped, extinguishing the flames from the sky—but not those that consumed the winged terror. The beast still writhed on the ground, smoldering and moaning in pain as it took its final smoke-filled breaths. Despite the pain in his chest and gash on his shoulder that was sure to leave a scar, Elucido had achieved victory. He was starting to believe that his skills in combat were growing and would be sufficient to see him through his journey. Straightening his shirt, he reminded himself not to let his confidence become his downfall.

With the creature felled and his pride firmly back under his control, Elucido carried on into the darkness of the valley in search of the light shard. Listening carefully, he heard no sounds aside from the bursting of the sulfur pits. "This beast may have been the sole cause of this destruction," he thought aloud. He felt safer now, though he took care not to let his guard down too soon.

Grasping at the light shards once again, Elucido followed their pull toward the depths of the valley and into a large rock outcropping that was filled with sand and pebbles. Feeling around on the ground for the shard, Elucido felt a thin, sharp object that cut his hand. He recoiled at the object's sharpness, then slowly reached back in and carefully picked it up, holding the light shard close enough to see the object. It was the empty shell of an egg. He was standing in the nest of the creature he killed only moments ago. If there were eggs, he thought, that must mean that more of these winged beasts could be nearby. He was not out of danger yet.

He pushed the rock, sand, and eggshells aside until he was able to find and extract another light shard from the nest. With renewed vigor, he raced back toward the entrance to the valley, listening for any additional airborne hazards. Reaching the edge of the valley, and continuing on for some distance, Elucido stopped to catch his breath. He had done what, to his knowledge, no one before him had—he had escaped the clutches of death in the Valley of Shadows with only a minor wound as a souvenir.

Lining up the shards and attempting to join them into a single orb, Elucido could see that his collection of shards was nearly complete, missing what appeared to be only one piece. Gazing upon the incomplete, shattered orb, he sensed the attunement of the shards and could feel an intense pull in a new direction. He paused, put the shards back in his satchel, removed and realigned them again, and re-tested their feedback. Again, the same response. Trying a third time, as if placing the shards back in his satchel might reset them and return a different result, he stored, then removed the shards, searching for direction. His heart sank as the results remained unaltered—this destination was the least desirable location on the whole of the continent. The shards were pointing him toward the ruins of the old fortress at Kaumaren.

The fortress was a place that haunted Elucido's dreams—it was his brother, Frater's, first and last posting with the Light Defender's battalion. Before the Great Battle, it served as an outpost near the tower of Ren. The Defenders of Light used this post to assess potential threats to the tower and issue early warnings to their commanders. All of that changed when Caligo's forces overran the fortress with darkness. While Elucido had no specific memories regarding the moments leading up to the Great Battle since he had awakened in the darkness, he knew with certainty that this stronghold was his brother's final resting place.

The ruins of the fortress had changed shape significantly during the battle. The creatures of darkness wreaked havoc on the structure, felling walls and razing watchtowers to the ground. All that remained standing were pieces of the stone wall, scattered in an array of useless fortifications. The ruins were still teeming with Nullblights, as if they drew strength and satisfaction from living in the aftermath of their destruction during the Great Battle.

Elucido had never visited the ruins. There was no point in risking the extreme danger—at least until now. In order to stand a chance against the barrage of enemies that awaited him, he would have to formulate a plan that offered a significant strategic advantage. Foolhardiness would not suffice in such an important encounter. He knew he'd been fortunate up to this point and that luck was bound to run out. The Shadow Garrison was too strong for him to risk his success to mere chance. Thankfully, his long trek to the ruins would provide him ample time to work out a plan and practice controlling the Red Elemental with more precision. Four days later, he arrived in a place he had hoped he would never have to visit.

Despite the fortress being on high ground, Elucido could approach from the south with relative stealth. Maintaining a reasonable distance so as not to be seen or heard by the creatures contained within, Elucido perched himself atop a large boulder in order to see if he could discern the layout of the ruins with what little light existed in the area. He could see nothing, at least not without risking being seen by his foes. The only way he could identify any strategic advantage would be in the heat of the moment, and at close range. That was, at least, what he initially thought.

An idea hit Elucido with absolute clarity. "What if I can create a distraction—an illusion of an attack with a larger force? If I can convince the enemies that I am not alone, the confusion would split their focus and allow me to pick them off one-by-one." Elucido had the power of the Red Elemental that he could summon now almost as naturally as he could walk. This would help him create the illusion of several attackers that would help distract his enemies. He knew that this power would give him an advantage against these creatures that made his plan for victory much more plausible. He would have to act quickly and make swift decisions to keep the illusion believable and divide the enemy forces.

After what felt like an agonizingly long several minutes of visualization and emotional preparation, Elucido was ready to strike. He moved his hands in the circular motion he was now so accustomed to, but before the red orb was ready to fire, he knelt down and tucked his elbows closer to his body. Rather than dispel the orb into a single fireball, Elucido built the energy up for longer than usual, withholding the energy of the fireball for as long as he could. When he felt that the power of the Elemental Orb was too great for him to contain, he stood up and thrust his arms forward, leaning into the push of energy. At this moment, a surge of several fireballs swirled forward, weaving around one another in a well-choreographed display of fiery beauty. The fireballs spread out in an array of heat and light, hitting the fortress in seven different locations. The fiery barrage lit up the sky with a ruddy glow, giving Elucido ample views to plan his next move.

The beasts scattered in all directions, trying to assess the threat, leaving a lone Nullblight at the southernmost entrance to the ruins. Elucido acted swiftly, sending another single fireball directly into the face of the lone confused Nullblight, killing it instantly. This gave him safe entry into the ruins, where he could now use the remaining structures as cover while he evaluated his next action.

Luck, as it turns out, would still play a role in Elucido's assault. He noticed a pool of tar on the edge of the ruins. Without hesitation, he fired another burst of red light toward the tar, igniting it with an explosive force, sending two nearby Nullblights into a deadly aerial spin far above the highest remaining point of the ruins. This cleared the way for Elucido to advance further. Taking a new position much closer to the burning tar pit, he saw three Nullblights approaching him. He caught two of them in the chest with fireballs, killing them before they could reach his position. The third, however, was now too close for an Elemental burst. He rolled forward on the ground toward the creature, unsheathing his dagger mid-roll. As the Nullblight dove over Elucido, they exchanged swipes of their pointed weapons. The Nullblight's claw grazed Elucido's back, creating a shallow, insignificant cut. The Nullblight landed on its feet as Elucido stood at the ready. Pausing for a moment, the Nullblight looked Elucido in the eyes, then fell to the ground, an excess of blood spilling from its soft belly. Elucido's strike had landed, and it now registered with him how successful his assault had been.

"That's five." Elucido said as the fifth foe dropped to the ground. Beyond the crackling of the burning tar pit, Elucido listened carefully for any other movement, while using the red glow from the blazing grounds to look for any living thing that could still be a threat. He stood for several seconds, chest heaving with breath, before reaching the conclusion that he had reigned victorious. His throat tightened, tears building in the corner of his eyes as he reflected on the significance of his achievement. This was the first time since his brother's death that the fortress had been under control of a Defender of Light, a title Elucido bestowed upon himself in this triumphant moment. This was not only a victory for Elucido's survival, but a symbolic victory against the forces of darkness. If Elucido could take back this fortification, it might be possible for him to take a larger stand and gain significant ground against the Shadow Garrison. But the weight of that burden overwhelmed him.

For now, he shifted his focus back to a simpler objective. The final light shard should be nearby. The light from the burning tar pits made it significantly harder to see the glow from the light shard, but he searched, nonetheless. After some time analyzing the fallen structures, he uncovered a wooden chest that lay underneath a pile of fallen stone bricks. Breaking the chest open with the back end of his dagger, he pulled the final light shard from within the ruins.

In the distance, a voice whispered quietly. While Elucido could not hear the voice, he felt the message all the same. The hair raised on the back of his neck and a chill ran through his spine as the message resonated within him. *"Let him come to me—I will efface this insignificant being from my land with rapture. His soul belongs to me now; this is the point at which his name ceases to exist."*

Chapter 7

Melding of the Light

Onymos watched as Elucido approached the tower of Ren. The moment had come for Onymos to begin his rancorous elimination of the emergent threat to his power. A rare look of pleasure crossed his face as he snapped his fingers, his dark minions quickly moving to their positions throughout the tower. They knew their role—weaken Elucido, but do not kill him. Onymos wanted him dead, but at his hands. Once Elucido was eliminated, he could report back to the Dark Lord in Umbra for his praise and what would likely be a handsome reward.

Elucido, fueled by his newfound ability to control the Red Light Elemental, and beaming with pride having found all the light shards on the continent of Ren, approached the tower with reluctant confidence. He was not sure what dangers may lie within, but he believed now, more than ever, that it was his destiny to reassemble the light shards to complete the Aether Orb and restore light to the continent. He was ready to face the danger, test his new powers, and conquer the darkness that had held a stranglehold on the continent of Ren for far too long.

As he approached the main tower, he found the door was locked with a complex mechanism of metal gears and panels. It appeared as though the mechanism could be shifted, but despite his best efforts, Elucido could not get the lock's gears to move. He hit it with a barrage of fireballs, yet still nothing in the lock would budge. "There must be a trick to convince these stubborn metal parts to move," thought Elucido as he pried upon the door, to no avail. Failing to find a way to move beyond the doorway, he pulled the shards of the Aether Orb from his satchel, hoping they would guide him in a new direction, as they had so reliably done in the past. As he moved the shards past the obstinate lock to illuminate them further, the mechanism surrendered with ease, following the light from the shards in an elegant pattern, resulting in the harmonious unlocking of the iron-clad door.

As the door slowly swung open with a smooth creaking sound, Elucido breached the entryway and crossed into the foyer at the base of the tower. It felt as if he was being invited into whatever hidden dangers were lurking in the darkness. In order to reach the throne room where the Aether Orb once sat upon its marble pedestal, he would have to climb each of the levels of the palace, uncertain how closely guarded the castle would be inside. Before he could reach the other side of the room, however, Elucido collapsed.

A man entered the empty throne room in the Palace of Ren in the dead of night. Resting in its place on the pillar near the center of the room was an Aether orb, fully intact. In his hand he held a tattered roll of aged parchment. Unrolling the parchment, he saw the structural makeup of the orbs with a newfound clarity. He understood their design and purpose as if he had made them himself. Tapping the orb gently with a metal rod, he listened to the ringing sound from the glassy object. It sounded like a tuning fork, resonating in a constant high pitch that seemed to last for an eternity before slowly fading back into quiet. Shining a red light on the orb, he tapped it again. This time, the pitch of the sound was different, lower than before. He continued to test the resonating pitches under different wavelengths of light, each one providing a unique sound. Combining all lights together into a bright white light, he tapped once more. It sounded as though each of the individual color's pitches resonated in perfect harmony, juxtaposed against one another in perfect composition. This was the confirmation that he needed—years of research had validated his theories—he knew that the one who controlled the Light Elementals would also control the Aether Orbs, and therefore, the fate of the world itself.

Waking from another evocative vision, Elucido understood it would be possible to re-assemble the Aether Orb and restore light to the land. However, to rejoin all the orbs in full harmony, he would need to uncover the secrets of the Light Elementals and harness their full power. His first goal was to reassemble the first Aether Orb and regain control over the darkness that continued its stronghold over the continent of Ren. He could worry about the other towers later.

It did not take long for the first danger to materialize. Four Nullblights entered the room, shrieking voices announcing their presence—an advantage that they rarely gave their prey. It was as if they were taunting him and pushing him to attack and make a mistake that they could pounce upon. He took the bait, only briefly wondering if his impulsiveness returned the advantage to the hungry Nullblights.

As he moved forward, the floor crumbled, giving way to gaping holes where his feet once tread; it was a trap. Moving quickly, Elucido analyzed his footing while approaching the Nullblights. A pattern of stable ground appeared as the stones gave way. Elucido knew that once he reached the enemy, a retreat would be difficult, if not impossible. He would have to play this round with an aggressiveness he was not sure he was prepared to take. His haste to advance had forced his hand, and he would have to live or die with the consequences.

Without hesitation, Elucido summoned his fiery friend in a bursting flame that orbited him in a protective crimson light. This provided a small radial barrier that would protect him from the flurry of attacks brought by the Nullblights. As they swung in his direction, he focused on maintaining a sure footing on the balance beam that was now the palace floor. Dodging glancing blows, Elucido was able to get small strikes in with his dagger, and the Red Light Elemental, but nothing significant enough to dispatch the creatures. He noticed, however, the creatures were not engaging him with the same vigor as their counterparts had in the fortress.

It was as if they had no intention of killing him—they were simply having fun torturing him.

This provided Elucido with clarity in his response. If the creatures were not aiming to kill him, it must be at the direction of some other authority. After all, Nullblights were well known for their swift and ruthless destruction. No one had ever reported them "having fun" with their prey. The advantage, as it would seem, shifted in Elucido's favor. He could leverage their unwillingness to kill by charging forward. He only hoped he was correct in this assumption.

Kneeling, Elucido folded his arms across his chest and summoned a raging burst of fire that moved outward in a perfect circle. As the fire spiraled into a tornado-like cylinder, it knocked all the dark creatures to the ground. Elucido pounced on the first with cat-like agility, plunging his dagger into its throat and releasing a fountain of blood onto the holy floor. Looking up, he saw the next enemy rising to its feet. Elucido made quick work of this foe, sending a large fireball directly into its face before it could come to a full stand, dropping it once again to the floor, lifeless. The two remaining Nullblights were slow to their feet, having taken the larger share of the forceful fire twister. They leapt toward Elucido, over their two fallen allies, spanning the gaping void where the stony floor had stood. As they reached Elucido's position, they were greeted by two pillars of flame, one in each of Elucido's clenched fists. Elucido's fiery punches landed firmly in the center of each Nullblight's chest, creating a shockwave of flame that radiated outward, exploding the chests of his enemies with a concussive blast of death and destruction.

The first wave of enemies had passed. Elucido gasped for air, as the encounter had ended so swiftly that he almost forgot to breathe. He had reached the other side of the open foyer and now found himself at the base of the stairs. "Upward is the only choice I have now," he muttered aloud, pondering what else awaited him on his dark ascent to the throne room.

The second floor of the palace had once been used to house foreign dignitaries and hold various meetings and diplomatic discussions. As such, there were several partitions and small rooms scattered throughout. Since the palace's conversion, started by Onymos after taking control of the tower, the rooms had been connected with a winding pathway that meandered in a zigzag of confusing corridors. Even worse than the confounding nature of the layout, the rooms were littered with traps that Elucido supposed only their designer and inner circle knew how to navigate. Elucido learned of these traps the hard way. As he took his first step into the pathway, an icy arrow zipped past his head, nearly embedding itself in the side of his skull. Staggering backward, Elucido ducked, now even more wary of the concealed dangers that lay ahead.

Snapping his fingers, Elucido summoned a small flame in the palm of his left hand, illuminating the corridor and allowing him to analyze where potential traps may be placed. As he rounded the first corner, he saw a small hole in the wall where, presumably, another ice arrow awaited his passing. Rolling past the hole's location quickly, Elucido dodged the projectile as it left its housing and whooshed past him. As long as he could see the traps, he stood a chance. In a well-choreographed sequence of dodging, rolling, sliding, and twisting, Elucido passed unscathed through the corridor and into a larger, open room.

There was something about this room that caused Elucido further pause. He felt an unusual chill about this place, as if the air itself was frozen. This was no ordinary cold; it was manufactured specifically for this space. Watching every heaving breath materialize in a plume of frosty vapor, his muscles tightened to the point at which they became nearly unusable. The piercing cold was nothing like the cold he felt in the glaciers of the north. It numbed not only every extremity in his body but seemed to paralyze even the core of his soul.

With what little movement he could muster, Elucido summoned the Red Light Elemental into a shallow orbit around his core. It provided the warmth needed for him to continue, albeit at a much slower pace than before. For now, at least, he could combat the inhospitable environment he now entered.

As he moved closer to the center of the frigid room, Elucido noticed the light from his Elemental behaving erratically. He watched the symmetry of the swirls decay into a random dispersion of light into the dark void that lay ahead. Slowly, the randomness took shape, re-assembling into a swirling pattern, but this time moving away from its comfortable orbit around Elucido, and toward a singular point in the distance. It was in this moment, Elucido could make out the vague silhouette of a monstrosity he hadn't for even a moment considered he would encounter. Forcing his brows together through their numbness, he could make out the shape with unquestionable detail. It was the creature he feared more than anything in the world—a Tenebrae.

Elucido had heard descriptions of these beasts, but had never seen one in person. The very mention of their name struck fear into all. Even the esteemed generals in the Shadow Garrison held these creatures in the highest respect, knowing that at any moment they could turn and devour their masters. Fearing that he was far outmatched, Elucido knew that the only way to reach the top of the tower and reassemble the Aether Orb was to defeat this beast. He held his breath, focused his energy, and started the battle.

The light from Elucido's Red Elemental was no match for this beast. Every carmine beam of light that he fired at it was swiftly absorbed into its swirling belly and quickly converted to pitch black. Every burst of flame he sent at the beast was consumed in the vacuous abdomen of his ignoble adversary. Even the powerfully charged bursts that hurled multitudes of blazing projectiles were no match for the beast. The spirals of flame entered a short orbit around the creature and were quickly absorbed into oblivion. The Tenebrae stared at Elucido, unfazed, yet still unwavering in following its directive not to destroy the palace guest.

Elucido and the beast exchanged blows—none of Elucido's strikes effecting the beast. Every strike from his Elemental was deflected or absorbed and immediately matched with a counterstrike. Elucido changed his position, circling the Tenebrae, searching for any points of weakness. Nothing he tried worked; the beast was simply too strong. After several fruitless exchanges, the beast charged at Elucido, losing its patience and abandoning its directive to leave Elucido unharmed. He evaded the beast's efforts to bring him down through a series of agile side steps and rolls, but he was tiring quickly. He needed to find a way to get the best of the Tenebrae, but he wasn't sure how he would manage. Time was running out, every passing moment bringing him closer to exhaustion and death.

"I need to bring this beast down," Elucido shouted, as if there was an ally nearby to aid him in his efforts. "Down!" he shouted louder in a much more exclamatory tone. He remembered the floor below had caved into a series of chasms that led to an endless abyss. If he could force the beast into one opening, he may end the tiresome encounter for good. He shifted his stance and charged his Red Light Elemental to full capacity. Rushing toward the Tenebrae in a sprint, Elucido caught it off guard—it did not expect this level of aggression from a mere human. It took one step backward as Elucido approached its position. As he neared the Tenebrae, Elucido placed the fully charged Elemental Orb on the floor and immediately shot a fireball at the Tenebrae's head. The confounded beast ducked beneath the fireball just in time for Elucido to dive over its head. As Elucido passed over the brute's position, he fired one more ball of fire—this time into the fully charged orb he had left at the feet of the Tenebrae.

The Elemental Orb detonated upon impact, creating a loud cacophony of fiery crackles and shrieks from the dark being. He had stunned, but not killed, the Tenebrae. That was inconsequential—Elucido had not intended to kill the beast with the blast. In fact, he assumed the explosion would not cause significant damage. As the enraged Tenebrae turned to face Elucido, it took a gargantuan step forward. However, as its mangled foot touched the cold surface of the stony floor, it caved in. The beast, unable to recover and gain its balance, tumbled through the rapidly expanding opening in the floor.

Elucido briskly approached the edge of his destructive blast. As he reached the perimeter, he saw the Tenebrae plummeting beyond the hard floor on the first level of the palace, and into darkness. Elucido fired a quick burst of fire toward the falling creature, knowing that the light would follow it on its way down. He observed the light of the fireball moving further away, its light slowly dying as it continued into the depths of the pit below. It was unlikely that the beast would be returning from the bottom of its cold grave. Collapsing from exhaustion, Elucido forgot for a moment how cold the floor felt upon his face.

He had done it—he felled one of the elite members of the Shadow Garrison. It had not been easy, but that made the achievement even more satisfying. Elucido's smile beamed as he thought of the pride his brother would have felt for him in this moment of victory.

"One more floor," thought Elucido. "The pillar in the throne room sits directly above me—I can assemble the orb soon enough. *Lux Superesse Est.*"

As he reached the third floor of the palace, the cold seemed to sharpen. It felt as if the temperature of the room itself was advertising how unwelcome he was in this place. The throne room appeared empty, the open windows allowing a breeze to pass through that was colder than the room itself. In the center of the room, precisely where Elucido remembered it, sat an ornate pillar of stone where the Aether Orb once rested, illuminating the continent of Ren. His objective was nearly complete; all he had to do was place the shards on the pillar and merge them once again.

"Hello there, Elucido." A feathery voice reached his ears through the sound of the wind in the room. "I would welcome you, but I truly don't enjoy having company. Still, I am looking forward to our encounter. I will tolerate your presence for the time being, but rest assured, your stay will be brief."

"Who are you?" Elucido replied.

"Ah yes, forgive me. I am not used to having guests in my home. I am Onymos, General of the Shadow Garrison, and one of Caligo's most trusted men. Have you not heard of me?"

Feeling a sense of familiarity about the man who now emerged from the shadows and into the center of the tower, Elucido furrowed his brow.

"I have no recollection of meeting you before," Elucido answered.

"Your knowledge of me is inconsequential—I shall kill you regardless, and then obliterate those pathetic luminous shards that you carry." Onymos laughed, continuing to move toward Elucido.

"Why do you want to destroy the light? What could you possibly gain from bringing hopelessness to the land?" Elucido's tone grew more erratic and fearful as he questioned Onymos.

"There is so much to gain from hopelessness. Don't you see? Without light, without hope, what remains is the purest power. With no one to love, you have no one to lose; and when you have nothing to lose, you have nothing to fear. Darkness is freedom. And I intend to annihilate the remaining light from the land and bring all of creation into that freedom."

"You're crazy!" Elucido bellowed. "No one believes that! Without hope, there is no meaning, no significance in life. You are truly a monster if you think that there is life in darkness."

"You and I are not so different," scoffed Onymos, his eyes locked intently on Elucido's. "If you were in my shoes, you would act the same way." He taunted Elucido, taking pleasure in his verbal torment.

"I would never stoop to your level!" Elucido spoke with rage in his voice, offended at the notion that he could be anything like the monster he stood before.

"Enough banter. My capacity for social niceties has diminished. I will end you and erase your name from history. I would tell you to prepare yourself for the inevitable, but truthfully, it does not matter how prepared you think you are. Your demise is imminent."

Onymos pushed his fists toward the ground and, in a swell of energy, a bright blue light formed an icy pattern on the floor at his feet. The blue light continued to swirl around him similarly to the Red Light Elemental Elucido had mastered. Could this be the second Light Elemental he had seen in his vision? If so, Elucido knew he may face an entirely different type of danger than he was prepared for.

"But why would Onymos be using the Light Elementals in battle if he is seeking to destroy the light?" Elucido thought to himself. The answer to his question, however important it may have seemed, would have to wait.

Elucido sent a blazing orb at Onymos to catch him off guard. As the orb approached Onymos, it was met with a powerful orb of ice. The two blasts collided in an explosion of fire and ice between the two adversaries. Onymos fired back, his burst of ice striking Elucido's chest, sending him hurling backward and landing flat on the floor.

The pain was trivial compared to the fear Elucido now felt. Adrenaline surging through his veins, he stood, shook the frost from his shirt, and charged another fiery blast. Back and forth, the two men threw Elemental Orbs in an exchange of flame and frost that appeared as though it would never end; each one landing an occasional hit on their opponent; each one counteracting the effects of the others' Elemental powers with their own. Try as he might, it felt like Elucido was not making any headway in the battle for the Palace of Ren.

"Give up the fight and give in to the darkness!" Onymos challenged Elucido, arrogance piercing through his aggressive tone. "There is nothing you can do to usurp my power. I am in complete control."

Elucido understood that control was the key element in this battle. Though Onymos had mastered his control of the Blue

Elemental, Elucido had enough control of the Red Elemental to hold his own in battle. As they exchanged blows, both Elementals seemed to meet with an opposing balance of force. Fire melted ice, and ice quenched fire in a harmonious exchange of power. There had to be another way to shift that balance in Elucido's favor. Remembering his visions, Elucido thought that perhaps gaining control over more than one Elemental would provide the edge he needed to defeat Onymos.

At that moment, Onymos fired another burst of ice in Elucido's direction. This time, rather than simply dodging or canceling the burst with an opposing fireball, Elucido tried something Onymos did not expect. Stepping slightly to his left, he lifted his arms outward to his right, attempting to gain control over the Blue Elemental's power. Failing, the orb struck Elucido in the shoulder, a shockwave of frigid pain traversing the length of his arm, numbing his fingertips. He shook his arms out, sending the warmth of the Red Elemental orb's energy through his biceps and down to the tips of his fingers, returning feeling and mobility to his frozen extremities.

Unwavering in his resolve, Elucido waited for Onymos to strike again, and repeated his attempt to overcome the icy powers of his enemy. As the ice bolt passed through his arms, he spun clockwise, capturing the ice in a new orbit around his torso. As he completed his spin, facing back toward Onymos, he combined the ice with an orb of fire, resulting in a steam bomb that he hurled back at Onymos.

The burst of steam hit Onymos in the chest, sending him staggering backward, briefly stunning him. Elucido capitalized on the opportunity to send a powerful blast of fire at his opponent, knocking him against the wall, drawing the air from his lungs and leaving him gasping to recapture his breath. Elucido let loose a flurry of fireballs, one after the other, meeting their target with savage force.

The flurry lasted only a few seconds before Onymos fell to the floor, lifeless. As Elucido watched his adversary for any signs of life, he felt the temperature of the room rise, warming to a tolerable condition, as the icy orb surrounding the Shadow Garrison general swirled around Elucido, yielding control of its movements to his will. There was no uncertainty in Elucido's mind—Onymos was dead, and he now possessed the power of the second Elemental.

Taking pause and struggling to regain his breath, Elucido delighted in the now warm breeze that passed through the open tower windows. He approached the stone pillar at the center of the throne room and laid the shards on the pedestal. He had time now to withdraw the tome from his bag and investigate the Aether Orb's composition, trying to reconstitute the shards. After hours of reading the text with painstaking scrutiny, he believed he had a way to bring light back to the continent of Ren.

Elucido joined the shards together as he would a jigsaw puzzle, placing the assembled pieces upon the pillar of marble. Each piece fell into place perfectly, taking the shape of a dark sphere with illuminated cracks where the edges of each piece came together. This assembly illuminated the throne room, but that was as far as the light reached. The rest, Elucido hoped, would come down to the incantation he found within the ancient texts. He recited the incantation, each iteration increasing in both clarity and confidence.

"*Congrega lucem.*" The light at the seams of the Aether Orb shards pulsed, each time growing in brightness.

"*Uniendis lux.*" The light spread from the seams of the orb, fusing into a solid globular radiance.

"*Lucem propagationem.*" With the final incantation, the Aether Orb's glow brightened with blinding intensity. In a singular explosive proliferation of light, the entire continent of Ren was brought back into illumination. The force of the expulsion knocked Elucido to the floor, his consciousness waning into yet another vision.

"Join me!" shouted the dark cloaked figure from the opposite end of the empty throne room. "If you wish to unlock your true power, you must embrace the darkness and give in to hopelessness. You will find that once you have made that choice, the world will be entirely ours. No one will question our decisions, our directives, and our control, for they will be unable to find a path toward hope. Our unchallenged power will be inevitable." There was something different about the way the cloaked figure spoke. Despite his gospel of hopelessness, his voice had an air of desperation to it, as if converting others to join his dark power relied, at least on some level, on the uncertain expectation that others would give in to the darkness. And yet, despite the uncertainty in his heart, his demeanor was commanding and

authoritative. His desperation, as it turned out, was altogether unnecessary—for his message of hopelessness would soon take hold.

Chapter 8

Reign of Darkness

Far away, on the sky continent of Umbra, a nameless figure entered the throne room of the Great Tower of the Palace of Darkness. He carried with him an overbearing presence that sapped the energy from the once bountiful hall. His heart was atramentous—black as the ever-present lifeless skies. He was calculating, cold, malevolent, and wanted nothing more than to see all light and hope drained from the land. They called him the King of Darkness, though none were aware of his true identity or origin.

"Gather the Generals!" he shouted with a commanding fervor; his servants quickly obeyed.

While waiting for his commanders to arrive, the King of Darkness paced the vacuous room impatiently. Idleness was not something he cared for. With every passing moment, he found his agitation growing.

It did not take long for the generals to arrive. The generals used the pre-existing Aether conduits between the palaces to traverse the long distances between the continents. These were the invisible conduits that transferred the light energy from the Aether orbs across the sky continents of Terrus, providing the light that humanity had enjoyed for thousands of years before the Dark Cataclysm. An unforeseen benefit of the Aether Orbs' destruction was the creation of such a means of expedited traversal. Travel and trade between the sky continents had been achieved via airship, taking several days—or even weeks if the weather was unfavorable—to reach a new destination. Now, however, the Aether passages bolstered the dark intentions of the king, allowing expediency in action, and protecting the secrecy of the commanders' communications; an optimization that gratified the king immensely.

"Onymos is dead." The king delivered the news to his surviving generals with a coldness that Onymos himself would have appreciated had he still been alive.

"He lived alone, he died alone, and I am happy to let him rot in his grave, alone." Dynamis, one of the Dark King's generals, spoke from the far corner of the room as he charged forward. While the Shadow Garrison commanders were aligned in vision and purpose, none saw one another as equals. It was no secret amongst those present that Dynamis had very little respect for his former colleague.

"He deserved death, though I would have preferred it be at my hand," replied the King. "His narcissistic pride was his unraveling. Any of you who fail me as he did should hope to be lucky enough to see death before I receive news of your failure. *Nox Praevalet*—night must prevail, at any cost."

Impenetrable as his generals' facades were, they flinched at the king's words. For as much as they desired power, their instinct for self-preservation dominated their emotions when in the dark ruler's presence. Not one of them dared challenge his authority; they understood that even the group of them working together did not have the skills to overcome the sovereign's overwhelming power. Subservience was their undisputed role in the king's domain.

"Find the Luxcreare. Tear him to pieces. I want a fragment of him displayed on every continent as a reminder to everyone who opposes me that I will destroy everything they hold dear. No one will survive my wrath. Fail me, and you will find pieces of yourself scattered through the darkness."

The generals dispersed through the conduits as quickly as they had arrived, each one returning to the palaces on their assigned continents. While none of them were capable of feeling joy or happiness, they experienced a strong sense of relief leaving the presence of the incensed king.

"I did not work this hard to fail at the hands of incompetence and pride," he muttered under his breath in the now emptied throne room.

The king's rise to darkness was not easy, nor fast. Years of research and development, recruitment, and arduous planning took place in his preparation to extinguish the light and steal hope from the land. The failure of one of his elite generals made him uneasy. He was familiar with the legends of the Luxcreare and knew the threat that they posed to his reign. Oppression, control, manipulation, and suffering were the king's instruments of power. News of the Luxcreare could spread hope to those still in hiding, and those who he used as his servants. Should that happen, his dominion would face significant challenges, or worse, rebellion. He needed to extinguish the Luxcreare's life as rapidly as the darkness engulfed the land when he had first destroyed the Aether Orbs.

For now, he only had one choice—a choice he hated more than anything else—to wait and trust his remaining generals to do their jobs.

Chapter 9

On Distant Shores

Elucido awoke on the edge of the sky continent of Vita, only footsteps away from falling off the edge of the terrain and into oblivion. Despite the darkness surrounding him, the sand at his feet told him precisely where he was. How he had arrived here was a mystery that put his nerves on end. He was unfamiliar with this continent—he only remembered visiting Vita a few times while working on his research for the Protectors of Light.

"How did I get here?" he mumbled, brushing the sand from his clothes and taking a few small steps away from the steep edge of the continent. "The Aether conduit must have pulled me in with the orb's reactivation. I had no idea that travel through the conduits was even possible. It's a miracle the energy did not tear me apart. But more importantly, now—where do I go from here?"

Since the darkness took hold, travel by airship was no longer possible. Even if an alternate means of travel were to become possible in the unlit skies, no organizations that survived the Dark Cataclysm would risk running such an operation. And now that Elucido was a very visible threat to the king, he knew that even if it were possible, travel by air would be far too dangerous. The Shadow Garrison would be hunting him with a new zeal after his defeat of one of their elite generals.

Vita was a continent with a very different composition than Elucido's home continent of Nomen. Sand engulfed the northern half of the land. It was Terrus' largest desert, and even in the abundant light before the Dark Cataclysm, this region knew scarce life. In contrast, the southern part of the continent contained vast bodies of water—a series of saltwater lakes known as the Magna Lacus. The one thing that brought the desert and the vast lakes together in harmony was a raging storm of electricity. Vita was infamous for its conductivity, often experiencing aggressive lightning storms. The dryness of the desert air made these storms even more treacherous, as static discharge could stop the hearts of large beasts, killing them in an instant. Elucido stood alone in the deserted darkness, pondering his next move.

The sand beneath Elucido's feet felt nothing like the golden shores on the northern part of Nomen. This sand was coarse, hot, and abrasive to the touch. Even in the absence of light, the energy from the continent radiated through the sand, creating heat that scalded any exposed skin that it came in contact with. Elucido longed for the sandy beach he experienced only a few short weeks ago, but the likelihood of reliving that experience was waning. He processed his new circumstances, his mind racing. Elucido now had to navigate an altogether unfamiliar—and dangerous—territory.

Elucido meandered aimlessly, searching for any clues or signs to give him direction. As time passed, the heat of the desert weighed on both Elucido's mind and body. He knew that the increased temperature could easily overwhelm him and send him into delirium and, eventually, death. He needed to find a way to combat the heat and traverse the sandy terrain, and he needed to do it quickly. In that moment, sweat pouring from his creased brow, lightheadedness overtook him. Elucido collapsed and fell to the ground, experiencing yet another vision.

In the midst of a great battlefield arose a warrior clad in the finest armor in the land. His breastplate remained unscathed; his helmet pristine. And yet, despite the seemingly unused nature of his armor, it was clear that this warrior was experienced far beyond a typical warrior of Terrus. An air of confidence surrounded him as he walked resolutely toward his enemies. One by one, he brought his foes down in flashes of red, blue, green, yellow, and purple light. His mastery of the Elemental Orbs was a wonder to those who observed his unmatched abilities. Wave after wave of enemies approached him, yet none prevailed. Then, as a large hoard of adversaries drew closer and surrounded the warrior, his knee slowly bent to touch the ground. In an instant, a flash of light radiated from the firmament, toppling every foe within fifty meters of the warrior, hundreds in total. As the flash of light swept over the battlefield, Elucido caught a glimpse of the nemeses destroyed by the fearless warrior. They were, much to Elucido's surprise, as human as himself.

Waking from his nightmarish dream, Elucido sat still, feeling unnerved as he pinched the bridge of his nose. His vision of a great warrior decimating a vast army of humans shook him to his core. Who was this ruthless warrior? Could it be that the King of Darkness would reveal his true form and destroy the last remnants of humanity in a great battle? What role was Elucido to play in the events that would unfold? It was clear that the power this warrior possessed was far greater than anything the world had ever seen. Whatever confidence Elucido had gained from his defeat of Onymos faded. His victory over the darkness yet again seemed hopeless.

After sifting through his thoughts, Elucido found his current predicament increasingly dire. The heat had become too intense for him to handle. His survival was in imminent danger. It was in this moment of realization that he took a deep breath, cleared his mind and pressed his hands together, focusing his energy into a manifestation of the icy orbs Onymos hurled at him in the tower of Ren. In an instant, a cool breeze surrounded him, as the desert beneath him turned into a refreshing, cool bed of powdered stone. In addition to his enjoyment of the now chilled air, he could gather the melting ice from the Elemental Orb into his canteen, providing him with the purest cold water that he needed to stay hydrated in this harsh land. Once again, the Elemental Orbs had saved his life.

Having re-assembled the Aether Orb at the Tower of Ren, Elucido now had no shards of orbs to guide him in his exploration of the vast desert. He needed an alternate means to navigate the desert in search of more shards that he could use to restore light to this continent still shrouded in darkness. He knew that the Palace of Light on Vita, known as the Tower of Ra, was in the southeast corner of the continent, in the depths of the Magna Lacus. Knowing that the desert occupied the northern part of the continent, Elucido surmised he would have to travel a substantial distance through the center of the desert to reach the tower. What dangers lie ahead were altogether uncertain.

With no other direction to follow, Elucido began his trek forward, toward what he believed to be the center of the continent. The assuredness he had earned through his trials on Nomen had dried up in the unfamiliar sands of the electric desert. He would have to find a way not only to obtain the light shards, but to regain his faith in himself. With unsure footing, the next phase of his journey began.

After hours of monotonous hiking over shifting dunes, Elucido spotted something moving on the dark horizon through the ambient light of the continent's electric storms. Gut wrenched, and fists clenched, he advanced to investigate the movement more closely. In sharp contrast to the dark beasts he had become too familiar with, the creature he now approached appeared to be fearful of him; with every step Elucido took toward the small animal, it took one step in the opposite direction. Comfortable that the creature posed no immediate threat to him, Elucido opted to take a gentler approach to reveal what he was seeing.

Elucido sat in the sand, reached into his satchel, and retrieved a small piece of food, a dried piece of edible moss that he had gathered from an outcropping of damp stones near his home village some time ago. While it was not the most satisfying to the palate, its nutrients and fiber provided sufficient nourishment in these dire times. He held his hand outstretched, breathing slowly and remaining as motionless as possible. Perhaps his desert companion would be interested in his offering of kindness.

The creature slowly approached, taking two steps toward Elucido, then quickly retreating one step in reverse. Noticing that Elucido was not moving, it gained a small measure of confidence with every cycle of its approach. After several minutes, it came close enough to smell the food in Elucido's gentle hands. With a beaming smile on his face, Elucido spoke with a soft whisper.

"Hello there, friend. How adorable are you?" The creature shifted its gaze intently toward Elucido, revealing its disproportionately gargantuan eyes, long whiskers, and soft mahogany fur that swayed fluidly in the warm desert breeze. With its head tilted and shoulders raised, it emitted a short burst of high-pitched squeaks that brought a surprising level of comfort to the Luxcreare. He had not felt companionship for so long. This small ball of fur felt like his new best friend. For the first time in a very long while, Elucido felt lighter, as if some measure of darkness had been removed from within him.

"I was in need of a friend, more so than I knew or even cared to acknowledge. I can't begin to tell you how comforting it is to share a meal with another living being." Joy was the emotion consuming Elucido. Joy. He had almost forgotten the feeling.

After sharing the dry, fibrous meal with his new compatriot, Elucido decided it was time for him to move on and continue his search for more signs of Aether Orbs. As allaying as this experience had been, he knew it could not last forever. Getting himself to his feet to continue his trek proved to be more difficult than he expected.

"I don't want to leave you behind, my friend. But sadly, I think it is time for me to carry on my search for the light shards. Most surprisingly, you have brought me hope in spades. I thank you for that, little one. Sincerely."

The creature squeaked several times, seemingly in response to Elucido's expression of gratitude.

Standing and shaking the sand from his trousers, Elucido began his deliberate, albeit slow, walk across the dunes. Something was different this time, however. With every step he took, he heard a short squeak. Step. Squeak. Step. Squeak. It appeared his new friend was not yet ready for Elucido to leave him behind. With a brief chortle, Elucido turned to admire his tiny confidant.

"I see you plan on following me. So be it. What should I call you then, little one?" Elucido spoke to the creature in a significantly higher pitched voice than he would any of his human friends. He didn't know why, but it just felt right, as if the creature would somehow understand him better in another octave.

"I know! I shall call you Amica—in my language it means 'friend'. That is, after all, what you are."

Though his interpretation was likely skewed by his desires, Elucido was confident he saw happiness in the colossal pearly eyes of the critter as it emitted a sequence of high-pitched "cheeps" at the mention of its new name.

"Friend indeed. Amica it is, then. Shall we carry on? We have much ground to cover."

Amica, growing in his trust of the much larger Elucido, quickly leapt from his place on the sandy ground, perching himself firmly on the right shoulder of Elucido's sweat-soaked shirt. As Elucido continued walking, his smile widened as he felt the gentle vibrations of the purring beast he now called friend.

Chapter 10

A Spark Ignites

Far away, in a tower of sandstone, General Dynamis sat and evaluated his options. He remained doggedly agitated at the failure of Onymos and resented the fact that he was left to clean up his mess. Dynamis, while impatient toward the failures of others, was very deliberate and pragmatic when it came to strategizing. He was comfortable waiting for a plan to take shape, but once the plan was in place, he was decisive, quick, and exacting in execution. For now, however, his nerves remained on edge.

Having witnessed the fury of the King of Darkness only moments ago, Dynamis understood the importance of his task. With Elucido landing on his continent, the responsibility to destroy the Luxcreare rested squarely on his shoulders. The King's report revealed that the Luxcreare had mastered the ability to control both the Red and Blue Light Elementals. Impressive as the speed with which he could attain his powers had been, Elucido's newfound faculty was of no consequence to Dynamis. He wielded a power that, at least from his perspective, was far superior.

"Sir, I have a report from the scouts on the northern dunes." A messenger entered the room without first requesting an audience with the general. It was a mistake that he would make only once. With a blinding flash of light and a deafening crackle, a white-hot bolt of lightning arced from Dynamis's fingertips into the chest of the ill-fated messenger. Dynamis approached the expired courier, chest smoldering, dead where he fell.

"I suppose I will have to obtain this information from another source," Dynamis scoffed.

A swarm of sizzling micro-sparks followed the base of Dynamis's cloak in a flurry of static discharge as he began pacing the floor of the throne room. He found the sound of every electric crepitation soothing. He didn't need the finer details of whatever report his scouts had prepared; he understood what was happening. The Luxcreare was moving toward the tower in search of shards of light. His intent was to bring light back to Vita and destroy Dynamis in the process. Dynamis would not allow that outcome.

Throwing the doors to the throne room open with another blast of electricity, Dynamis rushed past his servants, and into the basement to the heart of his research laboratory. Caligo had spent a tremendous amount of time leading up to the Dark Cataclysm creating the Tenebrae, but Dynamis had secretly been fabricating a beast of his own design. The desert was a perfect home for his colossal project. Dynamis had spent his time on Vita mastering the storm of electricity that consumed the continent. He augmented the power of the lightning with the fury of the blowing dust, creating a foe worthy of Caligo's praise.

"Prepare the capacitor!" Dynamis bellowed a set of instructions to his lead scientists.

As they opened a series of levers, a low drone of building energy sounded. A large cylinder in the center of the lab vibrated, small arcs of lightning emanating from its surface. After a few brief moments, the device reached full charge.

"Open the wind turbines and amplify the pressure in the chamber."

A blast of sand swirled in the chamber, energized by the high winds that now filled the cylinder in a cyclone of electric dust. Flashes of light consumed the growing storm as the pressure intensified.

"Nevermind the fool's plans; he is fully unprepared for what I have arranged for him. It is time to unleash the tempest!" The Yellow Elemental Orb swelled in Dynamis's clenched fists.

With a singular, focused blast of electricity from the orb, the chamber doors burst open, sending the voltaic monstrosity deep into the heart of the desert.

Chapter 11

Into the Storm

Back at the entrance to the rolling dunes of sand, Elucido continued his minacious journey. It was difficult enough navigating in the darkness, but the dunes were obfuscated further by blowing sand and waves of scorching winds that quickly drew the moisture from his weary eyes. Realizing the dangers of becoming lost in the waves of sand, Elucido formulated a plan to track his progress.

Elucido formed a small ball of red light in the palm of his hand and released it into the air. It floated at eye level, a small luminescent orb marking his current location.

"How long do you suppose those lights will last?" he asked Amica, as if he expected a response from the small creature resting on his shoulder. "Let's hope it will last long enough that we can navigate through this miserable desert."

An hour passed, with Elucido releasing a small beacon of ruddy light about every twenty meters. As he took a swig of the ice orb's melted essence and wiped the sweat from his forehead, he saw something faintly glowing in the distance. It did not take him long to identify the light; it was the orb he placed nearly one hour ago.

"Blast it! We are traveling in circles. I don't know which way to go, Amica. I fear we may be doomed to become victims of the relentless sandy dunes."

With a long squeal, Amica leapt from Elucido's shoulder and sprinted toward the ruby orb of light. Elucido pursued. Amica took the orb in its mouth and continued to move at a pace Elucido struggled to keep.

"Where are you going? Slow down!"

Thankfully, the glow of the orb provided sufficient light for Elucido to track his desert friend. He maintained chase, becoming increasingly winded as he struggled to keep the orb in his sight. Why he had chased his new friend with such fervor escaped his rational mind. Much to his relief, it did not take long for the captive orb's erratic movement to slow and eventually come to a complete stop. As he neared the orb's location, he noticed something else. A faint white light was pulsing from deep within the rugged dune ahead. He knew the rhythm of the pulsing light. It was a shard of an Aether Orb.

"Amica, I love you, my dear friend! Look what you have found! I don't know how you did it—and, to be honest, I don't even care. You have no idea how important this discovery is. You, sir, are a legend in a land of treachery."

Wind returning to his lungs, Elucido extracted the shard from beneath several layers of coarse sand. It did not matter to him that the desert's abrasiveness was grating the top layer of skin from his palms—he had found the first shard of light in this unfamiliar, barren land.

With the additional visibility provided by the shard of the Aether orb, Elucido climbed to the top of the tallest dune he could see in hopes of better surveying the land.

From the top of the mound, far off in the horizon, Elucido could see a flurry of light flashes, as a raging lightning storm illuminated the black sky with millisecond windows of near-complete visibility. At the base of the storm, he could make out an electrified isthmus connecting the vast desert to what appeared to be a depressed, barren valley. This was the only means of passage toward the Magna Lacus and the tower of Ra. Elucido's heart sunk; how he would overcome the trial of lightning was beyond his capacity to understand. Given his current pace of travel, he would have less than an hour's walk to figure something out.

Elucido approached the edge of the lightning storm with no idea how best to proceed. He looked to Amica for assurance, or even an idea of how to traverse the storm. Amica offered little help, crawling deep inside of Elucido's satchel upon seeing the power the storm exuded. The lightning bolts fell in a seemingly random assortment on the ground. The only thing that Elucido could discern was a consistent timing of strikes. That timing would not make much of a difference in his approach, however, unless he could find a way to ensure that the electricity did not choose to ground itself through his body.

In a series of floundering trials and subsequent errors, Elucido attempted to redirect the lightning strikes. He started with a Red

Elemental Orb—a blast of fire to see how the lightning would react. It had no effect. Again, he tried, but this time summoning a massive orb, scorching an area of ground near the epicenter of the lightning strikes. The lightning was agnostic when it came to the Red Elemental's powers.

Frustration mounting, Elucido shifted his focus to the Blue Elemental. Perhaps ice would elicit a different response from the electric barrage. He fired a burst of the Blue Elemental, creating a small, fractal ball of ice that shot forward with high speed into the storm's westernmost edge. Elucido noticed that the arcs of energy from the beams of lightning took a slight bend in the cobalt orb's direction before landing firmly in the sand below. He was on to something. If he could create a piece of ice large enough, he may be able to direct the current away from his path through the storm.

Taking a deep breath and centering his thoughts on the extreme cold of Onymos' throne room, Elucido summoned a swirling blue light that surrounded him, bringing with it an extreme frigidity. He didn't mind the cold, so long as it protected him from a most unwelcome shock. Pounding both fists into the ground, a large crag of ice sprung up from the ground with an impulse that shook the ground more than the electric storm's current terrestrial disruption. The ice column quickly grew to twice Elucido's height and reached nearly three times that measure in length. As the ice reached the pinnacle of its manifestation, the lightning struck it squarely in the center, causing an explosion of ice. Elucido quickly rolled to the left to dodge the shattered pillar's many pieces.

He had redirected the electric charges, but it brought with it the new danger of being torn apart by icy shrapnel. His timing and speed needed to match that of the lightning without fail. In a series of abrupt movements, Elucido placed a pillar of ice, rolled quickly aside, ran a few steps forward and repeated. If he wasn't so worried about the speed of his movement, he could have stopped to admire the beauty of the storm, arcing through the azure shards in an extraordinary glow of flashing blue light. The dazzling display lasted only a few minutes before Elucido reached the far edge of the storm and extricated himself from danger.

Looking back into the barrage of lightning that was now behind him, Elucido registered a remarkable pattern. There was a section of lightning that struck the same location time and time again. As the lightning faded to darkness, the center of the strike zone remained iridescent. While it was difficult to determine the precise hue of the remaining light due to the strain the flashing lightning placed on his eyes, Elucido knew this object needed a much closer investigation. He took a moment to visualize his movements and practice his timing, then he took off in a dead sprint toward the object. Throwing pillars of ice to the left and right of the object, he distracted the lightning's attention just long enough to snatch it from the ground. It was another Aether Orb shard. He didn't have time to dwell on his discovery; he needed to retreat before he became the focus of the lightning's next strike. Leaving a trail of ice in his stead, Elucido escaped past the edge of the storm and back to safety. He placed the shard in his satchel, hearing a loud squeal as he made his deposit.

"Amica! Oh my gosh, I am so sorry, I forgot you were in there!" Elucido had been so caught up in the storm's fury that he had forgotten that his new friend had taken shelter in his satchel. As guilty as he felt for dropping the shard on Amica's head, he was relieved to see that his companion had made the trek across the isthmus with him. But before he could complete his profuse apology to Amica, the creature shrieked in terror, jumped from the satchel, and fled deeper into the valley. At that moment, Elucido saw the shadow of a galvanic desert leviathan emerging before his very eyes.

Billowing air surrounded the stony creature, creating an eddy of vacuous space that revealed a faceless behemoth—Dynamis's voltaic monstrosity. The force of the gale obeyed the beast's every command, as it crafted an arena surrounding Elucido, forcing him to engage the beast in a gladiatorial fight, presumably to the death. Even if Elucido could elude the sandy hurricane that now enveloped him, the dust storm was wrought with an electric charge that cemented his position firmly in the center of the sandstorm colosseum.

The goliath wasted no time starting an onslaught of boulders hurled at Elucido's head. Rolling left and right, he dodged the first few tosses. The beast then pounded the ground with both stony fists, creating a tremor that knocked Elucido straight onto his back. It followed the tremor with a bolt of lightning that arced from its sternum right toward the center of Elucido's chest. Elucido reacted quickly, crafting a sheet of ice above his fallen torso, absorbing the blast of the electric bolt before it could reach his body. Icy shrapnel radiated outward, nearly shredding the flesh on his arms.

Elucido regained his footing and surveyed his surroundings. He saw no advantages offered by his environment, for the stadium in which he now fought for his life was empty. His only advantage would have to come from a misstep from his opponent. Summoning a powerful Blue Elemental Orb, he fired a blast of ice toward his opponent's feet, creating an icy trap that locked the beast's feet in place. This afforded him a wider range of movement, in which he could now attempt to find a weak spot on the seemingly unbreakable stony foe.

Circling the arena, Elucido observed small cracks in the rocky components of his combatant—what appeared to be seams, perhaps remnants of the being's construction. Elucido surmised he could use his powers to exploit those minute fractures to bring his adversary down. A barrage of fireballs had no effect. The Blue Elemental's icy power appeared to do some damage, though not enough to provide a significant advantage to him. After a series of failed Elemental strikes, the creature's feet broke free from their icy restraints, and the beast swung around to face Elucido and resume its bombardment.

The exchanges continued; Elucido locking the beast in place for brief moments while attempting to exact some measure of damage, the creature eventually breaking free once again to hurl more boulders and electric jolts at the Luxcreare. Elucido's chest heaved with every labored breath, his lungs on fire from exhaustion. While the Elementals responded to his commands with ease, his body could not keep pace. Elucido's options were dwindling. The exchange could not continue at its current pace. If it did, he would tire and perish at the mountainous rival's craggy hands. His pace slowing, Elucido let his guard down for a moment to catch his breath. The beast flung a large stone, nearly striking him. He ducked only a moment before being pulverized, his energy waning.

Elucido thought back to his traversal of the lightning storm. His icy pillars could act as conduits for the electrical energy of the storm. It was conceivable that he could leverage the conductivity of the ice to create a charged blast to fire at the behemoth. He froze the stony hoofs of the beast to the ground and circled like a predator hunting its prey. Positioning himself with extreme precision, he waited for the beast to fire another bolt of lightning in his direction. As the bolt charged toward Elucido's chest, he summoned a blue orb directly in front of him, absorbing the electrical charge. The Elemental absorption created a shockwave of electrified ice shrapnel that was directed back at the monstrosity, piercing and embedding themselves in the small cracks that lined the creature's surface. He followed the energized, frozen splinters with a barrage of highly effective fireballs. The heat from the Red Elemental Orb's power turned the ice to vapor almost instantaneously, creating a supercharged high-pressure blast that split the cracks in the rocky torso of the beast wide open.

While effective, this sent the beast into a furious rage. Swinging its stony arms wildly, it forced Elucido backward, step by step, toward the edge of the arena and what would most certainly be his death. The battle was not over yet.

Stumbling backward, scanning the damaged stone for any weakness he could exploit, Elucido noticed something quite remarkable. Exposed from the widening cracks, at the heart of the beast's chest, sat the shard of an Aether orb, glowing magnificently. The shock of seeing the treasure in the core of his adversary petrified Elucido. Whoever created this beast had obtained the shard and used it to enhance the power of an already incredible monster. He didn't have time to figure out who had created this beast, or how they had found the shard, he needed to survive and destroy the beast once and for all. His hesitation, however brief it may have been, allowed the beast time to charge its next attack.

Elucido could see the energy swelling in the arms of the beast. A surge of electricity was flowing from the core of its stony chest, building a powerful blast that Elucido feared he could not stop. Holding his breath, Elucido's chest tightened as he prepared for the worst. In that moment, he saw a fast movement headed straight toward the heart of the colossus.

"Amica!" Elucido shouted in disbelief, as his charming compact friend returned in an act of true valor.

The critter was far too small to conquer a beast of this size. That, as it turned out, was Amica's advantage. He moved at a speed that the behemoth could neither see nor match. In an instant, Elucido's furry friend flew through the crack in the chest of the stone adversary, snatching the shard of the Aether Orb from its rocky asylum. As Amica, and subsequently the shard of the orb, left the body of the beast through the large, exposed crevasse, its electrified charge quickly dissipated. With its primary source of power now removed, Elucido regained the advantage. He made quick work of the beast, repeating his electrified icy fusillade, blowing the cracks in the beast open further. In one final concussive blast, the goliath shattered into hundreds of small fragments that fell harmlessly to the ground at Elucido's feet.

"I thought you were gone, little buddy! How on Terrus did you know how to take that beast down?" Amica tilted his head slightly to the left, then abruptly to the right, focusing on Elucido's face as he spoke. "Nevermind, perhaps it was just your apparent love of the light of the Aether Orb shards that tailored your advantage. Either way, my friend, I am honored to see you resting on my shoulder once again."

Chapter 12

Magna Lacus

Three shards in hand and having obliterated the rocky gladiator, Elucido felt the surge of hope he had been missing since his arrival on Vita. Finding his new friend furthered his confidence and happiness in a way he had not expected. He was not alone in this fight. He suspected, as was the case on Nomen, that there were only a couple more Aether Orb shards to find on his journey to the sandstone tower of Ra before he could restore light to the continent of Vita.

Having survived the overpowering electrical storm, Elucido reached a place of relative safety. The terrain flattened, the air cooled, and the crashing thunder was behind him. What's more, he could still use the flashing light from the tempest to see more of what lay ahead. Though he did not have a specific waypoint in mind, the presence of the orb's shards drove him to the south, toward an old factory, no longer in service.

The ruinous factory sat in the south-central part of Vita, a short distance from the dust devil's colosseum that nearly ended Elucido's travels. It took almost half a day for him to traverse the flat desert plain. The factory sat in the region of the desert that possessed the optimal balance of accessibility, weather stability, and electric energy. The previous operators of the factory had to weather many storms, but that was a necessary hazard in order for them to enjoy the many benefits of the free power the desert storms generated. Of course, no one was using the factory for fabrication anymore. Since the Dark Cataclysm, the population on Terrus was decimated, trade routes were closed, and there was no need for mass production on Vita.

Though it was not being used for its designed purpose, the factory was all but empty. As Elucido approached the entrance, he heard rustling in the foyer. Elucido lurked in the shadows of the building's exterior, positioning himself so that he could see into the broken windows with each flash of lightning. He saw a horde of dark creatures of an unknown breed using the large, open building lobby as a training facility, engaging in tactical sparring rounds and combat drills. One such creature, caught up in the intensity of its training, bit his partner more forcefully than it found tolerable, which resulted in an aggressive response that left the offending creature's arm pulled cleanly from its body. The shriek of the injured being sent an intense shiver down Elucido's spine. It was more than evident that these monsters were serious about their methods of combat training.

Using his current position of stealth outside the factory, Elucido gathered information about the creatures' fighting style, physical composition, and demeanor. He noted these creatures were shorter than their presumed cousins, the Nullblights. What they lacked in height, they more than compensated for in muscle tone and aggression. Their need to stay as invisible in the darkness as the Nullblights was not as strong, given that the flashing lights on the continent provided both them and their opponents ample chance to visualize their position. As such, they moved with less covertness, taking heavy-footed steps, often growling and snapping at their fellow warriors. As far as the Shadow Garrison was concerned, these beasts were the belligerent muscle-heads that, despite their graceless presence, took care of business with definitive results.

Fortisblights was what this breed of dark minions were called, though Elucido did not know them by their formal name. Force was their modus operandi. And while Elucido did not know what to call them, their presence provided him sufficient grounds for fear. At least their unpolished and unconcealed methods afforded him the advantage of observation. And the knowledge that came with it provided him a chance for survival against the legion of gauche challengers.

Taking advantage of his vast supply of time in the safety of the factory exterior, Elucido's ability to analyze and formulate a plan kicked into full gear. He took his time identifying the plethora of unused, but seemingly functional, factory equipment. He noted that the switches providing power to the conveyor belts, power hammers, and waste disposal receptacles were still in an "on" position, indicating that they only needed a jolt of power to become useful once again. Carefully organized, precise activation of this equipment could make quick work of his opponents.

Using the powers of stealth that his foes lacked, Elucido harnessed the power of the Blue Elemental, placing small pathways of ice in the pattern of a circuit atop the roof of the dilapidated building. Then, with expert timing, Elucido captured a stray bolt of lightning using an ice crag at his location. The lightning bolt's energy, coupled with the frozen circuit board, was precisely what he needed to execute his plan.

In an instant, the circuit was completed, activating a series of machines that operated quite effectively. The first group of Fortisblights to be affected were standing on the swinging floor that covered the metal scrap shredder. The door activated as the winding gears that drew in the large pieces of metal to be macerated started turning. This machine made quick work of the fleshy beasts, devouring at least a dozen unsuspecting foes in a gratuitous display of mangled parts and splashing blood.

The next round of beasts were unlucky enough to be engaged in a petty rivalry at the time of the equipment's activation. Their infighting had positioned them directly underneath the hydraulic metal press. Seven more enemies were rapidly disposed of as the die crushed their bodies into an unrecognizable form. Elucido had not expected this level of carnage from his improvised scheme. It was more than his stomach could handle. As the metal press lifted, revealing the flattened sanguinary corpses of the Fortisblights, Elucido turned his head, his partially digested, rehydrated mossy lunch abruptly finding its place in the sand.

Various pieces of equipment maimed several more muscular beings. Arms caught in gears were torn from their torsos, legs were broken by flying shards of metal, while others were embedded from head to toe by copious volumes of shrapnel. The factory was active once again, though its safety record had now become contemptible.

Elucido recomposed his upturned stomach and charged into the carnage at full speed. He made quick work of the remaining Fortisblights, consuming them in a battery of fire and ice, finishing an occasional beast with the blade of his dagger. At this point, it all felt like a mercy killing as he put each of the snarling, screaming beasts out of their misery. Ultimately, the only sound that remained was the droning and pounding of the large industrial death machines.

Elucido headed toward the back rooms of the factory in search of the next Aether orb shard. Occasionally losing his footing on the slippery, blood-soaked floor, he approached what appeared to be the foreman's office. Sitting in the manager's chair, Elucido caught his breath and took a much-needed gulp of water from his canteen. Scouring the room for any sign of the shard's location, he saw a large safe in the back corner of the room. Elucido had never been trained in the art of safe-cracking, but he knew something about the structure of metal. Focusing the cold ice of a freshly summoned Blue Elemental Orb, Elucido super-cooled the metal, making it as brittle as porcelain. A quick strike on the lock mechanism with the back of his dagger's handle shattered the lock, allowing easy access to the vault. Inside, he found the fourth Aether Orb shard. He wondered—was the same person who hid the shard in the cabin on Nomen responsible for the safekeeping of this shard?

Pushing that thought aside, Elucido had a suspicion where his travels would lead him next. The draw of the shards proved his intuition. The next shard of the tower of Ra's Aether Orb rested near the base of the tower, nestled somewhere deep within the vast bodies of water of the Magna Lacus. Turning his head to the side, shielding his eyes from the consequences of his highly effective slaughter, Elucido left the factory and headed east toward the great lakes of Vita.

Elucido knew he needed to be more attentive as he neared the southeast corner of the continent. If the colossal rocky beast and the horde of Fortisblights taught him anything, it was that those in power at the tower of Ra were prepared for heavy combat and intended to meet any threat with the utmost force. Thankfully, the continuing electrical storm provided the visibility he would need to safely arrive at the lakes.

Five days later, as he neared the shore of the first lake at Magna Lacus, rain began to fall. The lakes were known for their "Virga," a unique weather phenomenon in which the rainfall from the stormy electrified skies evaporates fully before hitting the sand below. The dryness of the desert air gave the water droplets short life, while simultaneously creating a stunning pirouette of wispy, watery elegance hundreds of meters above the sandy shores.

Caught up in the weather's beauty, Elucido nearly forgot his mission. Somewhere in the labyrinth of inland seas rested another shard. Navigating the sand had been difficult enough, but now Elucido would have to take on the role of mariner and explore the watery surface for signs of light. Using the shards in his possession as a compass, he began his exploration of the coastline.

The pull of the Aether orb's shards had proven to be an accurate navigational aid on his journey thus far. Elucido trusted their guidance yet again and became much more in tune with their resonance the more he searched. He snaked his way around the many lakes, walking several kilometers before feeling the pull of the orbs intensify. Staying as close to the direction of the shards' counsel as possible, Elucido circumnavigated a single, rather large lake deep in the heart of the collection of bodies of water. Although the lake was littered with small islands, there was no way he could walk to this orb; there was too much lake in the way.

Elucido was not a strong swimmer, having grown up in a small village nowhere near any bodies of water large enough to justify the lessons. He feared that his failure to learn a skill common to most children on Terrus would prove to be the hurdle that cost him his success in his journey to restore the Aether Orbs. He hung his head shamefully, feeling the sting of regret. "If only..." he mumbled aloud. He knew he stood no chance of swimming to the heart of the lake without succumbing to exhaustion and drowning. But there were also no objects around that could be used to fashion any sort of craft that would be capable of remaining afloat and support his weight. He would need an alternative means to reach the shard.

Elucido could not just sit and wait—the shard of the orb would not travel to him, no matter how much he willed it. But how would he reach the islands on the lake and search for the orb?

"If only I could walk on water," he thought to himself. He then turned to Amica, looking for a response that may enlighten him.

"If only I could walk on water," Elucido spoke aloud. Amica chirped in agreement, as Elucido repeated himself a third time.

"If only I could—that's it! Perhaps I can walk on water." Testing his control over the Blue Elemental, Elucido crafted a small sheet of ice roughly one meter thick and nearly three meters in diameter. Gingerly, he placed his left foot on the icy rink, followed by his right foot. The ice sheet wobbled on the surface of the water, hardly stable. However, it remained afloat, even under Elucido's weight.

In a series of awkward, shaky movements, Elucido crafted ice sheet after ice sheet. The transition between each platform was tricky, and on more than one occasion, Elucido found himself submerged in the lake, having to carefully climb back up on the glacial platform. After nearly an hour of highly physical transfers, Elucido reached a small island near the center of the lake. His navigational aids had not failed him; he lifted the final Aether Orb shard from the sand and deposited it into his satchel. The only thing left to do was to head to the tower and face whatever dangers awaited. Elucido was ready.

Chapter 13

Tower of Sand

Upon his arrival at the tower of Ra, Elucido observed the sharp silhouette of a tall man, adorned in a flowing cloak, standing atop the sandstone obelisk. Flashes of lightning gave clarity and detail to his shape, revealing a strong, stoic, and what Elucido could only assume was a merciless soul. There was no presupposition of secrecy, no feigning of avoidance in his demeanor. The figure was inviting him in, although the invitation felt anything but warm. Elucido accepted the invitation as he entered the open doors of the palace with heightened trepidation.

"This, my dear friend, is where we must part." Elucido spoke to his fuzzy companion in a somber tone. "The dangers ahead are far too great. And while I am prepared to lose my life for this cause, I simply cannot risk yours."

Amica chirped a few short bursts, followed by silence. Elucido replied.

"Please. I cannot bear the thought of my actions leading to your harm. I would like to believe that you want to come with me, but I couldn't live with myself if anything should happen to you. I must handle this next fight alone."

As Elucido took a knee, his closest friend, and the only creature to offer him comfort in his isolation, jumped from his shoulder and onto the firm sandstone floor. Facing Elucido with his oversized umber eyes, Amica left him with a final soft squeak before turning and making his way back toward where they first met. Elucido's heart sank deeper into his chest, a clear sign of the grief he now felt at the departure of his friend. But this was something he had to do alone.

Elucido's nerves, already on edge, were electrified as he entered the palace and walked past two rows of Fortisblights lining each side of the long, golden carpet that stretched the length of the palace floor. The beasts displayed incredible restraint, doing nothing more than snarling as he made his way to the stairwell. Their orders were explicit—let the Luxcreare pass through, unharmed. Elucido knew that the self-control it took for these creatures to allow him to pass was a sign of their fear of their master. The fear they possessed transferred to Elucido with an unsteadying amplification.

The walk to the pinnacle of the tower was far less arduous than Elucido's climb of the tower of Ren. The silhouetted figure's invitation cleared the pathway for easy, non-violent progress. That offered little comfort to Elucido, for he knew the summons was not without expectation. He wondered what the general of the Shadow Garrison wanted from him.

"Please, come in," Dynamis gestured for Elucido to have a seat across the table in what appeared to be a large banquet hall. "You are most welcome here, for now," he added.

"I don't understand. Why the peaceful invitation?" Elucido asked, with a slight warble in his voice, expecting that the meeting could turn hostile at any moment.

"I have a proposition for you. Your performance in the desert against my stony creation has proven you to be most worthy."

"So, you're the one who created that behemoth? Wait—worthy of what?" Elucido's brow furrowed. On the one hand, he felt a sense of pride for being hailed as "worthy". On the other hand, Dynamis's overbearing presence made it clear to Elucido that he was being manipulated.

"I didn't expect your victory over the many hazards of the desert. But now I see your true strength." Dynamis stood from his chair, leaning in toward Elucido, palms firmly rested on the table. "You would fit in perfectly with the generals of the Shadow Garrison. Join us and make your power complete."

Dynamis had wasted no time presenting his proposal. Leaning back in his chair and folding his arms, Elucido replied. "I didn't survive the desert to be made a pawn in your game of oblivion." Elucido surprised even himself with the confidence and forcefulness of his assertion.

"There you are, I see you!" Dynamis bellowed back at Elucido, having registered the defiance in Elucido's response. "In fact, I see a lot of myself in you."

"You know nothing about me!" Elucido responded quickly.

"On the contrary, Luxcreare," Dynamis quipped. "I know exactly who you are. I know you are capable of greatness. Submit to the King of Darkness's authority and become the pride of his inner circle. You are alone in this fractured world, but your isolation is your own doing. The choice is yours, but I must warn you. The consequences of your choice are also yours to bear. Choose wisely."

"There is still light in this world. I will not submit to hopelessness and despair. Darkness cannot prevail. Lux Superesse Est." Elucido rose from his chair, knowing that his response would instigate the next, more violent, phase of his interaction with Dynamis.

With an explosive crackle of lightning, Dynamis shattered the wooden table into a splintery array that directed itself to the walls on his and Elucido's left and right sides, clearing a path between the two.

"You have made your choice. Your death is at your own hands." Dynamis shifted his stance and prepared himself for battle. Elucido mirrored the movement, confident that he could best Dynamis in this duel.

Swirls of fire and ice, illuminated by the flashing bolts of lightning, consumed the open spaces of the banquet hall in an epic display of the power of the Elemental Orbs. Both Elucido and Dynamis demonstrated remarkable mastery of their respective Elemental capabilities. The lightning Elemental's energy brought unmatched speed to Dynamis's movement. He darted from one location to another, expertly dodging Elucido's attacks. As hard as

Elucido tried, he could not hit the general with a direct blow, only grazing him periodically. Dynamis, having far superior speed, had no problems sending his assault directly to Elucido's position.

The only defense Elucido had against the onslaught of voltage was the brief period it took for Dynamis to charge his attack. He held his hands a short distance apart, creating a gap of air that acted as a capacitor, allowing the lightning to build in strength before discharging it. That charging time allowed Elucido to cast a wall of ice in front of himself, which absorbed the charge and dispelled its energy to Elucido's sides, sparing him the pain of a direct blast.

Elucido needed to regain the advantage over Dynamis. If he could slow Dynamis's movements, or use his speed against him, he might take control of the duel and bring Dynamis down. Calming his nerves and focusing past the anxiety he was feeling, Elucido shifted his focus, attempting to subvert the nimbleness of his electric foe. Waiting for the right timing, he took his chance.

As Dynamis fired a jolt of electricity and dashed to a new location, Elucido chose not to create an icy shield. Instead, he sent the Blue Elemental Orb toward Dynamis's presumed destination. Of course, that meant that Elucido had to take the brunt of the electricity. An excruciating burst of voltage arced between his limbs and the ground as his body tensed. Releasing a large shriek, and focusing through the pain, Elucido saw his plan was quite effective.

Dynamis, distracted by the excitement of landing a direct hit on the one he, himself, called worthy, arrived at his destination before he could see what was waiting for him. As he planted his feet firmly in his new location, the ice built up around his feet, trapping him and significantly slowing his movement. Elucido shifted his attention toward building the strength of the ice that now left his opponent unable to run.

Elucido deflected Dynamis's assault, all while maintaining the integrity of the ice that had gathered significant mass all the way up to the general's torso. He could see the electricity coursing through the block of ice, circling back into the body of its captive. Directing all the energy he was able, Elucido continued to build the ice, engulfing Dynamis completely. The ice itself acted as a superconductor, gathering an incredible amount of electric energy as Dynamis discharged the entirety of his strength in a futile attempt to break free of his icy prison.

Pressing his hands firmly together, Elucido used the swirling blue orb to compress the frozen block, raising the speed with which the electric charge built. When the supercharged ice could hold no more energy, it gave way with a blinding light and pulse that knocked Elucido backward into the wall at the far corner of the room. Dynamis, as powerful as he was, found himself unable to contain the pulse of energy that surged through his torso. In an instant, his body shattered, each piece carrying with it a bolt of lightning that illuminated the room for one final blinding moment.

Moving toward the center of the room, Elucido felt the static energy building around him, taking the shape of a small yellow orb that circled him, obeying his every command. The power of the Yellow Light Elemental was now under Elucido's control. Anxiety discharging from his body, he headed toward the throne room atop the tower, toward the pillar that once held the Aether Orb that provided light to the continent of Vita. Reaching the pillar, he gathered the shards of the orb he had worked so hard to obtain and assembled them using the same incantations he had learned on Nomen.

"*Congrega lucem.*" The Aether Orb shards emitted a faint light from the seams where they were fit together, with each pulse raising the luminosity of the room.

"*Uniendis lux.*" The energy of the light joined in perfect harmony.

"*Lucem propagationem.*" The orb was completed, with a great propagation of light that brought the desert into full view, revealing the treacherous path that Elucido had taken to bring light back to the barren continent of Vita.

As the light reached the far edges of the continent, Elucido could feel the pull of the Aether conduit draw him in. He knew he had no control over where the orb's energy would send him next. With the last moment he had on Vita before departing for his next destination, he looked at the path leading up to the desert entrance. In the distance, Elucido could see—or at least believed he could see—a small creature with large umber eyes dancing with joy.

Chapter 14

Illumination

An astonishing volume of light greeted Elucido as he exited the Aether conduit, and his attention was drawn to the skies that he had, until this moment, thought possessed no signs of hope. A wide glowing array of blue, green, and purple lights traversed the sky in a beautiful aurora, moving capriciously, as if the sky itself was alive. These were the Great Lights of Cor that he had heard of in his days as a young boy. He had never seen such beauty. Few had. The lights appeared above the continent of Cor only in extraordinarily rare circumstances, spurred on by the conjunction of electromagnetic energy released from the continent's core that resonated with the oscillations of the Aether Orb's conduit from the tower at the palace of Ib.

Perhaps, Elucido thought, the lack of light energy in the conduit due to the Aether Orbs' destruction slowed the frequency of the oscillations, facilitating the elegant display. Whatever the cause, he was awestruck that such beauty was present in these times. The lights, however, were not the end of the luminescent charm that Cor had to offer. Elucido turned his focus to a series of bright lights surrounding him. Despite the darkness that had overtaken the land, the life on Cor had found a way not only to survive, but to thrive. Plants and creatures alike had developed bioluminescent properties that only added to the immense allure the continent now possessed. Trees were filled with glowing blue leaves, effusing bright green light from the cracks along their trunks. Small creatures with purple light shining through the fibers of their fur scurried about freely, unafraid of predators. Lightning bugs covered the skies with a variety of neon colors swirling in a chaotic pattern of artistry. This was unlike anything the world of Terrus had ever seen. Elucido couldn't help but wonder what hold the powers of darkness had over this land, if any.

Overcome with wonderment, tears now welling in his weary eyes, Elucido fell to the ground. As he sat, trembling, he felt the sensation of his thoughts leaving his body, as if he could see himself from the outside, as an independent bystander. Unable to recapture his thoughts, he drifted into another vision.

Gather around the table, friends! The time is here—a great and dark power amasses strength like never before. It is time now for us to fight for our territory with zealous energy. Our objective is clear; we cannot falter. A battle for the very soul of Terrus will soon be underway. Join me in this fight, and do not fear. I, Elucido, will lead you to victory and freedom. Place your trust in me, and we will not fail!

Astounded and still quivering, Elucido rose to his feet. If his visions were to come to fruition, perhaps he could lead an army of Defenders of Light to take back control of Terrus and fully restore light to the land. But who were these allies, and where would he find them? Since the darkness took hold, humankind had very little presence on the continents. On his journey, he had found only one ally. And as trustworthy as Amica had been, the small creature did not possess the abilities necessary to confront the King of Darkness.

In that moment of wonder, a searing pain blindsided Elucido. It felt as if the life force within him was being violently pulled from his body toward what appeared to be a manifestation of darkness itself: the ghost of a cloaked figure, rapidly approaching his position.

"Hello, Elucido, it is good to see you again."

"I've seen you before in my visions. It can't be. You're the King of Darkness!" Elucido responded, his voice wavering with every syllable. "H-h-how do you know me? Why are you doing this? Can't you see the world is suffering?"

"Ah yes, so many questions, yet not enough time to illuminate you. For the time being, you will have to accept that my actions are not only necessary, they are for the benefit of Terrus. Life has always experienced great suffering. I am merely providing mercy and relief, freeing the world from its torment."

Elucido's stomach turned. "You cannot possibly consider this to be mercy—death and darkness are not the answer to the world's suffering. Hope and light are the means through which life can thrive."

"I don't expect you to understand my reasoning; it is beyond your feeble, broken mind." The phantom of the king swiftly turned his back to Elucido, the shimmer of the aurora visible through the translucence of his flowing black cloak. "I am here simply to warn you. My generals and I have had enough of your futile attempts to restore light to the land. Your victories on Nomen and Vita will be short lived. My dark dominion is most assured. Should you continue your pursuit of light, your death will be inevitable. Erasure of hope is the only resolution to this conflict."

Harrowed by the king's words, Elucido cowered, unable to find any words to reply. The presence of the King of Darkness, even if only an apparition, was overbearing. He now understood the loyalty the dark ruler commanded from his generals. If it were not for the vision he just had, he would not have believed that anyone could challenge the king's rule. For now, faith in his visions, and himself, was the only thing keeping him standing.

As he disappeared, the king shouted: "This is your only warning. The next time we meet, I will not be so kind." His shadowy ghost faded to darkness.

Fueled by fear and adrenaline, Elucido began to frantically move around the outer edge of the continent, searching for anything he could focus on to ground himself back to reality. Even if he wanted to turn back from his present journey, he did not know how to harness the energy of the Aether conduit for travel. He had to find his way forward—both physically and emotionally.

For now, however, that path escaped him. Elucido sat in silence, wondering if, perhaps, such a path even existed.

Chapter 15

Death Spiral

In the distance, thanks to the illumination the Great Lights of Cor provided, Elucido identified the shape of a small structure, near the edge of a marsh. He quickly traversed the distance to the structure to investigate further. The marsh was teeming with bioluminescent life—small insects and even a few minnows swirled about the small pool of water at his feet in a rainbow of color. A bright yellow light emanated from inside the nearby shack—a lantern, he presumed. The building was inhabited and, as far as he could tell, its resident was home.

Elucido knocked on the door three times, each knock slightly more timid than the previous. He took a large step back and waited to learn more about the shack's occupant, not knowing if friend or foe awaited him on the other side of the door. All he could do at this point was hope for a warm welcome. Silence. Elucido knocked three more times, but with heightened purpose and amplified intensity. On the third knock, the door swung open abruptly.

"I have been expecting you, young friend," said a soothing, well-aged voice.

"You have?" Elucido replied, his head tilting slightly off axis. He had no expectation of his arrival on this continent, nor any awareness of the individual that now looked him in the eye. The man couldn't possibly have known Elucido would knock on his door.

"Do not fear. You are most welcome in my home. Please, enter, have a seat. I will get you a drink."

Elucido, still uncertain of his host's intention and trustworthiness, cautiously placed his weary body upon the chair the stranger gestured toward. The cushion of the chair was worn, a clear sign it had been used for many years. Elucido didn't mind. In fact, he hardly noticed the tears in the seat's fabric. He had not been afforded the luxury and comfort of such a seat in quite some time. Still, he wondered, there had to be a catch to this kindness.

"Elucido, it is so good to see you again." The stranger handed Elucido a cold glass of home brewed mead, then gracefully sat at the table, entering the discussion with the calm effortlessness of two friends falling back into conversation after some time apart. "Won't you tell me, how has your journey been thus far?"

"I don't understand." Elucido gazed at the stranger, trying to gather information about who he was, or how he might know him. "You look vaguely familiar, but if I am completely honest, I can't place my finger on how we know one another."

"Well, you don't know me—not yet, anyway. I, on the other hand, am quite familiar with your work as a Protector of Light. I trust you found the shards of the Aether Orbs I safely stored for you along your path?" The old man winked at Elucido as he grinned at the support he had offered to the Luxcreare.

"Wait, it was you who stored the shards? Please, tell me—who are you? What do you know of the Protectors of Light? Are there more survivors? What of the Luxcreare? Are the legends true? Can the darkness even be defeated?" Elucido's questions sprang from his tongue with a swiftness that caught his elderly host off guard.

"Slow down, young one; I am far too old to field your inquiries with the same quickness and energy you present. I can provide you with some answers, but I must admit that there are details you are not yet ready to hear. I will tell you what I can—the rest, you must learn on your own." Leaning forward, the old man spoke with confidence and grace.

"Let us start at the beginning, before the battle for the Great Tower. In a time where light, life, love, and hope were the guiding rule of the land. Humankind was prosperous and free, with little conflict. Even in the height of Terrus's Age of Light, however, darkness found a way to move through humanity. Doubt, fear, insecurity, hopelessness are all emotions felt by even the fiercest Protectors of Light. Over time, the depth of those feelings grew stronger in some, even to the point of overtaking their way of life. That hopelessness—darkness, even—was destructive. As hard as the Palaces tried, many were lost to that hopelessness. At first, the rulers of the land thought these were small, isolated instances. As time went on, they learned it was much more of an epidemic."

"I have seen that hopelessness." Elucido quivered as he spoke.

"I am certain that you have, as have I," the old man replied. "When you live as long as I have lived, you see your fair share of suffering. Not only in those around you, but in your own life as well. I have seen loved ones succumb to the darkness, losing hope and purpose. That, I fear, is what has led us to our current state. The King of Darkness has propagated his hopelessness to the entire land. He has leveraged that despair to gather allies to his dark cause."

Elucido interrupted. "But I don't understand. No matter how bad things may seem, I cannot imagine reaching that level of carelessness and destruction."

"Of course you can." The old man assuredly replied. "If you were in his shoes—if you had shared the same experiences as him—you would certainly have faced the same choice as him. You, me, the King of Darkness—we are all the same at our core."

"What choice could he have possibly faced to lead him down this path?" Elucido asked the question as if he believed that there was no reasonable reply.

"The choice to give in to the darkness, or to fight for light. You see, we are all faced with that choice every day. Of course, it is not always as consequential as the king's choice, but nevertheless, we share the same experiences more often than we care to admit. You, Elucido, have faced the same choices, even if you have failed to see it."

The old man stood from his chair, grabbing Elucido's glass to refill it. He did not allow Elucido time to respond to his assessment. The man continued speaking.

"I have seen the effects that the king's choices have had on the world, as have you. I must warn you, however, that the places you have yet to visit have suffered a far worse fate. Those who survived now live in the hopelessness and darkness of the world. I often wonder if they would have been better off perishing in the battle that stamped out light from the land."

"I know things are bad, but there is still beauty—you have found your home amongst some of the most beautiful sights I have ever seen." Elucido's passions flared as he felt the need to defend this newfound beauty.

"Life on the edge of Cor is beautiful." The old man hung his head. "But if you pay enough attention, you see that beauty serves a much more sinister purpose. Look at the swirls of light more closely, Elucido."

Elucido stood and walked to the window, watching the movement of the lights. Their movement seemed to flow in a circular pattern, but he saw no indications of anything menacing.

"I don't see what you are talking about." Elucido turned to the man for a response.

"See, young one, how the lights move in a spiral pattern, with each iteration more closely approaching the center of the continent. Come, let us walk upstairs and have a better look."

Both men walked upstairs to the balcony of the shack, where they had a much clearer view of the continent. Cor was shaped much like a circle, with a great depression in the center of the continent. The path to the Tower of Ib was that of a spiral. The closer one got to the tower, the lower in elevation they found themselves.

"There. You see how the lights move toward the tower in a spiral pattern? As they get closer to the tower, they slowly fade, and life progressively turns to death and darkness. This light—this beauty you now see—it all serves to fuel the energy of the Shadow Garrison. The general, Sanguios, derives his power and energy by siphoning the power of other life-forms on the continent. The immense beauty of Cor is the very lifeblood the darkness feeds on."

This was not at all what Elucido expected to hear. The presence of such a destructive force was not surprising in and of itself, but the anger Elucido felt seeing how this beauty was being manipulated started his blood boiling. Feeling his emotions swell, the Elemental Orbs he controlled swirled about—red, blue, and yellow, all in perfect harmony.

"Whoa, that is enough!" The old man's abrupt interruption sufficed to break Elucido from his gathering rage. The orbs dissipated as Elucido turned to face the man.

"I fear that is all I can tell you. The rest of your story is one that you must come to understand on your own. I have faith in you." The old man returned down the stairs and back to his chair, where he sat silently.

Elucido, still feeling the anger within, responded. "I hate the king—he has taken everything from me!"

"As much enmity as I feel toward the King of Darkness," replied the man, "I feel the same for myself. I can't help but believe I had the power to stop this and sat idly by while darkness took hold. I am as much to blame as the king himself. Elucido, the power lies within you to change this. But in order for you to restore light to the land, you will have to first confront yourself. Your journey will only get more difficult from here. Trust yourself, Elucido; you are capable of more than you might think. But before you leave, I have something that I believe you are looking for."

Elucido looked puzzled as the old man gathered his leather satchel. Reaching into the pouch, the man retrieved a singular, glowing shard of an Aether Orb.

"I wish you the best, but my involvement must end here." The old man handed the shard to Elucido, left the common area, and entered his private quarters, gently closing the door on his way.

With an Aether Orb shard in hand, and perhaps more questions than answers, Elucido exited the cabin, turned toward the center of the continent, and began the next phase of his expedition to the center of Cor.

Chapter 16

Into the Cor

Elucido couldn't shake the uncertainty of his encounter with the stranger in the cabin. He had so many questions—not just about the man, but about what the future of his quest to restore light may hold. His encounter with the apparition of the King of Darkness weighed heavily on his mind. The burden of his thoughts, overwhelming as they were, would have to shift to the back of his mind to allow him to focus on the perils of his trek.

The path he now tread was gentle at first, caused by the beautiful flora and fauna that flourished at the edge of the continent.

"If only the remainder of the journey would consist of such beauty and comfort," Elucido thought. That wish, robust as it may have been, was not congruent with the reality he would soon face. He had seen from his view on the cabin balcony that the terrain would quickly degrade and become quite hazardous. What he did not see was how dangerous the trail would ultimately prove to be. Elucido's travel would take him in a counterclockwise direction around the continent, winding down a steep gradient toward the tower of Ib.

A bright green, glowing moss covered the rocks along the trail. Incredible phosphorescent ivy climbed the tall, rocky canyon walls as if it was confident in its ability to bring its light to the sky to spread across the land. Even the fruit growing on the trees provided a warm glow that seemed to brighten as the flesh of the fruit ripened. Elucido replenished his stock of food. This fruit was a marked improvement over his existing supply of dry moss, mushrooms, and hard, unmilled grains. As he continued his search for the Aether Orb shards, he moved slowly, unwilling to relinquish the company of life and light.

It only took a couple of kilometers for the trail to turn inward and quickly dissolve from a land of beauty into one of lifelessness. Elucido could see a clear delineation between the energy and light of his current surroundings, and the point at which the beasts and plants of the land had succumbed to the fact that their existence was no longer welcome. The siphoning of the energy into the tower of Ib had clear and drastic effects on the continent. How such beauty could be taken advantage of became the consuming thought of Elucido's mind as he continued down the main path. He couldn't help but feel his own energy and hope being siphoned off as well. He would have to fight the darkness with more fervor the closer he got to his destination.

While the path remained fairly linear, Elucido did not know where the shards of the Aether orbs lay. Thankfully, he was keenly aware of the power the shards held to provide assistance in locating the other components of their once whole orb. At this point, Elucido no longer required a physical grasp of the shard to feel its pull. His attunement to the energy of the Aether Orbs and their shards was becoming increasingly refined. Closing his eyes and focusing on the energy of the shard, he homed in on a direction—downward. He knew that the terrain lost a significant amount of elevation before reaching its center, but the gradient the shard suggested was far more extreme than the path he traveled.

"There must be a depression somewhere that I can descend into." Elucido had forsaken the effort to contain his thoughts to the inside of his head—he simply spoke to himself aloud. It provided some measure of comfort, as if there was indeed another individual with whom he could hold a conversation. Whether or not there was another companion was irrelevant. He was happy to be talking, rather than being consumed by his own thoughts.

Elucido was not wrong in his assessment—the only reasonable conclusion based on the draw of the shard's energy was that he would have to descend deeper into the continent, likely underground. The light from the residual aurora, coupled with the Elemental Orb light that surrounded his position, afforded him the ability to spot irregularities in the terrain. As such, it was easy to follow the shard's guidance to reach a cavernous opening in the earth. The subterranean chasm was wide in diameter, likely a kilometer by Elucido's best assessment. The width, however, was not the primary concern on his mind. The depth of the cavern was unknown, and based on his previous encounters with dangerous creatures, he was outright terrified about what may await his arrival at the bottom.

Elucido had no choice. He had to find the shards. Failure to do so would result not only in Cor's continued devastation, but would seal the fate of the world, enveloping it in perpetual darkness. Having seen no other Defenders of Light on his journey, he felt the burden of salvation was one that fate had levied solely upon him.

Despite the lifelessness of the surrounding area, there were still vines that wove themselves around the entrance to the cavern, creating an array of ropes, nets, and tightropes that held enough integrity to support Elucido's relatively light weight. He trusted his instinct regarding the vine's strength, and descended the first vine, using it as a rope to rappel to the first ledge fifty meters below.

As he reached the ledge, Elucido's arms grew tired. The descent was physically demanding, especially considering that he had no prior climbing experience. Nearing the end of his endurance, he arrived at a small mantel upon which he could rest. The ledge he now perched upon created a steep path he could follow for a short time. This not only moved him closer to the bottom of the abyss but provided his tired arms a much-needed rest. As he navigated the path deeper, Elucido encountered a pronounced dimming of his surroundings. The light from the aurora could not penetrate this far into the opening. He would have to rely on his Elemental Powers to continue to illuminate the path to the depths of Cor. As easily as flipping a switch on a lamp, he snapped his fingers, and the Yellow Elemental that he had obtained through his victory over Dynamis radiated a soft mustard light from his position that provided ample light for him to determine his next move.

A short distance ahead, he saw an array of vines that created a set of tightropes connecting the ledge he was on with another outcropping that appeared to lead to more opportunities to descend. Luckily, there were multiple vines at varying heights that afforded Elucido the luxury of having objects to grasp to maintain a better balance. He moved slowly, uncertain of his footing at each step. The longer Elucido stayed on the vine, the harder he focused on his technique and destination. As his focus intensified, he failed to notice the Yellow Elemental flickering—a direct result of his shift of attention. Instinctively squinting, not consciously aware of the consequences of his waning alertness, Elucido focused harder on the landing that was still at least two body lengths ahead as he took his next step.

In an instant, the Yellow Elemental's power flickered off, unable to sustain itself without the direct influence of its controller. Elucido's foot missed its intended landing spot, causing him to lose his balance and slip from the support of the vine bridge. Gravity took control at that moment, his feet dangling, arms outstretched, wrenching his weight forcefully against his weary wrists. His left hand gave way quickly, tearing small pieces of flesh from his palm as he attempted to hold on. The friction from his left hand, while not sufficient to stop his fall, was enough to slow him, allowing his right hand just enough time to clamp down on its vine.

Hanging from only his right hand, heart racing, and in nearly total darkness, Elucido's feet flailed, searching for a place to land that would support his weight and save him from plummeting to his death. After a few moments of panic, finding no footing at all—no vines, no platforms, nothing but air—Elucido knew he had to change his tactic. Pushing through the pain, he reached up with his bloody left hand and took hold of the vine. It gave him just enough grip to allow him to raise his legs upward and cradle the vine behind his knees. Re-instantiating the Yellow Orb, he could see that it would be an awkward and painful shimmy to the platform ahead. Uncomfortable as the traversal was, Elucido was elated to reach the outcropping safely. He lay flat on his back, staring up at the glow of the aurora, thankful that the light within himself had not been fully extinguished.

Elucido wrapped his bloody hand in a strip of old cloth and continued his descent. Despite the pain, he was able to amplify the Yellow Elemental and dedicate enough focus to keep it aglow.

Jumping over a series of short gaps, climbing down rocky slopes, and continuing his rappel down a series of vines for what felt like an eternity, Elucido reached the bottom of the fissure with only the injury to his hand. At the bottom of the opening, he saw the light reflecting from the surface of a great underground pool. Not only that, but he witnessed the glow of life teeming within. Fish, amphibians, and insects populated the reservoir, reminding Elucido of the beauty near the cabin where his aged friend offered him sage advice. The pull of the Tower could not reach these depths, preserving the creatures' energy and life. They were untouchable by the powers of darkness—and that brought the Luxcreare some measure of comfort.

Lux Superesse Est. Elucido confidently repeated the Protector of Light's mantra once again. He had always believed that light could survive in even the darkest of places. He now saw firsthand how well-founded that faith had been. There were limits to the power of the darkness, and he was looking forward to finding and exploiting those limits. His purpose remained unchanged from his days in the Palace of Ren—find what was driving the darkness forward and, by any means, find a way to push back with greater force. Light must survive, at all cost.

Emboldened by his revelation, Elucido focused on the energy of the Aether Orb shard in his satchel. It was an easy recognition for him—and after a short wade to the center of the sandy pool, Elucido held his breath, plunged downward, and reached to the bottom, effortlessly collecting the next shard. His hopelessness had, for at least the time being, subsided and given way to confidence and anticipation of what the world could once again become.

The exit of the cavern was not one of ease. He had learned from his mistakes on the descent and worked to ensure they were not repeated. He took his time, focused on his path—being careful not to lose focus on his Yellow Elemental Orb—and safely reached the upper edge of the void. Upon extracting himself from the abyss, Elucido immediately felt the burden of the darkness weigh down his shoulders. The siphoning of light and life had once again become an overpowering force upon him. He was aware, rationally, that this was a burden that he could fight to overcome should he reach the tower at Ib, but that provided little comfort in his current circumstances. He knew he had to continue forward to put to rest for good the power exuded by the dark forces that controlled the palace, and restore light to Cor.

The pathway forward proved to be entirely unambiguous. While there were rocky walls and small clearings on either side of him, the primary path was well worn and free of any obstruction. Elucido moved laboriously along the path—a labor not induced by the difficulty of the traversal, but by the immense extraction of energy from the tower's pull. With each step, he had to force himself to lift his knees and carefully shift his balance to ensure he did not stumble forward. Progress was slow, and the loneliness he felt in the absence of life amplified the struggle.

A few kilometers ahead, Elucido encountered a rather large obstruction in the trail. A nearby rock fall had shifted large boulders from their perch atop the cliff walls to the flat land below. Additionally, there were spots where the boulders had removed the pathway entirely when they made their way to the valley below, leaving gaping holes that were untraversable. Surveying the area, he knew he had to pass the boulders and cross the gaps on the path. There was no other means by which he could continue on the walkway to the center of the continent to reach the tower of Ib.

Elucido's frustration grew. He had traveled so far from his home, encountering many obstacles along his way. And while the current situation was not as dire as some of his other encounters, he found himself unable to cope with the emotion. He cried out in a loud scream that, had there been anyone within a kilometer, would have shaken them to their core. He clenched his hands into firm fists, fell to his knees, and cried out again. This time, his vexation was met with equal parts rage and bitterness. The combination of emotions stirred the Yellow Elemental Orb into a flurry of energy. It spun quickly around Elucido, accelerating with each orbit, culminating in a burst of electric energy that fired out in all directions with prejudicial force. A bolt of lightning struck a boulder directly, causing it to explode into a fine powder that filled the sky with a cloud of gray dust. Elucido was so angry that he didn't even notice. He continued to scream, curled up into a ball upon his knees. Another burst of lightning, another boulder decimated. This time, Elucido took notice. He had cleared the first two of a series of obstacles out of sheer indignation. His rage subsided. He knew that a solution to his predicament was, quite literally, at his fingertips. Elucido stood and pushed his arms forward, generating a blast of lightning that removed the last boulder in his immediate path.

Behind the boulders, however, was a new obstacle. He now faced a gap in the trail, where a gargantuan falling stone had removed the earth on its way to the bottom of the gorge. There were no vines along this pathway for him to exploit as he did in the abyss. He would have to find another way across. Having centered his emotions, he knew that his anger would not resolve the problem. His intellect, however, had proven to be his greatest asset in the past. He was confident that he could decipher the solution using the tools he had acquired along his journey.

He attempted to craft a sheet of ice to fill the gap using his Blue Elemental, but the ice was not thick enough, nor did it span the full width of the gap. Fire proved even less useful, as it did not change the constitution of the rocks, nor craft any solid surface upon which he could traverse. He didn't even attempt to use lightning for this solution—there was no way electricity played a part in this puzzle. The only other option was to combine the elements to see if their synergy would offer more clarity.

Recalling the power of the Red and Blue Elemental combination from his battle with Onymos, Elucido tried the steam bomb to see what effect it had. Summoning a swirl of red and blue near his chest, he sent the helix of Elementals into the ground above the gap where the boulder had made its descent. The ground absorbed the steam, transforming into a flowing wet bed of dirt and stone that started a mudslide through the hole in the trail. Seeing an opportunity, Elucido moved quickly. He blasted the front edge of the mudslide with a barrage of ice, solidifying the ground into a bed of permafrost. The remaining mud continued to flow, but now extended further across the gap as it covered the frozen ground beneath it. Continuing to blast the front edge of the mudslide with frozen energy, the path developed before Elucido's very eyes. As the mudslide subsided, what remained was a still-frozen platform that allowed him to easily pass over the gap and on to the remaining portion of the trail.

He had moved a tremendous amount of earth with this method, leaving a fresh array of small boulders and dirt above each gap he crossed. There was one gap, however, that moved more than just earth. As Elucido applied his frozen cascade of muddy earth to the gap, he noticed something quite incredible. As the ground flowed into the opening, he glimpsed a flash of light—a shard of an Aether Orb sliding out of reach. He reacted swiftly, fueled by the shot of adrenaline from observing such a high valued object moving so quickly. He lunged forward and snatched the shard from the mud just in time. Catching his footing on a slippery, muddy path, he was able to cross the gap, moving on to the next set of boulders ahead. His journey continued similarly, blasting boulders and crafting icy beds of permafrost, carrying on down the path toward the tower. Emboldened by his cleverness and swift reflexes, Elucido's stride had developed into somewhat of a strut.

Chapter 17

On the Cliffs of Ruin

Elucido now traveled along a clear path that widened into a shallow valley. Using an abundance of caution, he dimmed the glow from his Yellow Elemental to illuminate just his immediate surroundings so that he would be less visible to any potential threats. The reduced light surrounding him revealed a faint light in the distance, at the center of the valley. The glow moved swiftly from side to side. It was clearly not the glow of the aurora, whose light moved slowly, and nowhere near the ground. This was something else entirely.

Elucido commanded the Aether Orbs that surrounded him to extinguish their light so that he could travel under complete cover of darkness. He moved slowly, feeling his way along the path by shuffling his feet and, at times, crawling on all fours so as not to trip on obstacles lining the path. As he got closer, he could begin to make out the source of the light. From this distance, he could see the silhouette of what appeared to be a bioluminescent creature that, while not a giant, was significantly larger than the Nullblights he had encountered on Nomen. The creature was fast, with sharp claws and flowing fur that created a beautiful blur of blue and violet light as it moved from location to location. It seemed nearly impervious to the siphoning of energy from the tower, yielding only small amounts of energy to the skies above. Elucido could not make sense of it. How was the creature able to retain such an abundance of energy? One thing demonstrated by its survival this far from the edge of the continent was how incredibly powerful the beast must be.

Choosing stealth as his modus operandi, Elucido left the glow of his Elementals at rest. He waited for the beast to move to a new location before carefully taking shelter behind some rocks. This was considerably more difficult than anticipated, as his only view of the terrain was the glimpses he caught as the beast moved between its posts. One thing Elucido had not considered, however, was how the beast's hearing had adapted to the lack of visibility near the continent's center. It only took one stumble on a rock to send a sound wave's oscillations right into the ears of the nimble, effulgent quadruped.

It was clear from the creature's reaction that it believed Elucido to be a threat. Whether it thought he was the source of the attempted siphoning of its life force was irrelevant. The beast took offense to Elucido's very presence and moved fleetly toward his position. Elucido turned to face the beast, this time realizing that his objective was not solely focused on saving his own life. This creature, after all, appeared to be a victim of the same dark forces that he and the rest of life on Cor faced. Its beauty and brilliant coloring were not typical of a Shadow Garrison beast. This creature was native to Cor and, had its energy not been siphoned by the powers of darkness, may have posed no threat to Elucido. It wasn't fair that this creature's suffering should end in death, especially by his hand. He hoped to escape the beast and leave it, at least mostly, unharmed. Its suffering, he hoped, would end by freeing it from the grip of the King of Darkness.

As the creature reached him, Elucido crafted a sheet of ice at its feet, sending it sliding past him, tumbling to the ground several meters away. The flash of light from the beast's fur as it moved past him was both beautiful and blinding. The sheer beauty elicited mixed emotions from Elucido. He was awestruck by how incredible this animal was, yet he was filled with sorrow for how it was now forced to live—afraid and struggling to survive in a world of darkness. He couldn't help but project some of his own feelings of isolation and fear upon this magnificent soul.

Elucido had little time for pause as the creature righted its footing, moving once again toward him. He summoned a charged Red Elemental blast, crafting a ring of fire around himself. The creature, afraid of the light and heat brought upon by the shield of flames, danced around him, searching for a gap in his defenses that it could exploit. Elucido was certain that the flames would not hold forever; he would need to formulate another plan to escape the beast. He knew the animal's speed would be too excessive for him to overcome, even with the aid of the Yellow Elemental's powers; his best bet would be to slow the being long enough for him to escape to a safe distance, where the creature may no longer see him as an imminent threat.

As the fire dissipated, Elucido ran a few short steps away from the sprightly beast, contemplating his next move. Perhaps, he thought, the creature's natural light energy might make it impervious to a lightning strike, or at least reduce its effectiveness. This seemed like a reasonably safe experiment to test. Releasing a small flash of lightning from the Yellow Elemental, Elucido hit the beast with a moderate burst of energy. This was enough to stun the creature, causing it to stumble a few steps backward. Aside from the initial impact, it seemed unfazed by the electricity. Under other circumstances, Elucido would have seen this as a failure; after all, most of the enemies he had faced this far required a more deliberate dispatch than this innocent casualty of circumstance. He now had a way to keep the beast at bay, protecting himself while reducing the likelihood of harming the beautiful being beyond its ability to recover.

Charging the Yellow Elemental into a fractal burst of electric arcs, Elucido added the icy azure powers of the Blue Elemental, creating an incredible array of frozen lightning. The impact of the electricity stunned the beast, while the ice slowed its ability to advance its position. The frigid blast caused the creature's joints to move at a slowed rate of speed, and with much more difficulty. A few more blasts would be more than enough to push the beast back, stun it, and nearly immobilize it, all while leaving it without permanent damage.

This flurry of frozen voltage provided Elucido ample time to flee to a safe distance, away from the view of the animal. While running through the moderately lit valley, Elucido passed by what he presumed was the creature's den. He saw a glimmer of light, and while he did not have long to investigate before the stun of his barrage wore off, he sensed what awaited him at the back of the small overhang. He expedited his movement and hastily retrieved an Aether Orb shard that the creature had been storing in its den. Much like his friend Amica, it appeared this beast had been mesmerized by the glow of the shard. Having no time to reflect upon his success, Elucido carried on his attempt to escape the encounter with the bioluminescent beauty.

As he reached sufficient separation from the beast's position, Elucido was relieved by his assessment that the creature would recover from his attack and resume its life free from injury at his hand. At the same time, he realized that the only way to truly set this creature free would be to restore light to the land of Cor and give it a safe place to exist. It was not only this creature's fate that rested in his hands, but all life on the continent. With a newfound weight upon his shoulders, Elucido understood more than ever what was at stake in his fight to restore light to Terrus.

Advancing further along the path to the center of Cor, Elucido approached a tall canyon wall where the trail appeared to end rather abruptly. He surmised that the best way forward—if not the only way forward—was to climb to the top of the cliff. The rock was smooth, however, making an attempt at bouldering far too dangerous to consider. One failed handhold would surely send him to his death. He had no climbing equipment in his leather bag; he had not anticipated the need to ascend such a sheer wall. Searching for an alternate route, or some other form of help, Elucido found nothing aside from some frail, withered vines that were not strong enough to support his weight.

"If only the vines were alive, I could use them, and the climb would not be so bad." Elucido pulled on a dried vine only to have it break free from the canyon wall and fall upon his head, along with the dust of the fragile leaves that were previously attached to it. As a dead leaf floated above him, it brushed the Yellow Elemental Orb that circled his body. Upon making contact, the leaf briefly glowed with a bright turquoise iridescence. "The vines react to the energy of the Yellow Orb—of course they do! The energy of the planet has been providing their bioluminescent properties!" Elucido could see now that life on Cor was fueled by the Aether Orb's energy. It was as if the continent itself was unwilling to yield to the darkness.

The energy of the Yellow Orb must have a similar resonance to the Aether conduit. Elucido realized he should not be surprised; after all, the energy of the Aether Orbs seemed uncannily similar to the energy he felt from the presence of the Light Elementals. Leveraging his newfound knowledge, Elucido touched a dead vine that was still attached to the canyon wall. Gently driving the electric energy from the Yellow Elemental through his fingertips, he watched in amazement as the vine came back to life with a radiant neon array of green, blue, and purple light. Not only did the plant's luminescent properties return, but its structural integrity as well, as it rehydrated and thickened into a strong rope that Elucido was confident would now support his weight.

He climbed the vine to a shallow ledge above, stopping for a quick break. As he removed his hands from the vine, he noticed that the residual electric energy was consumed after only a few brief moments, and the vine shriveled back to its previous fragile state. Elucido would have to be careful not to withdraw the energy from the vines while he was using them. He continued to scale the wall by reanimating the next set of vines on the cliff face.

He made quick work of the first part of the climb, with the vines ascending between stable platforms. Elucido enjoyed the privilege of rest at each of the platforms; some were even wide enough for him to sit and stretch his legs while enjoying an incredible snack of iridescent fruit he had gathered from the tree near the cabin. The next section of the climb, however, proved to be more treacherous. Arrays of vines formed bridge-like connections between platforms. As long as Elucido maintained contact with the vines with one of his hands, he was able to maintain the life-bringing charge of energy to traverse the gaps—significantly reducing the concern for his safe passage.

Nearing the top of the cliff wall, the presence of a faint glow on a faraway ledge struck Elucido. There was no mistaking—this was another shard of an Aether Orb. The distance between the ledge he currently rested upon and that of the shard was rather far. Furthermore, there were no vines between the two ledges. He would have to find another means by which he could reach the ledge to obtain the shard.

Elucido surmised that the vine dangling near his feet could be his best means to manufacture a path to the ledge. He grabbed the solitary vine, mesmerized again at the life that flowed through it in the presence of the Yellow Elemental's energy. He held the end of the vine tightly and swung it like a rope to see if it was long enough to reach the shard's perch. It was not.

"How do I extend the reach of the vine?" he asked aloud. Pulling on the vine yielded no results. "Clearly that didn't work," he scolded himself. "If the vine can support my weight without breaking or stretching, there is no amount of pulling I can do to extend its reach." Swinging the rope again yielded no physical results. It did, however, spark an idea in Elucido's mind. "Here goes nothing," he shouted as he wound up for another swing of the glowing vine.

As the end of the vine reached the pinnacle of its arc, Elucido fired a blast of ice toward the far end of the vine using his free hand. The ice struck the vine as it met the wall of the canyon, anchoring the vine to the sheer face of the cliff. He leapt from his perch on the ledge, swinging on the rope as a primate would swing from tree to tree. As he passed through the trough of his swing, he charged a ball of fire in his free hand, ready for its release. Reaching the apex of his swing, he melted the ice by hitting it with the fiery orb, freeing the rope of its hold on the escarpment above his head.

Having mere moments to execute his next action, Elucido swung the vine again toward the cliff wall, this time closer to his destination. Crafting another ice shot as before, he secured the vine to its new anchor. The process repeated three more times, with each iteration becoming more efficient than the previous. The alternation between ice and fire in his free hand was mentally taxing, but his attunement with the Elementals had reached a level of mastery such that he could swap Elementals in time to avoid a treacherous fall.

On the last swing from the vine, Elucido's feet reached the new ledge. He released his grip on the vine but did so a moment too soon. As the vine withered back to its lifeless state, his right foot slipped, leaving the edge of his mantle. His left leg buckled under the pressure, and his torso met the hard rocky ledge with a force that pushed the wind from his already fatigued lungs. He reached his arms forward far enough to stop himself from falling completely, though he was not yet free from the danger of the steep drop. Catching his breath as well as he could, he leaned his head and neck forward, attempting to pull his leg up to the ledge to offer another point of stability. After three failed attempts, his arms began to shake. The words of the old sage in the cabin resonated within him—Trust yourself; you are capable of more than you might think. With a loud grunt and a final push of energy, he mounted the ledge, freeing himself from the danger. After pulling himself up to safety, Elucido grabbed the shard of the orb. The relief he felt masked the pain and exhaustion from his near-death experience.

As Elucido placed the shard of the orb in his collection, the enervation from his trials on Cor amplified the weight of his satchel. He had lost count of the shards he had been collecting. After only a brief rummage through his bag, he ascertained that this was indeed the fifth and final shard of the Aether Orb that once illuminated the continent of Cor. A short climb from the perch using some reanimated vines hanging above him, and he reached the top of the cliff, the tower of Ib clearly visible. From here, it was only a quick jaunt to face off against whatever awaited him in the tower's darkness. But before he took his first step toward Ib, he was struck with another vision.

A flurry of light orbs filled the air—a barrage of Elementals sent from frenzied palms, countering one another in a furious sequence of lights. Fire and ice collided in vast explosions of heat and steam. Lightning arced toward thickened walls of earth extruded from a bright purple glow. Combinations of Elementals—green, blue, yellow, purple, and red—engaged one another in the ultimate display of power and finesse. As the sequence neared its end, a cloaked man pulled his arms to his chest, retracting the Elemental Orbs back to his location in a swirl of light that moved toward what appeared to be a black hole. As the Elementals reached his position, he spun in a full circle and knelt to the ground, arms splayed. Clapping his hands together, a large black orb appeared in front of him. The Black Elemental vibrated in its position, as if it was struggling to escape the control of its summoner. As quickly as the orb appeared, the man pushed his hands outward, hurtling the orb forward. In an instant, the Black Elemental absorbed all the other Elemental Orbs, covering the entirety of the space in darkness.

Chapter 18

Life-blood

The tower of Ib was a symbol of power, constructed of thick limestone walls covered in a sprawling array of ivy. The energy that flowed into the tower from the outer edge of the continent imbued the ivy with a bright iridescence. Elucido did not expect such beauty and light could come from an otherwise barren, lifeless pillar of the Shadow Garrison. He expected, however, that the interior would not be filled with the same allure. Even so, he underestimated the darkness and danger that lie in wait.

The door to the palace was covered in foliage. Elucido used the fire from his Red Elemental to dispatch the organic covering that prohibited access to the door's lock mechanism. He waved the shards of the orb in front of the latch as he had done at the palace of Ren. The lock gave way under the influence of the shards' power, granting him unrestricted entry into the palace foyer. The entryway was dark and foreboding. Elucido noticed immediately that the darkness held more power here; the glow from the ivy just outside the main entrance did not even cross the threshold into the palace interior. It was as if the light had been commanded not to enter. Activating the Yellow Elemental Orb, Elucido attempted to illuminate the room to gain his bearings and navigate to the throne room on the top floor. The sheer intensity of the darkness impeded the orb's light, granting him a heavily restricted view of the palace interior.

Elucido could see that the interior of the palace was adorned with mechanized fixtures. The continent of Cor was once considered to be at the forefront of technological research. The continent's people, known as Corians, were responsible for the creation of the airships that began the free trade between the continents, as well as the communication equipment that allowed the Defenders of Light to transmit information regarding potential threats to the Aether Orbs. It appeared to Elucido that some of their technological research was on full display—if only the light could fully reveal it to those who entered its presence.

With boldness, and perhaps foolishness, Elucido sent a jolt of lightning toward one piece of equipment sitting on a nearby table, hoping it would activate it and allow him to identify its purpose. Sparks showered the table and metal parts swirled, making an intense whirring sound. In a moment, a flash of light blinded Elucido as the device burst into a pillar of flame and smoke. Behind the flash, Elucido had distinguished a shadow, a creature lurking in the darkness, watching his every move. He immediately took a defensive posture, and activated all three Elemental Orbs, commanding them into orbit around his torso.

The light from each of his Elementals swirled around him, but their residual energy did not remain in orbit. A beautiful helix of red, blue, and yellow pulled toward the creature hiding in the shadows. Elucido had seen this movement of light before. This creature was a Tenebrae. He puffed his chest, amplifying the energy of the Elementals to prepare for the battle with the magnificent force of darkness he now faced once again.

Elucido knew well that his Red and Blue Elemental blasts would not serve much purpose; the Tenebrae were far too strong to be affected by fire and ice. He did, however, have a new tool in his arsenal—the powerful Yellow Elemental. Elucido fired a bolt of lightning at his opponent. The beast absorbed the energy. The Tenebrae continued its charge toward Elucido, rapidly approaching his position. Elucido fired two more bolts of lightning, each one instantly absorbed. He did notice, however, that the lightning absorption slowed the Tenebrae, as if the pulse of energy stunned it, albeit only mildly.

The dark terror arrived at his position as he fired another jolt of electricity toward it. He then rolled to his left, dodging the swing of the enemy's jagged claws. While the lightning had some effect on his foe's movement, he needed more power to fuel his assault. Taking a step backward, he bumped against a table, knocking an old piece of equipment from the surface, sending it crashing to the floor. He recalled only moments ago that the device he sent an electrical charge at had exploded, unable to handle the voltage the Yellow Elemental provided. If he could get one of these objects inside the swirling core of the Tenebrae, perhaps he could damage it from the inside.

Elucido sprinted to the far corner of the room, as far away from the powerful Tenebrae as he could. He hoped that would give him just enough time to set up his plan. He sent a gentle red orb of light toward an object on the table to his left, infusing it with an almost soothing glimmer of crimson, while simultaneously infusing an object to his right with an indigo glow. The light from these objects followed the pull initiated by the core of the Tenebrae, carrying the objects from their position on the table on a trajectory directly toward the beast's center. Elucido had to move fast to strike the objects with electricity before the belly of the enemy fully devoured them. As the objects neared the center of the Tenebrae, he sent the most powerful burst of lightning that he could muster straight at them. The voltage reached the objects just in time, sending them into a frenzy of movement, noise, and vibrations. He could not see the progression of the object's reanimation as the gravitational pull had drawn it deep inside of the Tenebrae's core. The effects of that charge, however, became visible rather quickly. The dark core of the beast swelled in all directions, tearing into a series of vertical fissures that spanned its height. From those fissures spewed viscous fluid and large chunks of tissue—presumably the intestines of the monster being forcefully expelled by the separation of the mechanical object contained within its core. It was over in an instant; the beast exploded, leaving Elucido covered in the remnants of the monster. His destruction of the Tenebrae was far more effective than he had anticipated. Wiping the mucosal sludge from his face and suppressing his growing urge to vomit, he continued to the next room of the palace.

Elucido found that a locked door sealed the entrance. This door was sturdy, mechanized, and had a complex lock system that seemed to be connected to a power source on the adjacent wall. Fearing that the control mechanism may explode with a high voltage strike, Elucido summoned the smallest amount of energy that he could from the Yellow Elemental. It was easy to throw all of his rage into a powerful blast, but controlling the energy to limit its output took all the focus he could muster. Placing a very small charge of energy on the control panel illuminated the panel's lights ever so slightly, but the door did not open. Controlling his energy like a rheostat, he gradually turned the voltage up until he heard a loud click. The door's locking mechanism sprung to life, moving an array of pinions and annular gears until the door swung open, granting him access to the large banquet hall.

Sending a bolt of lightning into the depths of the room, Elucido hoped to gain a sense of its layout before entering. He was provided with a moment of illumination, upon which he noticed something strange. The floor near the center of the room, it seemed, was moving, as if it was alive. He cautiously entered the room, taking considerable care to avoid the innermost point until he had time to assess the strange movement. Reaching only a quarter of the way across the floor, he tried to see if he could discern what hazard might await him. In that moment, the alarm on his face amplified, every muscle in his face stretching outward as he raised his weight onto the balls of his feet; the floor was moving closer to him. He summoned a bolt of lightning and discharged it to see if its light could tell him more.

The movement, as it turned out, was not the floor itself, but a swarm of small creatures. They were swift, thin, nimble, and looked like miniature Nullblights. The Shadow Garrison called these monsters Veloxblights. They were known for rapidly swarming their victims and shredding them with their razor-like teeth. When their victim had been cornered, it took them only a matter of seconds to clean the flesh from their bones. They were now forming a circle around Elucido, beginning their deadly assault. With a near-instinctual reaction, Elucido discharged as much electricity as he could. An array of small lightning arcs formed and radiated outward from his position. As the electricity reached the small creatures, it quickly dispatched them. Fierce as they were, their small hearts could not handle the amperage of the Yellow Elemental. One dozen of the beasts fell to the ground, dead in an instant; however, still hundreds more made their approach.

Elucido crafted a circular array of ice that surrounded him, making it just tall enough that the creatures could not jump the barrier. Taking advantage of his shelter, he sent a blast of fire over the barricade that he used as a flamethrower, torching the Veloxblights. Their bodies thrashed for a moment, generating a chaotic pattern of movement and illumination on the floor of the banquet hall as the smell of burning flesh filled the room. Elucido fired several more blasts of fire around the space, summoning not only the power of the Red Elemental, but also death. He continued his defense using the Yellow Elemental's powers, zapping the miniature dark beings in small groups, a handful at a time.

Having only dispatched roughly half of the creatures, and fearing that his wall of ice would soon be overtaken, Elucido attempted a new tactic. He combined the power of the Yellow and Red Elementals, crafting an electric firestorm. The explosively charged arc of firebolts consumed the entire volume of the room and annihilated the remainder of the Veloxblights in an instant. The room was cleared of danger, though the bodies of his foes remained, covering the floor in a sheet of burnt flesh that crackled beneath his feet as he walked to the mechanical hoist at the far side of the great hall.

The Yellow Elemental's electricity easily powered the hoist up, and Elucido rode to the top floor, prepared for whatever might appear when the heavy steel doors opened. As the pull of the cables slowed, Elucido took an aggressive stance, ready to enter the highest floor of the tower and bring the fight to his enemy. The doors creaked, opening slowly enough to amplify the anxiety Elucido felt. He rocked back and forth until there was enough of an opening in the doorway for him to escape the steel cube and enter the open atrium adjacent to the throne room.

He fired a bolt of lightning toward the entry to the throne room to reveal any immediate danger. Two Tenebrae stood near the palace's royal sanctuary—one on either side, acting as the guards of General Sanguios, who calmly stood at the center of the throne room, ready to witness the destruction his protectors would bring upon the Luxcreare.

Elucido made extraordinarily quick work of the Tenebrae by infusing two mechanical objects attached to the atrium wall with a bright red light that was absorbed by the beasts. Even if they knew what his plan was for the small machines, there was nothing they could do to stop the light from entering the black holes at their centers. They were designed, after all, to consume all the light in their presence. Another burst of powerful electric energy entered the two black holes at the Tenebraes' cores as Elucido struck each object with the Yellow Elemental's power. This time, Elucido took an additional step in his relentless execution of the Tenebrae; he crafted a wall of ice in a semicircle around his position to avoid being struck by the aftermath of blood and sinew forcefully cast away from the position where the foul beasts once stood.

"Well done!" A voice echoed from the throne room a small distance from Elucido.

"I have no fear of you," Elucido lied through his clenched teeth. "I am here to restore light to the continent, and to take back the power that the king stole from Terrus. I will do whatever it takes to conquer the hopelessness and fear brought on by darkness. *Lux Superesse Est*."

"Calm down, my boy, there is no need to rush the inevitable. Let's get to know each other a little before I annihilate you. I am Sanguios, general of the Shadow Garrison, trusted servant of the King of Darkness." The general circled Elucido's position while maintaining the formal pleasantries and traditions of the palace court.

"Unlike some of my associates, I enjoy the company of others. You see, I gain energy from being surrounded by life." Sanguios chuckled, knowing that Elucido understood he was using that surrounding life to siphon power for his own gain.

"You don't enjoy others; you enjoy the power you get by increasing their suffering!" Elucido's rage swelled once more, the Red, Blue, and Yellow Elemental Orbs pulsing with the same tempo as his accelerating heartbeat.

"I do love that power; you are correct." Sanguios took a less relaxed posture as he continued. "But you see, I don't view it as one-sided. I gain power while their suffering ends. It is a symbiosis in which both parties gain. There is nothing barbaric about it; it is a purely logical exchange."

"It is only a reasonable exchange if all parties are willing to participate," Elucido shouted, blood rushing to his face as the anger rose within him. "You think you are doing them a favor by ending their suffering, but you have given them no choice in the matter. They have a voice too; their desires are no less important than yours!"

"You are naïve, my boy—can't you see that life is most beautiful when on the precipice of death? It's the desperation for release—the anticipation of freedom that is the purest expression of oneself that I admire so dearly; and I am happy to provide escape for those in need. It is that exchange that fuels my soul and gives me purpose." Sanguios, aware that his words would not convince Elucido of his barbarous position, initiated a swirling bright purple light around his feet.

Elucido, reaching the same conclusion that his words held little weight in this conversation, flexed his arms, bringing the Elemental Orbs in front of his body in preparation to defend against whatever terrifying power Sanguios possessed. The Shadow Garrison general matched his posture, and initiated the battle for the Palace of Ib.

Slamming both fists on the stony floor in an amaranthine glow, Sanguios generated a platform of dirt and rock that rose and covered the breadth of the throne room. The newly formed earth moved outward toward the walls like a conveyor belt. Elucido did not expect the ground beneath his feet to lurch into motion—he stumbled to his knees as he began his involuntary transport to the outer wall of the sanctuary. Sanguios' mastery of the Purple Elemental had granted him the ability to manipulate the earth in a most powerful and striking manner.

Elucido hurled a fast ball of fire toward Sanguios. The commander didn't flinch—in fact, he didn't even move. He stood motionless, taking the fireball strike directly to his chest. His shirt burned, revealing a shallow wound where the Red Elemental had met its target. Both men stood silent, staring at each other, motionless. Not all things remained still, however. After a few moments of anticipation, the wound on Sanguios' chest began to heal as a faint glow of purple radiated from his core. The Purple Elemental provided its wielder with the ability not only to control the earth, but also to heal themselves. Now, more than ever, Elucido believed that the one who could control each of the Elementals' powers possessed the ability to save or destroy Terrus—whichever they desired.

Emboldened by the display of his incredible abilities, Sanguios swung his right arm, the Purple Elemental in his palm, resulting in the creation and tossing of a large boulder aimed at Elucido's head. Reacting with speed, Elucido struck the boulder with a bolt of lightning, shattering it with such force that a fine powder of dust filled the air, slowly depositing itself on both warriors' shoulders.

The earthy conveyor continued to push Elucido away from his target, making it increasingly difficult for him to aim his Elemental shots. He was able to stop the movement of the earth for a brief time by crafting a sheet of ice at his feet, freezing the earth in place and preventing its advance. He began his onslaught of Elemental shots to find Sanguios' weakness.

"I will never give in!" Elucido shouted as he sent a barrage of fireballs upon Sanguios. A few hit their target, doing minimal damage to his bloodthirsty foe.

"It is futile to fight the darkness when you know, in your core, that it will rule over all the land." As Sanguios taunted Elucido, he sprung pillars of sharp stone from the ground at Elucido's feet, knocking him off balance and drawing blood as his feet and legs were struck by the rising earth.

"You may have mastered the Purple Elemental, but you cannot possibly believe that you possess the ability to rule this land." This time, as Elucido replied, he switched to a combination of ice and lightning that embedded small pieces of ice shrapnel in Sanguios' flesh. The damage, widespread as it was, was superficial. The general healed quickly, as if the blast had never occurred.

"My powers are strong. If you think you can stand against Sanguios, general of the Shadow Garrison, show me what you can do!" Stalactites of stone dropped from the ceiling as the general continued to provoke Elucido; skewers of earth just missing their intended target as he rolled along the earthy conveyor.

"You have no right—no authority—to siphon life from this continent. These creatures are innocent and deserve to thrive. I will defend that right with all the strength I have." Elucido saw that even his strongest flurry of attacks could not create sustained damage upon his powerful rival. He needed to extend the duration of the damage from his Elemental bursts in order to stack the damage he was causing. Perhaps then, Sanguios could not protect himself.

Elucido constructed a blueprint in his mind. Watching the pace of Sanguios' movements, and the rate at which he crafted the airborne stone spheroids, he charged his next counterattack. As Sanguios drew his arm behind his head and gathered the Purple Elemental's powers, Elucido discharged a combination of Red and Yellow Elementals that merged into a supercharged pillar of flame. However, this time, the blast was not aimed at his foe. The yellow-red swirl of light and energy collided with the newly crafted stone as it hung directly over Sanguios' head. The extraordinary heat and voltage transformed the stone into a globule of molten lava that escaped the general's control.

The heavy magma hovered above Sanguios for only a moment before pouring itself upon him from above, not only burning him, but sticking itself to his flesh like a thick syrup. Crying out in agony, Sanguios flailed, trying to escape his fiery prison. Try as he might, however, he could not remove the lava from his skin. He focused his healing powers, and for a brief moment restored some of the integrity of his flesh; but the lava's persistence was too powerful for him to counter. Snaring this opportunity, Elucido continued to fire a flurry of Elemental bursts toward Sanguios, each one amplifying the damage caused by the sticky molten prison that fully engulfed his enemy.

"The darkness cannot hide the light—for the light penetrates everywhere it touches. Your time on Cor ends here. It is time for the light to bring life back to those from whom you have so callously stolen. It is your death now that will return power to this land." Elucido stood at attention as the floor's movement slowed. The earth beneath his feet faded back to a cold limestone floor. As he walked to the far corner of the room, toward the pillar that once housed the Aether Orb that illuminated Cor, he could hear Sanguios's faint wheezing. The wheezing lasted only a few moments before fading to silence as the cooling lava solidified, encasing the corpse of the fallen Shadow Garrison general in a tomb of metamorphic stone.

Approaching the pillar, Elucido collected the five shards of the Aether Orb from his bag and placed them on the flat surface. The shards assembled themselves, hovering above the pillar as if they had a life of their own. The incantation used to reconstitute the structure of the orbs was almost natural for Elucido to recite.

"*Congrega lucem.*" The Aether Orb's shape finalized as the glowing shards fused together into one unit.

"*Uniendis lux.*" The orb's light pulsed, increasing its intensity with every beat, as if the heart of Cor beat within it.

"*Lucem propagationem.*" A brilliant burst of light flowed from the center of the tower of Ib, throwing its energy in all directions, reaching even the deepest parts of the continent. As the light energized Cor, the plants were restored to life and all the beasts of the land glowed with a bolstered bioluminescence that filled the land with incredible color and beauty. Cor's life had been restored.

Elucido took a knee, knowing that he would soon be transported to a new land. He focused on the words of the old man in the cabin. *In order for you to restore light to the land, you will have to first confront yourself.* As the Aether conduit pulled him in, however, he heard a new warning issued by the sage, spoken as if he was in the throne room with Elucido. *Your journey will only grow more perilous and darker from here. You must take considerable care not to let the darkness poison your heart. Remember—the light shines brightest in the darkest of places.*

Chapter 19

A Dark Fire

Far away, in the dark tower of Sheut, a sweeping black orb spiraled around the exterior of the palace, gaining elevation with every pass of the obelisk's circumference. As the orb approached the spire above the throne room, a scream of rage burst from within.

Blasts of dark energy shattered furniture and decor throughout the palace, as the king's frustration manifested itself in a deluge of ashen ardor. He threw the doors of the throne room open, entering a chamber filled with a legion of Tenebrae. Understanding the danger they were in, the Tenebrae attempted to flee the room in fear of the destructive force heading in their direction.

The King of Darkness flexed his hands, summoning a powerful burst of wind that threw several Tenebrae from the window, plummeting to their deaths hundreds of meters below. He then focused a dark orb—the Black Elemental—around a group of the powerful light-consuming monsters. The energy lifted the Tenebrae and suspended them, dangling them above the ground like puppets being controlled by an obsidian marionette. Waving his hands from side to side, the king flung the Tenebrae into one another with concussive force, breaking every bone in their bodies. The creatures let out a shriek of pain as they were pulverized in a weightless battering until they were nothing but lifeless husks. Having turned their bodies into a gelatinous pile of flesh, he threw their corpses from the tower to join their counterparts on the cold ground below.

"In the name of Darkness, how has he done this!" The king furiously shouted at the remaining commanders in his presence. "His power grows, and you stand here waiting—for what? Take control of your powers and defend your palaces! Don't make me regret trusting you to use the Elementals to destroy the Creator of Light."

The Dark King's antipathy toward the Luxcreare swelled as he struggled to contain the anger within. He approached Caligo—the only general under his command who could calm him and return him to rational thought.

"My Lord, rest assured that the Luxcreare's powers are nothing compared to your mastery of the Elemental Orbs. Onymos, Dynamis, and Sanguios were weak, and deserved the pain they suffered. Their elimination has culled the weakness from our ranks. There is no chance of him reaching the tower and, if he does, I will dispatch him prejudicially." Caligo spoke firmly, with authority and confidence.

"I should have expected his powers to grow—the Elemental Powers resonate as strongly within him as they do myself." The king's frustration subsided. Caligo calmed his nerves, saving the palace from further destruction. Caligo's history with the king had bonded them deeply, building a strong trust unique to the pair. He had been with the dark ruler since the creation of the Shadow Garrison, and their confidence in one another was unwavering.

"Animus!" The king summoned the general who was charged with protecting the palace of Ba on the continent of Spiritus.

"Yes, my lord?" Animus cautiously approached the king's position, half expecting the rage to continue at his expense.

"Your power is far superior to Sanguios's. Return to your tower and continue to refine the power of the Green Elemental. Use it to infect the Luxcreare with doubt, fear, and hopelessness. Poison his soul. Convince him that the only way to survive is to succumb to the power of the darkness."

Animus left the presence of the dark ruler and returned to Spiritus to carry out his orders. That left only two men in the room—the King of Darkness, and his most trusted general, Caligo. The two men made eye contact, nodded, and parted ways to begin preparations for the potential arrival of the Luxcreare, should Animus fail his objective.

Chapter 20

Entropy

"You cannot defeat me!" Two figures simultaneously shouted at one another with indignation. They squared off, face to face, shoulders forward, fists clenched at the ready.

"I have worked too hard for you to stand in the way of my dominion." A figure cloaked in darkness took a step forward, raising his posture to gain a height advantage over his counterpart.

The dark figure's castigator stood taller, mirroring his opponent's stance. "Your dominion means nothing if the world loses hope. Can't you see your actions will lead to the end of humanity as we know it?"

The two men swirled around the room in a seemingly choreographed dance of movement and declarations, neither willing to release the hold they had over one another. It was as if they were bound by fate itself. It seemed, at least in that moment, that one could not exist without the other.

The cloaked enigma spoke once more. "If you continue to stand in my way, I will destroy you. Your existence has only opposed my will. I can no longer stand for it. This power struggle ends here—it is time *for the world to finally realize the power that emptiness can bring. Brace yourself and prepare to be engulfed in the darkness."*

Elucido felt the anguish and tension that existed between the two men in his vision. The crushing hopelessness tried to gain hold in his heart. His torment, however, was more than just psychological—the environment he now found himself in was affecting his body. The Aether conduit had transported Elucido to the continent of Spiritus, home of the Palace of Ba—Terrus' once thriving center for philosophy and ethics. His body ached from head to toe. He felt nauseated, weak, and his flesh was covered with small blisters that burned and itched feverishly. He noticed, through the thickened mucus now plaguing his eyes, that the continent itself was in a similar state of infection, its once lush landscape plagued with toxic overgrowth and gaping fissures in the earth.

Spiritus' once thriving glades had deteriorated into a series of toxic, malodorous bogs. The ground itself had also collapsed, wrought with open pits with no discernable foundation. The once fertile land had broken into many small islands, separated by vast arrays of skies—a darkened, seemingly infinite void of despair. Death and decay were the rule of law in this place, where entropy held dominion over the land, bolstered by the passage of time. It was as if life had abandoned all desire to persevere, unable to find purpose amongst the rampant putrescence. Traversing the shattered continent to reach the palace would be nearly impossible, as there was no way to cross the terrain in its collapsed state.

The more immediate concern for Elucido, however, was his own health, which seemed to be in a similar state of rapid decline.

As he rose from his prone position on the toxic soil, the blisters on his skin tore from the tension placed upon them by his movement. He winced in pain, rising only to one knee before stopping to catch his breath, gasping in agony. His lungs inflated with decreased elasticity, while the air they took in burned deeply—a consequence of inhaling the virulent chemicals propagated by the harsh winds. He needed to find a means to heal his body before the pain became too much to bear.

Mustering all the strength and dexterity his arms could find, Elucido carefully crafted a Purple Elemental Orb—a gift bestowed upon him through his defeat of Sanguios at the Palace of Ib. The gentle glow of the orb cooled his skin and provided a soothing sensation similar to that of the Alorcus plant on his home continent of Nomen. The orb brought not only a comforting relief, but began to repair the blisters on his skin. He flexed his pained muscles, watching the purple light intensify. He took a deep breath, feeling the relieved expansion of his lungs as the healing power of the Purple Elemental took full effect. Elucido sprang to his feet, feeling healthier and more ebullient than he had in years.

The relief, however welcome as it had been, was short-lived. Before his very eyes, the Luxcreare could see the boils forming on his flesh as his chest tightened, lungs filling with noxious fumes once more. The environment was so toxic he would have to fight its effects with every step he took. And while he had reached a level of mastery of his Elemental powers, their use consumed physical energy and required a great deal of mental focus. Elucido was not sure that he could sustain the violet glow of the Purple Elemental for as long as it would take to find the Aether Orb shards and restore light to Spiritus. This would be a test of endurance, whether he felt prepared for it or not. Focusing his energy toward finding the next Aether Orb shards, he reminded himself of the importance of his objective—*Lux Superesse Est*. Casting a translucent mauve sphere that encompassed his entire body, Elucido transformed the healing protective powers of the Purple Elemental into a shield that centered itself around his torso, following his every step as if it had been commanded to couple its movement to his own. This shield would have to hold in order for him to safely traverse the continent without succumbing to the toxicity that pervaded the land. He felt healthy enough inside the protection of his Elemental powers; it was now time to begin his search for the shards of the Aether Orb that once rested on the pillar inside the throne room of the tower in the Palace of Ba.

Not knowing where to begin his search, Elucido surveyed the small sky-island where he now stood. The earth extended from his position only a few hundred meters in any direction, ending in a sheer drop into the dark, abysmal sky. There was no vegetation, and the ground's makeup was relatively homogenous, with little change in elevation. The only features of note were a series of small, glowing green pools filled with a liquid he could only assume was caustic due to its neon color and faint glowing steam rising from its surface. He approached one of the larger pools as closely as he felt was safe to investigate. The liquid was thick, almost mucosal in its constitution, and it glowed a bright green, illuminating its immediate surroundings in a vivid lime-colored luster.

Elucido moved closer and leaned over the pool, mesmerized by the luminescence and surprising beauty of the bright liquid. His thoughts became lost in the reflection on the surface. The viscosity of the fluid prevented ripples from forming, resulting in a nearly untarnished mirror image of his weary face. He had not seen his reflection in some time. The sight of his dirty, scarred face came to him as a shock. He could see the physical effects of his journey, not only in the injuries he sustained battling to restore light to the land, but in the visible weight of loneliness and isolation. It was as if the burden of hopelessness transformed his face into something he no longer recognized. The memory of himself had somehow abandoned the visage he now saw clearly in his reflection in the glassy surface. Memories of the joy of his youth—time with family and friends—came flooding back into his mind. He couldn't help but tear up thinking about the merriment of the way things once were. He sat on the hard, cold dirt and slowly fell into a trance-like reflection of his past.

"Boys, come inside—it's time for dinner!" A beautiful young woman shouted to her two children playing in the yard. Her auburn hair caught the light of the setting sun, reflecting a lovely saffron glow as she returned to the house to finish setting the table for the family gathering.

"But Mom, Frater and I are defending the palace from the monsters!" Elucido and Frater continued their mock duel, wooden

swords clacking together against the tree stumps—or, as they imagined, monsters—lining the yard. As was typical, the young boys had been playing on the lawn for hours, every burst of energy they spent building layers of memories and dirt.

"Elucido, enough! Listen to your mother!" A stern voice reminded the boys to respect their mother's request. Rex, the boys' father, commanded authority when he spoke—but never at the cost of gentleness and love. The boys responded well to his charge and rarely pushed back when he issued direction. As the boys entered the house, they were reminded to take their shoes off and wash their hands.

"You would think that after the hundredth time, you two would not need to be reminded," their mother, Solati, scoffed; a faint smirk on her rosy lips. "Perhaps there is still hope that one day you will learn." She grabbed Elucido as he attempted to run past her, gripping him in a firm embrace and kissing his forehead.

"Yuck, Mom. You're embarrassing me!" Elucido winced as though he was in pain from the attention, but the giggling her affection extruded from him indicated quite the opposite.

The table was set humbly—the family was not of means, but they were blessed to have everything they needed, nonetheless. A series of candles were lit along the center of the table, as the sun would soon set on Nomen, and eating in the dark was a messy affair that Solati did not want to manage. Pasta with homemade tomato sauce and meatballs filled the room with a pleasant aroma that quickly distracted the boys from the fact that they still had monsters to deal with in the yard.

The family sat at the table and ate their dinner. Laughter filled the room as they shared stories of their days and teased one another lovingly. Life was simple, but simple was good. With their bellies and hearts full, they cleared the table and began preparations for bed.

Elucido shook himself from his trance, eyes filled with tears. Every memory of joy and happiness was met with an equal measure of sorrow—a reminder of the way things had been, and the hopelessness of how they may never again be restored. Now, more than ever, he longed for his home and the days of his youth. The pain of isolation was wearing on him. He wasn't sure how much more he could handle. Feelings of despondency built, giving rise to anger and resentment, directed squarely toward the monster who had ripped his life from him. The King of Darkness destroyed all that he loved, all that he held dear. He had stolen his future—his plans, hopes, and dreams. Elucido had never felt this broad of a range of emotions at one time. Depression overlayed with anger, fear, hopelessness, and resentment all simultaneously acted as thieves to the happiness and joy he felt reflecting on the memories of his youth. His current pain was amplified by the possibility of darkness taking permanent hold of the world he held so dear. He found himself more homesick now than ever.

Elucido wondered if it was even worth pushing through toward his objective of restoring light to the world. Maybe, he thought, the world had suffered for long enough, and surrendering to the darkness would give reprieve to the suffering and madness. The physical and emotional toll this journey had taken was perhaps beyond Elucido's capacity to endure. For a moment, brief as it was, the thought of giving up lifted a weight from his shoulders, giving him a sense of peace and relief. Fighting through the tears, he reminded himself of what the world once was, and what he hoped it could be returned to. The love and light the world once knew only stood a chance if someone fought for it. He took a deep breath and vowed to himself that he would do whatever it took—pay whatever price was necessary—to restore that joy to the world so that others might once again experience the same love he and his family had shared. He had to endure, for his family, and for light's sake.

Chapter 21

Across the Void

With his determination renewed, Elucido now needed to find a way off the small batch of floating islands he stood upon. They made up a constellation of stony platforms, a sort-of atmospheric archipelago that he hoped held the shards of the Aether Orbs that would restore light to the continent of Ba. Standing on the edge of the island, he fired a sequence of Elemental Orbs to act as flares to provide better visibility to aid him in identifying a path to the next island. One flare that traveled downward impacted a large area of ground, spreading its light across the rocky outcropping. Elucido estimated the vertical distance to the unfamiliar territory was roughly one hundred meters below—not an incredibly far distance, but farther than he could jump.

As he peered over the edge of his position, he wondered if the Purple Elemental's power could provide a means by which he could reach the ground below. During his fight with Sanguios, Elucido had seen the Dark Lord's minion craft a sheet of moving earth beneath his feet. Troublesome as that treadmill of stone had been for him at the time, it might be recreated with a less sinister application. Concentrating on the experience he had fighting Sanguios, Elucido formed his hands into a bowl shape, engaging the power of the Purple Elemental, filling the void in his grasp. As the power of the Elemental grew stronger, he continued to focus its strength on a concentrated area, building both its mass and density. In a bright flash, the periwinkle glow transformed into an oblong piece of granite that floated just above his hands as if gravity had no hold on it. It slowly and weightlessly spun as Elucido stared at it in wonder. A few short seconds later, the granite spheroid transformed instantly into a fine powder, gravity regaining its hold on the dusty particles as they fell to his hands.

Elucido could feel his hands shaking. He had the ability to craft a set of steps that could reach the ground below—but a single misstep could cost him dearly. He tested the plan at least two dozen times, crafting a series of small stones mere centimeters from the stable ground of the island. He quickly stepped across the stones in an awkward, barely balanced run, occasionally slipping from his stone perch and stumbling to the ground. As he practiced his skills, he was able to move between the stones without falling, but he could feel that he was on the edge of control of both the Purple Elemental Orb, and his ability to maintain balance. Practicing as long as he could without exhausting himself—and having no other options—he stepped to the edge, created the first step toward the ground below him, and began his dangerous descent.

As he reached each stepping stone, Elucido had only a moment to craft the next step and move to its position. If he took too long, the platform would turn to powder beneath his feet, sending him to certain death below. He crafted seventeen steps in total before his rhythm was staggered. Maybe it was a momentary lapse in concentration, or perhaps the exhaustion of the stair hopping set in, but as he leapt to the eighteenth step, Elucido's foot missed its target. His heel caught the edge of the stone, sending his body into an awkward rotation as he fell past the step. He had just enough wherewithal to create another stone below his position, but he didn't have enough time for the precision of its placement. The new stone disrupted his momentum as his chest bore the brunt of the force of his fall. This slowed his cascade and changed his rotation abruptly in the opposite direction. One more step crafted—and one more impact—and Elucido no longer had the energy to summon another stone. The last fall was nearly five meters. Elucido landed squarely on his back, creating a plume of dust that he watched rise above him as his vision blacked out.

Waking to an incredible amount of pain, Elucido attempted to sit up, only to find that he could barely move his arms, and his legs remained motionless, no matter how much he focused on their engagement. He coughed, tasting the blood in his mouth as he gasped for his next breath of air. Boils formed on his flesh in the absence of his healing shield. He knew he was in trouble and needed help quickly. Elucido had enough presence of mind to engage the healing power of the Purple Elemental that had kept him from being eaten alive by the toxicity of the land. He moved his fingertips as much as he was able, stirring the Purple Elemental's powers gently at first. The healing power of the orb restored mobility to his hands and arms, allowing him to amplify its powers further. One joint at a time, Elucido used the Purple Elemental powers to heal and rebuild his body. It took some time, but he was able to shift himself to a seated position, breathe deeply, and feel only a small measure of residual pain. He stood up, dusted himself off, and thanked the powers of the Aether Orbs for saving him from what was far too close a call.

Still shaken by the emotion of his near-death experience, Elucido surveyed the island on which he so dangerously took occupancy. This aerial atoll was much larger than the previous. It contained numerous pools of the viscous green ooze, significantly larger than the first he had encountered. These pools, however, were not as still as the last. A sequence of low-frequency ripples moved as though in slow motion, creating an oscillating glow just above their surface. Feeling no wind, Elucido feared that there must be something else creating the movement. Anything that could survive the hazardous viridescent sludge would clearly be a threat.

As quickly as he came to that realization, something emerged from the liquid and rapidly approached him. He glimpsed a six-legged creature, long and muscular with a tail as long as its body. Its skin was spiny and thick, a clear measure of protection against the toxicity of its abode. Seeing the creature's head made it apparent to Elucido that it was the apex predator in this land. The creature had strong muscular jaws, lined with hundreds of sharp serrated teeth it bared menacingly as it thrashed its head from side to side. From its throat it emitted a low, aggressive gurgling sound that startled Elucido more than he already had been.

Having six legs allowed the creature to pursue its prey while simultaneously swinging the enormous claws on its forelimbs to tear flesh. Here, Elucido was the target. As the aggressor swung toward Elucido's core, it let out a large snarl. Elucido leaned back, barely avoiding evisceration, the nail-like talons tearing his shirt and drawing a small line of blood from his chest. He met the beast's second swing with a frantically crafted stone—the Purple Elemental reacting swiftly to his command. The stone maintained its integrity just long enough to stop the blow from the creature's large claws. The force of the attack pulverized the rock into a small cloud of dust that filled the darkened space between the two.

The exchange continued—each swing of the beast's claws met with a firmly placed boulder shield. One after another, Elucido's stones protected him from a grisly gutting. The creature continued its assault, with each swipe pushing Elucido back two steps. He quickly retreated to the edge of the atoll, and a drop that he could not survive. Elucido took a more offensive action with the next shield, pushing it forward with a blast of fire from the Red Elemental. As the beast struck the boulder, the stoney object collapsed into a fine dust that was accelerated by the firebolt directly into the creature's eyes. The burning powder temporarily blinded the beast as it bellowed a raging roar at Elucido. It staggered backwards a few steps, writhing at the surprising bath of rock particles that had caused the gritty pain it now felt in its fierce scarlet eyes.

Elucido, lacking the cleverness and time to craft a more sophisticated plan, continued to summon small boulders from the power of the Purple Elemental. He thrust each orb upon his enemy's head in a barrage of blunt force that rendered the beast unable to recover. The bludgeoning continued much longer than necessary—Elucido didn't want to risk the creature surviving and coming after him again. After nearly a dozen strikes from the granite armament, the foe's skull had caved, its contents flowing from its eye sockets with a consistency that matched much more closely to the thick, oozing green fluid from which the beast had emerged.

After securing his safety from the six-legged brute, Elucido scoured the island for any signs of danger. The rest of the area was barren. Seeing no sign that an Aether Orb shard was nearby, and no other clues for where to find one, he knew he needed to move on to the next island to continue his search. This time, however, he saw no islands below when firing a series of Elemental flares around him. The only new territory he observed was on the western edge of the island, several hundred meters above his head. He would need to gain significant elevation without the considerable risk his stony steps had posed on his previous descent.

Elucido sat and searched his mind for ideas. He found it difficult to focus his thoughts due to his constant battle with the noxious fumes from the bright green pools. While the Purple Elemental could protect him from inhaling too much of the vapor, enough seeped into his lungs to cause a significant amount of fogginess in his head. Every time he felt like he was able to engage his brain in clever thought, his mind would wander back into memories of his past. Those memories, in this case, seemed at least adjacent to his current circumstances. He found his thoughts centered squarely on his youth—the days when he and Frater would play in the trees in the forest just outside of his hometown. On one occasion, he and his brother foolishly crafted a parachute from their rain cloaks and attempted to land a jump from the top of an Aspundula tree. Elucido was too scared to leap from such a height, but Frater, who had always been far braver than Elucido, took charge and jumped first to show his younger brother that everything would be fine. Bold as Frater had been, the boys misjudged the height, and Frater's leg buckled under his weight when he reached the ground, broken just above the ankle. He screamed out in pain, grasping his leg with both hands. Elucido had to quickly climb down the tree and help his brother limp back to town for medical attention. Traumatic as that childhood experience had been, Elucido now chuckled to himself, wondering why they ever thought that such a dreadfully crafted parachute would have any effect on the safety of their landing.

Perhaps the notion of a parachute—or in this case, a paraglider—was not as witless now as it was in the days of his youth. Practically speaking, however, construction of such a device would be a challenge. He had no materials to fabricate something with enough surface area and structural integrity to generate the air resistance needed to glide between destinations. The Blue Elemental could create a sheet of ice with enough surface area, but it would be far too heavy to be pragmatic. The Red Elemental was powerful, but it served its purpose by reigning fiery destruction on the environment. The Yellow Elemental charged the skies, but created no tangible objects he could use to build a glider. The Purple Elemental seemed useful primarily in the creation and manipulation of earth, and for its healing properties—neither of which would be of particular benefit in these circumstances. Elucido concluded the Elemental Orbs, as powerful as they were, may not be useful for crafting such a lightweight and strong sail. He would need to find another way.

Elucido returned to the stinky bog where he had defeated the leather-skinned beast to search for a solution to the problem of creating a paraglider. He realized that the beast's flesh was tough—tough enough to hold up to the air pressure needed to generate lift, yet light enough that it would not weigh him down. The large ribs of the beast could be used, he surmised, to construct a frame upon which he could stretch the tough skin. Confident in his design, he began his meticulous deconstruction of the animal's body, starting by taking his dagger and skinning the torso to obtain the large sheets of leather he would need for the sail. The smell emanating from the beast's intestines was far stronger than the stench of the bog. As the flesh peeled back from the bones of the beast, a putrid odor of sulfur and bile filled Elucido's lungs. His stomach turned as the color in his face matched the olive color of the acidic morass.

When it came time to retrieve the rib bones for the paraglider's frame, his dagger was not strong enough to saw through the bone. Instead, Elucido fashioned a serrated tool made of stone using the Purple Elemental power. This tool made quick work deconstructing the rib cage, separating each bone from the sternum as he sawed through with relative ease. The job was messy, and the amalgamation of slimy fluids from the beast's chest cavity made it difficult to maintain hold of the stone blade after only a few bones had been removed.

As Elucido cracked the fourth rib free from its position, a faint glow shone through from behind the creature's heart. As unexpected as his whole encounter with the beast had been, he had even less expectation of finding an Aether Orb shard in the beast's chest—and yet, here it was, securely stashed. How the shard had found its way inside the beast was perplexing—perhaps the force of the shattering Aether Orb during the Great Cataclysm had propelled it with a high enough velocity that it struck the creature, embedding itself beneath flesh and bone. Elucido could only speculate the plausibility of such a scenario. What was more important to him was the existence of the shard altogether. After reaching his arm elbow-deep into the chest cavity, he removed the shard. He then summoned a small Blue Elemental orb to create a micro-cloud that rained just enough water for him to clean the bio-sludge from his arm, and to rinse the Aether Orb shard clean before placing it in his leather satchel for safe keeping. He considered himself most fortunate in this find.

After obtaining all the raw materials he needed to craft his glider, he began its assembly. Tying rib bones together using tendons harvested from the creature's legs, he constructed a sturdy frame. He then stretched the hide over the frame, using the Red Elemental to tighten and dry the flesh to make it both strong and lightweight. After the sail was formed, all that was left was to attach handles to the frame. Retrieving the orbital bones from the otherwise gelatinous skull of the animal proved to be relatively simple. The sockets were of ample diameter for a solid handle, and the bone was strong enough to support his weight, having survived the battering Elucido exacted upon the skull moments ago. He tied the handles to the frame with more sinew, completing his sail.

As he approached the edge of the terrain and looked up toward his new destination, Elucido realized a foolish flaw in his plan—there was no wind he could employ to gain elevation using his newly crafted paraglider. He could wait and hope that the winds would return or devise an alternative means to facilitate his ascent. Elucido knew he could use the Yellow Elemental to initiate an electrical storm, but he could not control the direction that the winds from that storm would blow. If he could create an updraft, that would provide him with sufficient means to rise to the island above. He carefully blended the power of the Purple and Yellow Elementals to see what effect the combination might produce. As the storm built in strength, the Purple Elemental power added a measure of earth to the mix—specifically a cloud of dust that quickly swirled into a large dust devil. The sooty tornado moved violently, creating a powerful updraft. The strong winds caught Elucido off guard, nearly tearing the sail from his hands. He bolstered his grip on the glider just in time—a gust lifted him from the terrain as he accelerated upwards in a rather ungraceful aerial ballet. He tumbled in the air, nearly dropping his glider and falling to the earth below. Righting his position with an awkward mid-air roll, he caught another burst of air, providing him with sufficient elevation to then lean forward and exit the air current, gliding safely to the ground on the next island. Elucido landed and strapped the glider over his shoulder, wearing it like a backpack to free his hands while it wasn't in use. He grinned, thinking about the cleverness of his new tool and how proud Frater would be that it worked as well as it did.

Elucido found that the island he landed on was desolate—no life, no light, not even pools of neon muck to examine. He summoned the Yellow and Purple Elementals into another flurry of wind and glided to the next island in the chain with significantly more control than his first flight. The next island revealed itself to be as barren as the last. Elucido traveled to three more skerries, each providing no Aether Orb shards, no clues to their whereabouts, and no landmarks of note. He could sense, however, that he was approaching the center of the archipelago, where he expected to find the tower at the Palace of Ba. The single shard he gathered from the heart of the monster began pulsing, giving him confidence that he was headed in the right direction.

Not seeing any islands in the immediate vicinity, Elucido created a column of air and rode his glider to a great height. At the apex of the glide, he fired a chaotic array of lightning from the Yellow Elemental in all directions, searching for his next landing target. He could make out the faint silhouette of an island far to the East. Having no other locations to travel, he generated another blast of air—this time pointed diagonally in the direction of the land mass. The burst sent Elucido toward his destination at high speed; much faster than he intended. What he had failed to see in the flash of light that revealed the island, however, were a series of small floating boulders that lined the sky along his path.

The first boulder whooshed past Elucido's head, catching him off guard. He reacted quickly, firing a bolt of lightning to illuminate the thoroughfare and show him what other obstacles he needed to avoid. Flexing his torso and changing the angle of the paraglider, he was able to roll in the air, narrowly missing another stone. He stowed his glider on his back, his momentum carrying him forward, and fired two bolts of lightning—one from each hand—in a fork, shattering two obstacles headed straight at him. As he reached the peak of his trajectory, he began to lose altitude. Retrieving the paraglider from his back and firing another burst of air, Elucido was able to change his course upward, away from a large cluster of rocks, saving him yet again from an impact. His quick reflexes allowed him to continue to adjust his path, fire bolts of electricity at boulders, and maintain safe passage.

Between two of his rapid bursts of lightning, Elucido recognized a familiar residual light adjacent to one of the larger floating stones; it was an Aether Orb shard. He had just enough time to modify his pathway toward the faint light. With only a brief window of opportunity as he flew past the boulder, Elucido reached out with his left hand, sacrificing control over his flight path, grasping the shard and swiftly placing it in his bag before securing his grip once again on the glider. Within moments of gathering the shard, Elucido exited the barrage of stone obstacles and arrived at the largest island on the archipelago, where he used the power of the air current once again, slowing his approach, allowing him to glide to the surface and land confidently on his feet, a small cloud of dust forming where his sandals met the dry, barren dirt.

Chapter 22

Toxic Nihilism

A sullen figure sauntered aimlessly through the halls of the Palace of Ba. Animus, one of the Shadow Garrison's most powerful generals, was known for his nihilistic brooding. Nothing brought him joy. He paced the floor of the tower until finally taking his seat in the center of the throne room. Even when seated, his legs bounced on the floor with anxious energy, as if he would never find rest. A servant brought him his dinner, treading softly as he entered the room. The cold scowl Animus sent in his direction was the best reaction the frightened man could hope for—Animus was known for doing far worse to those who he perceived to be beneath him.

"Pointless, trivial burden of a human," Animus muttered under his breath as the attendant exited his chamber. "Though I suppose we all are, aren't we?" he continued his solo despondency as he consumed the beige sludge that filled his platter. Food was, in his opinion, not something to enjoy, but simply a means to fuel one's body. "We grind along the ever-moving pathway of life, marching slowly to a meaningless death. What are we but fragile piles of bone and flesh? In the end, none survive, and just as many are remembered."

When it came to the King of Darkness' selection of his generals, each had his place. Animus, nihilistic as he was, proved to be one of the key personnel when it came to obtaining—and maintaining—the king's hold on Terrus. It was Animus's view of the meaninglessness of life that allowed him to impose an extreme authority over those around him. People were disposable, and anyone who opposed his will was quickly disposed of. While this was not an inspiring approach to controlling his palace, it provided the motivation his subjects required to fall in line. The King of Darkness closely monitored Animus's approach, mimicking his methods to facilitate the creation and recruitment of the most powerful army Terrus had ever known.

Another strength that Animus brought to the Shadow Garrison's dominion was his experimentation in developing the monsters that the king used to amass his army. Animus had created magnificent beasts that were as exacting in their approach to destroying the enemy as he had been in designing them. His designs, however, came with a cost. His experimentation often led to half-finished constructions—piles of flesh that writhed in pain and suffering as they tried to spring forth into full beings. Animus saw these creations as failures, but did not feel any compassion toward them. If they were tortured by his unsuccessful attempts to finalize the formation of their bodies, it was none of his concern. He knew that all life must eventually perish, and as such, all of his creations—especially the insignificant ones—were disposable.

Finishing his dinner, Animus stood up and threw his plate against the wall. "Let the Luxcreare come! His existence is no more significant than anyone else's." He paced around the throne room, becoming increasingly agitated. "We fuel the world through our labor, then we die with nothing. Our purpose serves no benefit to any of us. Humanity is a poison on the planet and deserves to be eradicated." A faint green glow surrounded him as he raised his voice even further. "I will end the Luxcreare's suffering. Yes, as an act of mercy. All is lost, and that will be the salvation of humanity; that all things, including suffering, have an end. I will accelerate that end for us all, starting with the cursed Luxcreare!" He sat back down on his throne and took a deep breath, legs still anxiously jouncing.

Chapter 23

Stormy Skies

Two figures sat, shrouded in darkness, drawing plans on the tattered parchment at the center of the table. Next to them sat the Elementum Potentia torts, one for each color of Elemental. They consulted the texts while discussing what were clearly plans for a great battle.

"We mustn't allow hope to persevere—its survival represents the possible failure in our objective to stamp out all light from the land." The first man looked at his counterpart for reassurance.

"You are correct, but it is critical that we have a plan set in place for the arrival of the Luxcreare. We are amassing an army of terrible beings that serve our will without question. Their deployment should create enough of a threat to deter him from restoring the Aether Orbs and cement our victory."

"A most excellent point," the leader responded. "We must control the Luxcreare in order to bring victory to the darkness." The two men continued to sit in silence, drawing plans on their parchment and cross-referencing their research materials.

It was clear to Elucido from his visions that the King of Darkness and his generals had undertaken a great deal of thought and planning in their rise to power. They were, no doubt, continuing to strategize as he progressed toward the Palace of Darkness on the king's home continent of Umbra. For now, however, he had to continue to find a way through Spiritus to restore light to the land through the tower at the Palace of Ba. But the events he observed in his vision reminded him of the dangers that would await him if he reached his final confrontation with the King of Darkness. He did not know what plans the dark leader and Caligo were making to prepare for his arrival.

The atoll Elucido stood upon was considerably larger than any of the others he had seen along the series of sky-islands. A river of the bright green sludge flowed, albeit quite slowly, through the center of the land, falling from the edge of the earth in a rhythmic precipitation of large oblong blobs. He decided the best course of action was to follow the river upstream and see if anything significant was contained near its source. Approaching the river's edge, he noticed something quite remarkable. The vale contained a thick undergrowth of green, yellow, and purple plants. The vegetation was drawing fuel from the caustic fluid and had somehow adapted to survive its toxicity. It existed in what appeared to be complete opposition to the entropy that permeated the land.

He stepped closer to examine the beauty of a kaleidoscopic array of flora that had draped itself over a large boulder. It was bewitching, grasping his attention and garnering his admiration. At the end of the vine was a large discoidal green attachment that shifted its shape slowly in an oscillating manner, always staying close to its original shape, but transforming nonetheless. Elucido could not help himself; he reached out to touch the plant, suppressing the feeling in his gut that told him it was a bad idea. In an instant, the kidney-shaped pod transmuted into a vicious, snapping malformation. Elucido's reaction was quick; just quick enough to avoid being maimed by the sharp thorny fangs the plant had revealed as it attempted to defend itself. Beauty, he was reminded, is often used to mask the true nature contained within. Elucido shook his head in disappointment at his foolhardiness, while chuckling aloud.

"Alright—you almost got me." He shook his finger at the plant and turned his attention upstream. He could see the glow of the emerald channel reaching the far end of the valley at what appeared to be the base of a cascading series of falls. After a brief hike along the riverbed, he reached the outpouring.

The viscous fluid cast itself over the edge of a wide rock ledge above Elucido's head, creating an eerie laminar flow of glowing ooze. The sound the liquid made as it reached the shallow pool at its base reminded Elucido of the sound his mother's sticky rice pudding used to make as it hit his plate—a combination of a dull "thud" and a gentle, wet "slap". He was amazed at how this virulent toxic hazard could somehow make him homesick and hungry, yet here he was—both. As he stood before the sheet of falling sludge, he caught a momentary glimpse behind the falls as the wind pushed its way through the previously unbroken wall of liquid.

There was an opening; a deep cavern that beckoned Elucido, as if taunting him to discover the secrets it held within.

Elucido crafted a large rock from the Purple Elemental, roughly the size of his body, that he placed near the upper edge of the falls, where it began its descent to the oozing river below. It was large enough to bifurcate the flow of the cascading sludge, creating a v-shaped gap just big enough for him to pass through, untouched by the caustic river. He cautiously entered the depths of the cavern, summoning the bright light of the Yellow Elemental to guide his way. Only ten meters into the darkness, he encountered his first hurdle.

Before his weary eyes, in a place devoid of any human presence, Elucido gazed upon a stone door. Surrounding the door was a series of runes—a clear indication that the passageway was not of natural origin. The runes, however, seemed strange to Elucido. They were similar to the ancient languages he studied during his apprenticeship in the Palace of Ren, yet they seemed less refined. He could not decipher their meaning at first glance, but he was convinced of one thing; he would be unable to open the door if he failed to decipher their message.

While he was frustrated at his lack of understanding of the runes, Elucido was grateful to be challenged with a riddle. After all, his prowess had always been in the intellectual realm, and the burden of physical combat had become rather tiresome. He was eager to flex his mind once again, even though he was uncertain whether he was capable of finding the solution. Elucido channeled his energy to brighten the glow of the Yellow Elemental Orb he had been using to illuminate the passageway. He counted five runes in total, spanning the breadth of the arch. Under the bright yellow light, Elucido recognized the topmost rune and quickly deciphered its meaning—'kerditheis', or in modern language 'earned'. The other runes, however, he did not recognize. They seemed familiar, yet somehow incomplete. "What could the word 'earned' mean?" he thought.

After staring at the remaining engravings for some time, Elucido was at a loss. How could he understand what wasn't there to see, especially with no context? He tried a different approach, summoning a bright heliotrope glow—the Purple Elemental—to see if he could use its earth-controlling powers to shift the heavy stone door from its closed position. Under the bright purple glow, he pushed, harder and harder, with the orb. The door vibrated, but did not change its position. It was futile to try to force the door open. Elucido glanced once again at the topmost rune, searching for other clues; however, as his gaze focused on the rune, he noticed it was now only partially completed. Perplexed, he tilted his head to see if a change in angle would also lead to a change in perspective. The rune remained unaltered. He scanned the remaining runes, and much to his surprise, the fourth rune was now completed. It read 'thysia', which translated into Terrus' modern language as 'sacrifice'. This unnerved Elucido greatly. 'Earned'. 'Sacrifice'. What was needed to get beyond this door? And what could be hidden behind it?

Elucido now had two of the five runes decoded, but he still did not know how he had revealed either. The only thing he had done was fail to open the door with the Purple Elemental. Failing seemed an unlikely means by which the runes revealed themselves. He subdued the Purple Elemental Orb and re-ignited the Yellow Elemental's powers in order to brighten the room more fully. He noticed that as the violet glow subsided, the fourth rune lost elements of its makeup, hiding a large part of the rune. However, the topmost rune completed itself as the yellow light took hold of the room.

"It's the light!" Elucido sprung from the rock he sat on, a grin beaming from ear to ear. He had done it—the color of the Elementals' light brought the runes into full view. He swapped the Yellow Elemental out for the Red Elemental, bringing the cavern into a sharp, cerise glow. Precisely as he expected, the first rune was now completed, revealing to him the word 'perasma'—which translated as 'passage'. A quick switch to the Blue Elemental provided the next clue, 'prosvasi'—'access'. The message, so far, read 'passage', 'access', 'earned', 'sacrifice'. He snapped his head toward the final rune and immediately came to the realization that he only had control over four elementals—Red, Blue, Yellow, and Purple. The fifth rune's translation was outside his grasp.

"The passage access is earned through the sacrifice of... what?" The final piece of the puzzle was perhaps the most important. What sacrifice was required to gain access to whatever was hidden in the egress? Sacrifice was far too strong of a word for him to attempt trial and error to determine. He sat back down and scratched his head, searching his thoughts for what the mystery oblation might be. Nothing stood out to him as a viable option;

at least nothing that he was confident enough to sacrifice without confirmation. If he wanted to reveal what the offering was, he would have to find a way to illuminate the last rune. He reflected on what he knew of the Elemental powers. Back on Nomen, he had a vision—a vision in which he controlled the powers of the Elemental Orbs. He closed his eyes and replayed the action in his mind. He watched as the memory of his vision revealed him cycling through the Elementals; from Red to Blue, then to Yellow, Purple, and finally ending its cycle in a transformation to the Green Elemental.

"Green light is what is needed to reveal the final rune." Elucido was certain that the Green Elemental's power would allow him to decipher the last rune and gain access through the door. That confidence, assured as it was, did not help Elucido. He did not control the Green Elemental's power, nor did he know how he could obtain it. He pondered for a moment. "I suppose, though, I never technically used the Elemental powers on the runes to reveal them. It was the glow of the light that divulged their full shape. But still, I don't have a green light to shine upon the runes." Elucido strained his mind, searching for a sophisticated solution to find a green light. As he had a habit of doing in school, he was entirely overthinking the problem.

"By the love of Terrus!" Elucido grabbed his face with the sweaty palm of his right hand. "How could it take me this long to figure it out? Yellow and blue make green. I am a colossal idiot!" He chuckled while he scolded himself, shaking his head from side to side. In his right hand, he crafted a small Yellow Elemental Orb, initiating a golden light. In his left hand, he crafted a Blue Elemental Orb of similar size, bringing an azure glow to augment the light he held in his right palm. Moving his hands closer together, the colors merged into a beautiful emerald glimmer at the center, while keeping their individual yellow and blue lights around their perimeter. All that was left was for Elucido to position the light in front of the fifth rune. As he did so, the final rune came into full view, displaying the word 'aima'.

"Blood." A surge of adrenaline sliced through his veins as he spoke the word. "The passage access is earned through the sacrifice of blood." He took a deep breath and returned to his seat. At the center of the door, he took notice of a small stone basin that, at first glance, appeared to be decorative. It was clear, however, that the purpose of the minute reservoir was to collect the byproduct of self-immolation from the one who sought entry to the depths of the cavern. He stood and approached the door, unsheathing his dagger as he reached the cold stone. Fighting through the adrenaline, trying to focus his mind on anything else, he clutched the blade of the dagger with his left hand and hesitantly pulled his right hand toward his hip. His hesitation only heightened the pain he felt, as his poniard left an uneven, jagged tear in his flesh. Instinctively, Elucido pulled his hand back and grabbed his wrist, blood flowing from his wound and striking the ground at his feet. Resisting the urge to collapse from the pain he now felt, he thrust his injured hand forward, directly above the stone receptacle. Blood flowed freely from the deep wound in his hand, filling the basin.

The warmth of the blood met with the cold stone, resulting in a gruesome, steamy pool of sanguine fluid.

A loud crackle erupted as the door began its movement and freed itself from its stagnant position. It creaked as it swung inward, granting access to the one who had been willing to make the blood sacrifice. As Elucido stepped inside, he swiftly employed the Purple Elemental's powers to seal the wound on his hand and dull the pain. It took only a moment to heal the gash. But the memory, like the scar, would stay with Elucido forever. He brightened the room with the Yellow Elemental's light and cautiously continued his entry into the depths of the cavern.

Chapter 24

The Prophecy of the Luxcreare

A set of stairs descended into a small room beneath the antechamber. It was a subterranean gallery of graves lined with tombs, each covered with a flat sandstone plaque with heavily worn engravings. Clearly, those buried in the catacombs were important; they wouldn't have been given the honor of such a ceremonial burial if they were insignificant. Unfortunately, with the lack of remaining markings on the tombstones, Elucido was unsure if he would ever know the identities of those contained within.

He thought it was important for him to identify at least one occupant to see if he could learn anything about who they were, or why they were buried in the depths of the catacombs in such protected graves. It took little effort for him to shift one tombstone aside and reveal the contents of the chamber. It was empty. He pushed another plaque aside to find yet another empty grave. The third attempt, however, yielded a different result. Elucido pushed the block aside to find a solitary skull with brightly glowing eyes. Startled, he took a step back and sharply inhaled. The skull was not attached to anything—in fact, there were no other bones in the tomb. Either the bones had been removed, or the skull was placed in isolation deliberately. Either way, someone had manipulated the graves with a specific purpose. Elucido reached out and lifted the skull, the brightly lit shard of an Aether Orb dropping from within. He retrieved the shard of the orb and placed the skull back in its resting spot. Satisfied with his find, yet still perplexed at the circumstances surrounding the placement of such a treasure, he determined it was time to pass through the catacombs and continue into the depths of the chamber.

In the next room, a series of pictographs lined the walls on both sides in what appeared to be the telling of a great story. Elucido could not identify where his trust originated. Perhaps it was the age of the ruins, the required mastery of the Elemental Powers, or the necessity to shed blood to enter, but he believed the tales contained on these walls were inerrant. The academic in him was thrilled by the opportunity to study the images and learn more about the power of the Elementals. He read the text that was written on the wall closest to him, starting at the beginning—a history of the creation of Terrus.

In the beginning, when all that existed was the Great Void, the world was formed from the Aether. A series of continents came into existence, each afloat in the vastness of the sky. All that was formed existed in darkness. From the earth, life sprung forth, as if the spirit of the land itself created plants and animals, each in kind with the continent's composition. As life emerged, the Aether provided the final element needed for the world to survive—light. Out of the Great Void came five glassy orbs that hovered effortlessly in the skies above each continent. Each Aether Orb brought with it a powerful light that illuminated the land and allowed life to thrive.

The five continents existed in perfect harmony for thousands of years—life flourished and the light shone brightly. But there was something missing from the world. As beautiful as it was, Terrus had no one to foster its development. The cycle of life had remained unaltered, and the Aether grew weary with its stagnation. In a flash of blinding light, the Aether formed humans from the powerful energy contained within. Each continent was populated with a colony, and each colony was entrusted with the care and development of their newly gifted land.

For many generations, humanity cared for the land and the creatures, revering the Aether and the life it provided. But something happened the Aether had not anticipated. As bright as the Aether Orbs' lights were, they could not cover the darkness that had started to grow in some people's hearts. It began slowly at first, as the pain of watching loved ones perish became more than some could bear. The sting of loss led to a desire for more—for greater fulfillment, more power to control circumstances, and the ability to shape life according to one's own will. And while people's intention to improve their lives seemed noble in their minds, they failed to realize the effect that wrestling control away from others would have. The longing for authority pushed them to take advantage of one another to better *their own lives—greed festered in their hearts, and no matter what they had, it was never enough.*

Over time, the darkness overtook some completely, leading to war and famine across the land. What the Aether had borne had become corrupted and broken. There were, however, those who still clung to the ways of light. The five palaces—Ren, Ka, Ib, Ba, and Sheut—were formed, one on each continent, by the group that called themselves the Protectors of Light. The Aether Orbs were tethered from their place in the sky and transported within the tower of each of the palaces in order to protect them from the darkness. With this, the Protectors established their purpose, Lux Superesse Est—Light Must Survive.

Elucido was astonished at the level of detail in the texts. He knew the theories surrounding the foundation of the Aether Orbs, but to read confirmation of how the world had come into existence struck him powerfully. He felt validated; all the work he had done in the Palace of Ren had meaning and purpose. He was one of the Protectors of Light. He was fighting to preserve the sanctity of the world and restore it to the beauty the Aether had intended. If he was fighting for the purpose of the Aether itself, how could he possibly be wrong? He shifted his attention to the wall opposite of the detailed history of Terrus. A series of runes at the top of the wall clearly read 'The Prophecy of the Luxcreare'. Elucido's chest tightened, his stomach rising to his throat in anticipation of the answers the augury would provide.

In a world marked by despair, the skies have fallen, and the land is barren. Darkness has consumed all hope, and the world is at war with itself. The land is broken, and light is the scarcest resource. But legend tells of a hero, worthy of the light. One for whom the darkness breaks, who will bring hope to the people. A hero with the power to restore life to a broken world. But the darkness will not relinquish control of the world so easily.

A foe greater than the world had ever seen has amassed his power in secret. None saw the forces of darkness taking hold so strongly. From the darkness rose a potent king. His ascension to the throne was hidden from the world—a secret kept by some who had previously sworn to keep the light safe from the despondency mired in the hearts of humanity. For the darkness dwells within us all, unforgiving and relentless. It takes hold and captures our every thought. Even those sworn to protect the light are vulnerable to being consumed by its hopelessness.

However, darkness exists solely as a lack of light. The Luxcreare alone has the power to break free of despair and restore hope to the land of Terrus. He will wrestle with the darkness contained within his own heart—a darkness fueled by hopelessness and fear. However, the future is not written in stone; if the Luxcreare should fail in his objective, the world will be thrust into unrelenting darkness and the power of the Aether will fade forever. For the Luxcreare to overcome the darkness, he must first embrace its origin. Not only will the Luxcreare need to confront the King of Darkness, he will have to come to understand...

The last section of pictographs was missing. The wall's surface was broken and ragged, destroying the conclusion of the prophecy. Elucido was shattered; he felt weightless and weak at the revelation that he would not know the full extent of the prophecy. He wanted confidence that the story of the Luxcreare—his story—had a happy ending. It was clear that the Luxcreare had the power to restore the world, but that future was not guaranteed. What was it that he was meant to understand? He knew what was at stake; he would have to fight for his life against the powers of darkness. The world could not afford for him to fail.

Elucido searched the remaining portion of the cavern walls for more pictographs that might help him obtain the missing information from the prophecy. All that he saw was a pile of rubble amassed in the far corner of the room. He searched the rubble for additional insights, perhaps even a shard of an Aether Orb. What Elucido found in the rubble, however, was of far greater significance to the Luxcreare's journey. He reached down and picked up a small item—a mere trinket to anyone else. But to him, it represented much more. He closed his eyes tightly, re-opened them, and checked again, hoping that what he saw was nothing more than a myopic distortion. However, his eyes were not deceived, and the object remained unaltered by a fresh view. Elucido was shaken to his core. The blood drained from his face as his legs weakened. He looked away, as if removing it from his sight meant that he had not discovered it. The only instinct was the intense desire for flight. His legs took over, sending him rapidly out the door of the cavern and back into the darkness of the sky.

Chapter 25

At Arm's Length

Chest heaving, heart pounding, and adrenaline running on an open tap, Elucido exited the passageway back to the river basin. As he withdrew from the underground chamber, he heard a noise from the depths of the catacombs. He paused, listening for any additional sounds, but heard nothing more. Having convinced himself that the noise was a mere auditory apparition, a result of his already frayed nerves, he continued his trek forward toward the Palace of Ba. As he reached the edge of the hill, he peered over his shoulder back toward the cavern, where he believed he saw a faint glow moving slowly in his direction. The luminosity's movement seemed to couple itself to him. When he moved, so did the glow; when he stopped, it mimicked. While the glowing mass appeared to have an interest in Elucido, it remained at a distance that caused no immediate concern to him. As long as it posed no threat, he did not want to risk a direct confrontation with it. He carried on, looking over his shoulder every few paces to ensure the danger did not amplify.

Elucido now had three shards in hand. Two more, he presumed, and he could enter the Palace of Ba and restore light to the land of Spiritus. What now stood between him and the tower was an immense bog with narrow pathways that meandered through it in a convoluted maze of rock and viscous green ooze. A sea of clouds lined the sky above the swampland, emitting a shower of acidic rain—the source of the fluid that flowed through the land. As he approached, a droplet landed on his hand and gave way to an immediate burning sensation as it ate through the flesh, reaching the bone in a matter of seconds. He took three paces backward, recoiling and shouting in pain as he crafted an umbrella of plum light, borne of the Purple Elemental, to stop the droplets before they reached his flesh.

He navigated the marshland with extreme care, making sure not to step on the muddy earth and sink into the caustic fluid. The Purple Elemental was strong in its healing powers, but he feared it would not be strong enough to protect him from full immersion in the mordant mire. There were sections of the bog where Elucido needed to craft sheets of earth to traverse—temporary bridges of rock that allowed him safe passage. Toxic plants lined the passageway, adding to the care in which he tread along the path. Despite all the dangers, the guidance of the Aether Orb shards allowed him to make quick time through the exterior of the maze, where he eventually found his progress halted as he approached a large acidic lake at the center of the swamp.

The caustic rain droplets landed on the surface of the lake, creating small ripples that subsided almost immediately due to the thickness of the fluid. The lagoon was expansive, extending to the horizon, where Elucido could make out the faint silhouette of the tower at the Palace of Ba. He felt the shards of the Aether Orb pulling him toward the tower. While he only had three shards in his possession, the strength of the pull reassured him that the remaining shards were on the path.

With the large lilac umbrella protecting him from the acidic rain, Elucido shifted his focus to crossing the large lagoon. He was able to use the Purple Elemental's powers to craft small land bridges between the many pockets of terrain surrounded by the sticky fluid. That allowed him to move closer to the center of the wide pool while avoiding the hazards that the liquid presented. Elucido noticed that as he moved closer to the nexus of the lake, one precarious step at a time, the magnitude of the ripples on its surface amplified. He paused, watching the reflections of the light move across the surface as each ripple radiated. The rhythm of the movement was hypnotizing, briefly distracting him from his surroundings before he snapped back into reality. With the recent memory of the large six-legged monster that emerged from the bog, he readied himself for whatever behemoth could be causing such a disturbance.

Elucido felt a strong grasping force wrap itself around his ankle, sweeping him off his feet. Before he could turn his head to see what had taken hold, he was dragged along the hard, dusty ground and into the pool of caustic emerald ooze. He had no time to take a breath before finding himself completely submerged. Adequate oxygen supply was a secondary concern—the thick fluid was quickly dissolving his flesh. He instinctively engaged the Purple Elemental powers to shield him from the liquid while initiating the regenerative powers to restore his body. It took all the power he had to ensure his protection from the acrid immersion.

Having protected himself from the toxicity of the lagoon, he now shifted his focus to escaping the grip that ensnared him and reaching the surface to catch another breath of air. He withdrew his dagger and plunged it into the flesh of his captor, causing it to release its hold on his leg. He surfaced close to the land from which he was snatched, allowing him to quickly pull himself up onto safe ground.

No sooner than he regained his footing on the stable earth, Elucido was knocked off balance as a monstrous kraken surfaced from the depths of the green ooze. The beast had twelve long tentacles, each covered with an array of suction cups as big as Elucido's head. The kraken had more eyes than Elucido could count, arranged around its head in concentric circles, always watching, always ready. Its skin was bright purple and covered in thick scales—an adaptation surely meant to protect it from its toxic habitat. But one feature above all struck Elucido. At the end of two of its tentacles, it held two bright objects that he immediately recognized as shards of the Aether Orb.

He sprung back to his feet, Elemental powers at the ready. With no hesitation, he crafted a large boulder that he threw at the kraken's sizable head. The beast was fast. One of its tentacles caught the stone and sent it tumbling back toward him. Elucido rolled to his right, avoiding the projectile as it removed a large portion of earth beneath where he once stood. He cycled through his Elemental powers, firing a burst of flaming energy from the Red Elemental toward the beast's foremost limbs. It struck its target, doing minimal damage to the hardened flesh. The beast lunged forward, angered by the Luxcreare's aggression. A heavy swing caught Elucido in the gut, sending him hurtling backwards onto the small parcel of land he had crafted as a safe platform. He stopped his momentum as he reached the edge by summoning a rock barrier that battered his ribs as it abruptly ceased his movement, preventing him from re-entering the acidic lake. He rolled to the side, just missing the smashing movement of the tentacle targeting his skull. Elucido sent a barrage of deep blue light at the swinging tentacle, freezing it into a scaley icicle that the aquatic behemoth could no longer move. As fast as he froze the tentacle, he summoned a large boulder that he hurled at the point at which the tentacle attached to the beast's body. The impact from the stone shattered the tentacle into an icy purple powder, removing it from the creature's arsenal of limbs.

Eleven. There were eleven more tentacles to contend with. The beast, however, was smart. It swung at Elucido with much more care, painfully aware of the consequences it would face should its arms be trapped in another frozen prison. But the care it took only slowed the rate at which Elucido could freeze and destroy its limbs. One by one, the Luxcreare pulverized the kraken's arms using the combined powers of the Blue and Purple Elementals. On the rare occasion the beast made contact, Elucido was able to heal his wounds, regroup his thoughts, and continue to reign destruction upon his foe. It was easy for him to collect the shards of the Aether Orb as the arms holding it were blasted into oblivion. In this battle, Elucido was now the heavy favorite. When the monster's arms had all been dispatched, Elucido sat on his foundation of stone and watched as the helpless creature sank into the depths of the gelatinous lake of neon ooze, shrieking in pain, disappearing from sight. He had, once again, proven his worthiness to control the Elementals and fight to restore Terrus to its former beauty.

Once the beast was out of sight, he stood and continued his expedition through the marsh. As he approached the tower, all five shards in hand, Elucido looked over his shoulder once more to find that the glowing light that had followed him was now close enough to observe in more detail. He discerned it was not a singular light, but rather a swarm of individual lights. It appeared to be a colony of radioactive monsters, rapidly approaching his position.

Chapter 26

Before The Throne of Ba

The Tower of Ba was grand, reaching higher than any of the other towers Elucido had visited in his quest to restore light to the land of Terrus. It was constructed from large granite blocks, bolstered by rusted iron bracing and surrounded by a wide moat of the viscous emerald fluid that permeated the land. The same toxic green goo seeped through the cracks in the tower walls, creating a bright glow that spanned the height of the palace. A small section of the tower walls had been reduced to rubble—a likely consequence of the battles that led to the Shadow Garrison's conquering of the continent. The assemblage of stone had no pattern or purpose to its creation, but that did not stop it from being of use. The rocky ruin provided a safe passage across the viscous moat. Elucido pounced from rock to rock as nimbly as he was able. For a moment, he reminded himself of the sprightly movements of Amica, his adorable, umber-eyed friend from the continent of Vita. With the image of his trusted ally and friend in mind, he made the final two leaps with heightened liveliness, emitting a small chirp as he landed firmly on the ground before the main gate of the palace, as if to tell his former compatriot that he had succeeded in his crossing. The moment of levity, brief as it was, distracted him from the horde of beasts that were in pursuit, providing a restorative energy to Elucido's soul.

As was the case at the other towers he had visited, the main doorway's hearty lock relented at the power of the Aether Orb's shards, granting him access to the Tower of Ba. The palace was empty; there was no furniture, no decor, nothing of note. The former glory of Ba had been stripped of all that had given it life. Elucido pivoted his head, surveying the circumference of the grand foyer, expecting to find—and fight—the palace's first line of defense. He completed his sweep three times, finding no signs of any monsters to oppose his entry to the building. Nevertheless, Elucido walked slowly through the first floor, prepared for the worst.

Despite the barrenness the tower displayed, Elucido could feel a potent energy pulsing through the room. The air itself was cold and sapped the energy from his body, leaving him searching for vigor and purpose. Somehow, the emptiness was enough to drag the Luxcreare's spirit straight to the lifeless stone floor. He felt alone and afraid—not of the dangers that may lie ahead, but afraid of what it might mean if he were to fail. The despair he felt in this tower could not be permitted to overtake the world. Perhaps this is what the prophecy meant when it said *"The Luxcreare alone has the power to break free of the despair and restore hope to the land of Terrus."* If he could not break free of the power that existed in the Tower of Ba, Terrus had no hope for survival. He had to restore light to the land of Spiritus before it was too late and the darkness took hold. His spine shivered as he worried the darkness would take control, not only of the land of Spiritus, but of his own heart as well.

Elucido climbed the wide staircase that led to the top of the tower with relative ease. The lack of Shadow Garrison forces made his ascent swift. Though there were no enemies here, he felt that the darkness in this place was significantly greater than any he had encountered on his journey thus far. Nothingness had a hold on this alcazar, and Elucido knew that the power of nothingness was indeed one of the strongest enemies Terrus had ever faced. As he reached the opening at the top of the stairs, he noticed something strange behind him. A dull sage glow appeared to be working its way up from the base of the stairwell. He had momentarily forgotten about the strange band of creatures that had followed him from the catacombs. It appeared to him that he was now trapped between the unknown illuminated mass below and the power of the unrelenting darkness above. At this point, Elucido did not know which danger he preferred.

"I see you have released my legion of toxic creatures, my Rutilanblights." A low, calm voice echoed from the depths of the palace.

Elucido turned and echoed in reply, "I am not afraid of your creation. I have mastered the powers of the Elementals and can easily defeat them." Despite his presentation of confidence in his ability to control the Elemental Powers, Elucido was not entirely certain that he had what it took to challenge such a mass of unknown monsters.

"I am sure you have what it takes. After all, they are but a mere mistake, a failure of my early experimentation into creating an army of mutant monsters for the Shadow Garrison. They are nothing to me—garbage, disposable, meaningless. They have no value." The dark outline of a slouching man appeared on the far side of the room.

"Why trap them in the catacombs, then?" Elucido's voice softened, his heart now feeling some measure of compassion for the creatures that his shrouded foe claimed posed no threat.

"Why not? It makes no difference to me how they die. They will perish eventually, regardless of the means."

Elucido moved toward the brooding voice and away from the stairwell that was now beginning to swarm with Animus's malformed abominations that had been pursuing him since the catacombs. They had also found a way to cross the viscous moat and enter the palace, catching up to him. Though the general dismissed the threat the Rutilanblights posed, they continued to approach Elucido, thrashing and clawing their way toward him. He could not take the chance that they would attack him. There were far too many of them for him to attend to, especially while dealing with the danger posed by the emerging Shadow Garrison leader. He quickly constructed a wall of stone and ice, leveraging the combined powers of the Blue and Purple Elementals. The barrier was sufficient, at least for the time being, to contain the glowing mutated bodies that amassed at its threshold.

Animus's Rutilanblights had been his attempt at creating powerful, submissive, dark minions to fight for the Shadow Garrison during the Great Battle. Ironically, the powers of darkness he used to subdue them had infected them with a toxicity that caused them to radiate a strong pulsing, glowing illumination. And while they were held at a distance behind the stony wall, Elucido could feel the radiation they emanated affecting his own body. The strength of his healing powers could not overcome the sheer magnitude of their numbers. He would have to make quick work of Animus and re-activate the Aether Orb to have any hope of escaping the tower before he succumbed to the degradation of the powerful radioactive anathemas.

"How could you treat life with such disrespect?" Elucido's voice quivered as his emotions stirred. "Can't you see they are suffering? All life has value. And while you may not understand it, all life has purpose."

Animus was mostly unaffected by the Luxcreare's words. The only thing that seemed to register in his emotions was the mild irritation that someone had called his nihilistic values into question. He seemed to take offense at the presupposition that life had meaning or purpose.

"What do you know about purpose?" Animus snapped at Elucido. "Life has always existed in an endless cycle of birth, suffering, and death. To avoid life is to bypass suffering. Nothingness is the only true escape from torment."

Elucido could feel the weight of the general's words. He wasn't wrong, after all. Without life, there would be no suffering. But he also knew that without life, there would be no joy, no love, no hope. All of his experiences on Nomen would not have existed without life. His family, friends, the satisfaction he took from his research with the Protectors of Light—all made possible, regardless of the suffering that life sometimes thrust upon him.

"Suffering is real. I won't deny it. But the joy and happiness that life can bring makes it worth living. To sacrifice all the goodness the world offers would be foolish. You are a fool for giving in to nothingness." Elucido advanced toward his cloaked adversary, knowing that he needed to dispatch him swiftly to escape the Rutilanblights clawing at the barrier behind him.

As Elucido moved toward the heart of the empty room, Animus's body radiated a bright green light. Elucido deduced that this was the power of the Green Elemental. No sooner than he recognized Animus's control of the Elemental, he saw the full force of its powers. Animus hunched his shoulders, palms down, hands trembling as he brought forth a surge of toxic fluid that precipitated from the ceiling of the throne room. Quick thinking, along with a sheet of hovering ice, protected Elucido from the onslaught of acid rain. As the olive rain dissolved the ice, Elucido clapped his hands together forcefully, creating two pillars of rock that bared down upon Animus. The Shadow Garrison general took an enormous step backward, narrowly avoiding being sandwiched between the two cold stone slabs.

Elucido followed with a barrage of fire and lightning. Animus seemed unfazed by their impact. It was as if the pain brought him amusement. How the Elemental cannonade did not damage the nihilistic combatant was nothing short of miraculous. It appeared Animus had found a way to embrace pain and hopelessness at the Elemental level, nullifying any effects of their damaging capabilities. Elucido tried again, this time with ice and stone. Again, no effect on the commander aside from mild gaiety.

Elucido had tried every weapon he had at his disposal, to no avail. Taking a moment to compose his thoughts and devise a new plan, he left himself vulnerable for too long. The power of the Green Elemental spun from Animus's fingertips, sending a concussive blast of toxic radiation through Elucido's body. The impact alone caused him tremendous pain, but worse yet were the effects of the radiation. Elucido's body transmuted as it warped into an increasingly mangled array of fleshy limbs. He collapsed, writhing in agony as the mutation amplified. He pivoted his emotions, embracing the pain and fear and channeling his panic into a healing orb that circled his body at a fierce pace. The violaceous orb sent forth a propagating burst of healing energy. The mutation was allayed as the Purple Elemental's power expanded and Elucido's body started to rebuild. As the wave of restorative energy surged through Elucido and past Animus, the general fell to his knees. Elucido took note—Animus's embrace of the pervasive toxicity of the land had generated a new weakness within him. Healing powers drained him of his energy, elegantly counteracting his toxic abilities.

A flurry of Elemental exchanges between the two men carried on at a feverish pace, the Luxcreare now holding his own against the incredible prowess of Animus's fighting style. Corrosion and healing powers commingled as the balance between decay and restoration waxed and waned in an almost poetic exchange. Elucido had matched Animus's powers but still found himself unable to overcome his sheer strength and reach victory.

Animus, now beginning to feel the fatigue of the protracted battle, became uncharacteristically frantic. He knew that if the battle continued for much longer, he stood a reasonable chance of losing. In his heightened desperation, he fired a barrage of caustic sludge blasts in all directions, hoping to land a blow upon Elucido that would, at a minimum, stop him from his onslaught of restorative magic. One pilaster swooshed past Elucido, nearly striking him in the face. As the blast continued its trajectory, Elucido turned and watched it collide with the wall of stone he was using to hold the Rutilanblights at bay. He had no time to react. The barrier rapidly dissolved under the acidity of the fluid. Before he could shift his focus to the Purple Elemental's earth-shaping qualities, the rampart gave way to a flood of Rutilanblights, each moving swiftly toward his position. Elucido took a step back, stumbling over his own heels, falling flat on his back as the creatures approached. Instinctively, he covered his face with his arms, preparing to be overcome by the weight of the mangled beings.

The first disfigured beast arrived quickly. In preparation for the pain he assumed would follow, Elucido curled his body and winced, expecting the worst. As the beast leapt over his body, however, it did not strike him. Instead, the beast carried on its awkward sprint straight toward Animus. The remaining beasts echoed that movement, each one passing by Elucido and swarming the creator who had imprisoned them so callously in the catacombs. Elucido watched in terror as the creatures pulled the flesh from Animus's bones piece by piece. As he observed them maliciously devour their architect, he noticed something strange about their movement. It seemed unsettlingly similar to the movement of humans.

Elucido stood and entered the heart of the palace tower, screams of terror echoing from the antechamber behind him as the palace host was torn to shreds by the very creatures he had disposed of. As Animus took his final breath, Elucido discerned a light smile on his face for the first time, as he greeted death with open arms. Elucido moved quickly to reassemble the Aether Orb, uncertain of what the Rutilanblights may do now that they were free from the oppression of their maker.

"*Congrega lucem.*" Elucido peered over his shoulder at the Rutilanblights as the Aether Orb's shape completed, shards merging into their original form.

"*Uniendis lux.*" Light seeped from the fused cracks in the orb, glowing with increasing intensity.

"*Lucem propagationem.*" As a tremendous burst of light emanated from the center of the Tower of Ba, a faint purple hue covered the land. Pools of bright green ooze clarified into beautiful blue lagoons, teeming with plant and animal life. The broken continent shifted back into place, merging once again into a lush tropical forest filled with the graceful songs of beautiful birds. The Rutilanblights quietly took a seated position, allowing the healing properties of the purple light to restore their broken bodies, their once-human forms regaining shape. Spiritus had once again become a thriving sanctuary of life and light.

As the Aether conduit began to open and initiate its transport of the Luxcreare, Elucido took hold of the object he recovered in the depths of the catacombs. He looked in anxious disbelief at what now rested in the palm of his trembling hands—the broach of the Defenders of Light that had once belonged to his brother, Frater.

Chapter 27

In Service of the King

Elucido arrived on the continent of Umbra via the Aether conduit's expedited travel. And while he had made the traversal through the conduit several times, he still emerged dizzy and disoriented, swaying back and forth as he established his footing and evaluated his surroundings. Umbra was once known as the lively hub of the world, not just a bustling metropolis, but an example to the world of how to experience the fullness of life through community, entertainment, and opportunity. Energy, abundance, and hope were the lifeblood of this continent. It was by far the largest of the sky-continents of Terrus, easily doubling the size of Elucido's homeland of Nomen. Though the territory was familiar to the Luxcreare from his past travels, so many of the details appeared obscured to his weary eyes. The changes to Umbra, drastic as they were, registered in his mind secondarily to the recognition of his brother's broach that he now held securely in his hands.

"What could this mean?" Elucido stared intently at the jeweled medallion, Frater's name carefully engraved on the back, hopeful for the implications its existence brought to his mind.

"Could Frater still be alive?" He paused, hesitant to allow his hopes to rise at the possibility that his brother could have survived the Dark Cataclysm when the light was stamped from Terrus. After all, it was believed that Frater had perished at the hand of Caligo's dark forces, as had all of those in his battalion on that fateful day. The legion of Tenebrae had descended upon their position swiftly, overcoming their defenses and leaving little more than a field of blood-soaked turf behind as they marched toward the tower of Ren. No bodies were found, leaving little doubt in Elucido's mind that his brother had been among the dead.

That belief shifted now that Frater's broach had appeared in the depths of the tomb on Spiritus. It could not have been a coincidence that an object that was so sacred to the Defenders of Light had made its way to the catacombs. It was left behind—intentionally, Elucido thought—discarded as if it were no longer valued by its owner. Or perhaps, its owner desired it to be found by the Luxcreare.

"Frater would not have left his broach behind, not while he still had breath left in his lungs." Elucido's rationalization of the provenance of the broach convinced him once again that his brother was no longer among the living. "It was far too important to him to abandon in the darkness of the caverns of his own volition."

A flurry of possibilities spun through Elucido's mind, starting with the simplest explanation; the broach had been picked up by a Tenebrae and merely dropped in the cavern. He quickly abandoned that notion as extraordinarily implausible. There was no way that a Tenebrae would have carried the object for such a long distance. The Tenebrae had no desire for such treasures. Their job was simply to destroy light and all who stood in their way.

Perhaps, he thought, one of the king's henchmen would have stolen the broach as a trophy. But again, why would they discard such a prized emblem, especially in that location? It made no sense; there had to be another reason the broach had been abandoned for Elucido to recover. He struggled to find a reasonable explanation for the discovery. For now, he thought, he would have to accept the mystery and move forward toward restoration of the light on Umbra.

Elucido had visited Umbra many times before in his capacity as researcher for the Protectors of Light. He knew precisely where he was, and the significance of the continent to those who sought to protect the light. Standing only a short distance away from his position was a gray-bricked building, aged but well maintained. Its windows were blacked out—a condition that had been imposed far before the darkness had taken over the land. Its owners desired secrecy, as the activities that took place in the structure were not intended for the public's view. This building was known as the Abattoir—or, more commonly, the slaughterhouse. It was home to the primary meat processing plant, used for production and distribution of food to the housing district. While there was nothing inherently evil about its purpose, it remained veiled to the people. Leaving a layer of ignorance about the means by which the fleshy nutriment arrived at the dinner table helped maintain humanity's desire for both its purchase and consumption.

With a loud creak, Elucido opened the front door to the plant. The shrieking door caught him off guard, causing him to flinch and raising the hair on the back of his neck. He didn't believe in ghosts, but the aura surrounding this building created a palpable tension he could not ignore. He took a deep breath, glanced over his shoulder, and tiptoed slowly into the foyer.

It didn't take long for him to recognize the source of his chills. The walls were still coated with a spatter of dried blood, the floor covered in a thick maroon crust that crumbled beneath the weight of his feet. The smell of iron turned his stomach, and though his visibility was limited, he could clearly see that death had been quite comfortable in this place. He paused abruptly as he heard a noise coming from the main production floor in the adjacent room.

Elucido identified the sound as that of chains being dragged along the floor, rhythmically paced with each step their carrier took. The heavy clinking sound moved slowly from one end of the room to the next in a seemingly laborious crawl. Fearing what creature might be pulling the chains across the bloody ground, he cautiously crept to the threshold of the entryway and peered around the corner to investigate.

There was nothing there—he saw no creature, no chains, no evidence that anything had traversed the floor where he was so certain to have heard the sound. This only amplified the fear he now felt as he carefully took a step into the room. In the center of the space stood a small display stand with a glass case perched securely atop. It glowed with a familiar luminescence—that of the shard of the Aether Orb contained on the pedestal. Elucido was shocked that an object of such importance was so openly displayed for anyone to take; and yet, here it was, placed with purpose and intentionality.

He cautiously moved toward the pedestal, uncertain if it had been exhibited as a means to ensnare unwelcome visitors such as himself. With every step he took, he glanced over his shoulder, alternating the direction in which his attention was focused. Nearing the glass case, he could see a small plaque at its base. Having moved close enough to read, he spoke the words on the display aloud.

"Remnants of a broken world—displayed here to remind humanity that it, too, has been broken."

There could only be one purpose for such a message. The King of Darkness had placed this memorial to remind any survivors of the control he held over the darkness that now consumed Terrus. Wasting no time, Elucido snatched the shard from its glass housing, secured it in his leather bag, and turned to explore the slaughterhouse further.

As he pivoted from his stance at the podium, he recoiled as he found himself face to face with another human—or what at least appeared to be one. The man's eyes were vacant, obscured by scaly, white cataracts. Though there were clear heaving breaths in the man's chest, Elucido thought for a moment that he was lifeless. The shock of his appearance caused the Luxcreare's fight-or-flight instinct to kick in. He thrust his shoulder against the man's chest, pushing him aside, and then ran as fast as he could through the room and into the adjacent packing facility.

Stumbling on a small step as he entered the room, he nearly fell flat on his face. The room was dark, musky, and cold, the hard floor sending firm vibrations through his knees with every weary step he took. Elucido couldn't see more than an arm's length into the frigid space. He felt the anxiety and panic rising in his body at the combination of seeing the strange man, and the eerie feeling the slaughterhouse projected. Fear rising, he hastily summoned the Yellow Elemental's powers to illuminate the room. As the light permeated the depths of the chamber, hundreds of cloudy white eyes shone back at him, reflecting the rays of the yellow light. He took a large step backwards, falling on the small step he had avoided tripping on moments ago. His heart bounced from his chest straight into his dry throat as he landed in a seated position on the cold, bloody floor.

He tried to call out to the people now revealed in the center of the mill floor to warn them to stay away, but no words left his withered voice. He sat motionless, watching what he could only describe as mere shells of human beings carrying out a well-rehearsed routine. They were transporting canvas satchels of meat product to the assembly line, where the large portions of carcass were steadily dissected into smaller rations. At the end of the line, a group of hunchbacked, mangled monsters carried the packages of food away, presumably to be distributed to the beasts the Shadow Garrison had employed for their calamitous purposes.

No one so much as turned their heads at the presence of the Luxcreare or the bright light the Elemental powers provided. Their hearts were beating, their bodies moving, but none of them had any semblance of free will or independence of thought. They were serfs, bound to the prison of labor for the king's armies, unable to separate themselves from his dark dominion. They existed only as empty vessels, void of the personalities that once shone their vitality. The cataracts in their eyes, Elucido assumed, were inflicted intentionally by the Shadow Garrison to control them. Not only did the darkness restrict their movement, but their vision was damaged so severely that even in the presence of light, they could only repeat the same routine—providing sustenance to those who had condemned them to a life of subjugation. Their demeanor was the ultimate manifestation of depression and hopelessness.

Elucido was sickened by the entrapment of his fellow humans into the servitude of the dark ruler. The shard on the pedestal had served the purpose of holding them firmly under his control, as none appeared willing to stage an escape.

Elucido's desire to free them grew as he formulated a plan of attack. Firing two fireballs at the small monsters transporting the food packages dispatched them with ease. They were not bred for fighting, which was made clear the moment their bodies disintegrated under the extreme heat of the Red Elemental's blazing power. Elucido ran headlong to the workers at the front of the room.

"Let's go, make a run for it!" He shouted at the people, begging them to break free of their captivity. "I can protect you; I just need you to follow me!" The serfs continued to work, either unable to hear his charge or unwilling to respond. Elucido grabbed one of the young men by the arm, pulling him toward the door. The man was unresponsive, carrying on his movements toward the production line as if Elucido wasn't even there. He tried with all his might, to no avail—screaming, crying out, and pulling on the captives had no effect. He sensed that there was no way he could free his fellow men and women from their hopelessness. Unless, that is, he could restore light to the land and end the reign of the king.

By the time he realized that his rescue attempt was futile, a large mass of factory guards had descended upon his position. These creatures, unlike their smaller counterparts, existed to protect the food supply of the dark army against any enemies that may intrude upon the abattoir. They were large, thick-chested, and tall. Their long arms dragged on the ground alongside their bodies as they moved toward his position. There were just too many of them for him to contend with. Not only that, but Elucido feared that any altercation with the guards could turn his fellow humans into collateral damage. He had no choice but to flee.

Running through the assembly line, Elucido pushed past the servants. He traversed the hallway, taking a hard left into a room filled with the sharp tools used to break the carcasses down into more manageable portions before they were carried to the conveyor for their final packaging. The blood in this room was not dry, as it had been in the foyer. He could feel the heat and humidity of the hematic fluid that was still dripping from the large steel table at the center of the room. The warm moisture passed through his nose, allowing him to experience the metallic taste in his mouth as the dampness reached his tired lungs. Elucido could hardly breathe, a consequence less of his exhaustion from the run he had just taken, and more related to the mugginess and foul stench of the air in the room. He followed the wall to the other side, taking care not to slip on the wet, sticky floor. Stabilizing himself on the shelving that lined the far wall, he reached the rear door just before the guards arrived.

As Elucido entered the next room, the blood instantly drained from his face as he wretched up a steady stream of vomit. His knees weakened, and his head felt as though it had lifted from his shoulders into a feeling of complete weightlessness. He had entered the room in which they sourced the meat for processing. As his vision began to white out, he registered with absolute certainty that the pile of bodies being deconstructed to fuel the Shadow Garrison were human.

Chapter 28

Home is Where the Heart No Longer Lives

Elucido had encountered countless monsters on his journey to restore light to Terrus, but none as sinister as the King of Darkness himself. How anyone could treat human life with such disregard was beyond his capacity to understand. Fleeing the slaughterhouse, he struggled to find his footing, still fueled by adrenaline, fear, and now a burgeoning rage. He looked over his shoulder to see if he was being followed. The guards did not pursue; their duty ended at the boundary of the abattoir. Elucido was free from their presence, but not from the effects of the tragic scene he uncovered in the blood-soaked chamber. His anger fueled his resolve. He vowed to fight the darkness with every breath he had left in his body.

Elucido continued his passage toward the tower of darkness by moving through the center of Umbra near the housing district. Many of his friends at the research center on Nomen grew up in these homes. He approached the edge of the precinct, uncertain what carnage may await. Elucido could make out a vague silhouette of the roofline along the horizon, jagged and torn. The buildings were in a state of heavy ruin, damaged, worn, and abandoned. His gut twisted into a knot so tight he could barely breathe. This used to be a place of happiness, joy, and memories. Where families once thrived, there were now no signs of life. Where there was once love, only loss remained. Approaching the first building, he could feel the warm breeze blowing across the chilled skin of his arms. It would have been refreshing if it weren't for the emptiness it carried with it.

Entering the first building, Elucido left footprints in the dust that had gathered during the time the home had been empty and exposed to the elements. Windows had been shattered, and holes punched in the roof, exposing the interior of the building to the boundless darkness above. He covered his mouth with his shirt to avoid inhaling the thick powdered grime. While there had been no one in these homes for quite some time, he could feel the memories of the families that once dwelled within. He could see the faces of children playing with their parents, laughing lovingly as their fathers hoisted them high into the air, time and time again.

Now, in the absence of life and love, those memories shifted. Elucido could sense the pain of loss; fathers murdered in cold blood by the Shadow Garrison, mothers crying as they desperately tried to feed their starving children, unable to find food in the cold, dark world; sons and daughters searching for reason and comfort at the loss of parents and siblings, now left in somber isolation. Elucido felt the same pain of loss, the same hopelessness of the struggle to survive alone in a world of darkness. The King of Darkness had stamped out all light from the land, but he was guilty of so much more. He eviscerated hope and love from humanity's core, leaving them desolate in their solitude.

Elucido climbed the stairs to the second floor of the building, where empty bedrooms lined the hallway. The home had been ransacked. Walls were damaged by large, unforgiving claw strikes from dark monsters; doors torn from their hinges with such brutality that sections of the wall were removed alongside them. It was obvious to him that the Shadow Garrison's forces had cleared the district of all remaining human presence, likely to gather them as servants, or worse—as rations.

The third bedroom down the desecrated hallway caught Elucido's attention. It was adorned with pale, pink walls, and carpeting that would have been quite soft, if not for the dust and water damage it had sustained in its exposure to the elements. Hanging from the ceiling near a gaping hole, he saw an arrangement of small trinkets attached to a metal ring. It spun in circles as the gentle breeze moved through the room. Shiny objects clinked together, creating a soothing jingling sound. It was an infant's mobile. In the corner of the room lay a small crib, undamaged by the brutality of the beasts in their quest for destruction. Somehow, this delicate cradle had survived the carnage.

It was strange to Elucido how calm it seemed standing in this domicile in the aftermath of such devastation. He felt an almost eerie tranquility. Perhaps the loneliness and isolation of the structure provided him a small break from the constant struggle against the enemies of darkness. Or, perhaps, it was the fact that he found himself in a home, once again surrounded by walls—broken as they were—shielding him from the terror of the outside world. Whatever the reasoning, he welcomed what he could only describe as a fractured yet familiar normalcy, inching him at least a modicum closer to the comfort of a former life. He took a deep breath into his lungs and allowed himself a moment to enjoy the silence.

Starting his retreat downstairs to the main floor of the home, Elucido entered the dining area. He noticed the table was still made; plates of food unfinished, now nothing but dehydrated reminders of the bounty humanity once celebrated. The Shadow Garrison beasts had torn through these homes relentlessly, with no consideration for what they were destroying. The remnants that persisted served as a reminder to Elucido of the comforts he feared he may never again experience.

Moving into the main living room, he heard a noise not of his own making. He froze, silent, to avoid detection from whatever was moving through the room ahead. Peeking around the corner of a heavily damaged wall, he saw a small monster stooped over the fireplace. It was cradling something in its grasp, admiring the object it had found within its bed of ash and coal. He took no pause in his next move, blasting the creature with a powerful combination of the Green and Yellow Elemental powers. A discharge of bright viridescent amber energy surged through the back of the beast, instantaneously exploding its body into dozens of pieces that disintegrated in a glowing green dissolution of flesh and bone as they dropped slowly to the ground. In the fireplace, beneath the remains of the fragile foe emerged the familiar glow of an Aether Orb shard, adding a second piece to his collection. Kneeling and reaching for the shard, Elucido was struck with another vision.

Elucido stood face to face with the King of Darkness. The two locked eyes, as if gazing into the depths of one another's souls. The Luxcreare could see his reflection in the dark pupils of the one who ushered in the age of darkness. While neither man spoke, their message to one another was clear—concession was not an option. Elucido was unwavering in his opposition to the powers of darkness; his counterpart had already fully surrendered to it. They both knew the consequences of the choice to embrace the darkness—perpetuating an infinite void of nothingness and despair upon the world would plunge one's soul into eternal darkness, from which there would be no redemption. The dark lord had made his choice. The only thing left to do was for the two men to square off in the battle to determine whether Terrus would live in the light or perish in the everlasting shadows.

The strength of the opposition he faced struck Elucido with increasing clarity with the revelations that each vision provided. He knew his resolve would be tested, though he was uncertain precisely how. The search for the remaining shards would not be easy. Elucido could sense their presence, and feared for what may await him near the end of his journey on Umbra.

Having no other choice but to press onward, he shifted his travels to the southwest, toward the Temple of Illustratio. He had visited this temple before. All of those who were committed to research within the Protectors of Light made a yearly crusade to the sanctuary dedicated to veneration of the Aether Orbs that brought life and light to Terrus. Though it wore its age quite well, the temple had existed for thousands of years. A group of monks living at the temple dedicated their lives to the maintenance and protection of this holy place. Generation to generation, new monks were trained in the ways of Aether worship. Even now, despite the terrible tragedies that played out during the Dark Cataclysm, the temple grounds were pristine because of their dedication and allegiance to the light.

Not everything at the temple, however, was as it had once been. Legend had it that the King of Darkness had stormed the temple following the Great Battle, intending to destroy the building as a demonstration of the power that darkness now held over the land. However, as he entered the sanctified chambers where the Protectors of Light gathered, he had unexpectedly shifted his target, focusing instead on the monks that acted as caretakers to the grounds. In an instant, the king had sent a surge of Black Elemental lightning that arced in a propagation of darkness toward each of the oblates. Their lives were spared—the king had not desired their death. The monks' punishment was, in the dark ruler's mind, much more severe. The dark energy burned their eyes, fusing the very skin of their eyelids shut. They had dedicated their lives to the protection and worship of the light, and now they were forever unable to revere its beauty. They had been relegated to a life filled with darkness. The king was pleased with their suffering. He left them to tend to the temple day and night, watching as they continued to toil over the care of the building, despite their permanent anopia. Their pain did not affect their commitment to the light, but it served as a reminder to the king of his belief in the futility of their devotion.

Elucido entered the temple with trepidation. What he once viewed as the holiest of grounds was now a reminder of the control the darkness had claimed over Terrus. His emotions were equally torn between the reverence of the light he was accustomed to in this holy place and the fear that he might fail in his quest to restore the glory of the Aether Orbs. He couldn't help but feel a small measure of guilt as well. Guilt at the notion that he could stand in such a sacred place and still be filled with such doubt. *Lux Superesse Est*, he thought. Or would it?

At the far side of the room, Elucido saw a group of monks diligently working. As he watched them carry out their devoted tasks, he tried to suppress the ignominy of his disbelief. He was the Luxcreare, and if the world was to survive, his confidence needed to be buttressed. The steadfastness of the monks' faith was precisely the reassurance he needed. They did not speak. Their silence, however, was not a vow they had taken voluntarily. Perhaps their muteness was a direct consequence of the pain they felt having let the great temple of the Aether fall into darkness. Or perhaps their voices had been stilled by the force of the king's powerful electric blast. For now, all Elucido could do was watch them work, finding inspiration at their allegiance to the light regardless of the tragedies that had befallen them.

Following the carpeted aisle down the main hall, Elucido walked past the laboring monks and approached the altar to reflect. The silence of the temple comforted him as he took the familiar walk to the chantry. Every feeling of conviction from his past replayed in his heart—every step building confidence that he would, in fact, be able to defeat the King of Darkness. Kneeling at the marble block at the back of the chamber, he spoke once again, with unwavering assurance. "*Lux Superesse Est.*" He declared once again, this time louder than the last. "*Lux Superesse Est!*" He stood, proclaiming as loudly as his voice would allow. "*Lux Superesse Est!*" At the sound of his final decree, the altar shook violently, splitting in two with a jagged fault down the center of the stone. Much to Elucido's surprise, contained within the broken altar was the third shard of the Aether Orb he had been searching for.

The light from the shard illuminated the room in a beautiful shimmer. The pristine stained-glass windows once again shone their glory throughout the temple. Elucido was struck by the peacefulness the rainbow of colors brought to the chamber, a reminder that even a single ray of light can cut through the depth of the darkness. He was emboldened—the Aether had clearly trusted him with the power to control the Elemental Orbs—a direct sign that he was worthy of being called the Luxcreare, and more than capable of dispatching the darkness to bring glory back to the Aether. His resolve was stronger than it had ever been. Even if this would be the final pilgrimage of the Luxcreare, he knew with the fullest of confidence that he had what it would take to save Terrus.

Chapter 29

Bloodshed

Elucido held three shards in his weathered hands. He was nearing the point at which he could restore light to Umbra, and hopefully the whole of Terrus. He knew, however, that the next stop on his journey might prove to be the most challenging. He was on his way to what the Shadow Garrison now called "Castellum Nox". It was the remnants of the military complex that the Defenders of Light had once used to train for conflict. It was where Frater had lived for years as he rose through the ranks of the Defenders, mastering his skills with traditional weaponry and elite battle tactics. The buildings at the facility had been modified to suit the Shadow Garrison's needs, but they retained largely the same purposes. Infiltrating the grounds and dispatching the soldiers within would require Elucido's utmost mastery of the Elemental powers. Precision, expert timing, and perhaps a bit of the luck he had experienced along his journey would all be critical to his success.

He approached the facility from the south, climbing to the top of the hills the Defenders of Light once used to run practice incursions. The mounds of earth were tall enough to offer Elucido the necessary cover to advance toward the walls of the fortress while remaining undetected. He observed the movement of the enemy forces within the boundaries of the complex. They were not concerned with covertness—after all, they were the greatest army Terrus had ever known. They could afford to be cavalier in their training activities. And while they likely knew the Luxcreare was on his way to confront them, they were supremely confident in the sheer magnitude of the force they represented.

Having seen how the multitude of beasts operated, Elucido formulated what he believed to be the best plan of attack. His incursion would begin first by breaching the walls at the southeast end of the institution. The barricades that were intended to protect the Defenders of Light from enemies had been damaged during the Great Battle. Elucido used this to his advantage, approaching a weak spot in the large stony wall. He needed to remain as quiet as possible to prevent raising alarms and calling attention to his position. With extreme finesse, he summoned the power of the Purple Elemental to gain control over each rocky particle within the lowest block of the facade. He vibrated each piece of dust, removing one grain at a time. After a few minutes of focused action, he had carved a hole just large enough for him to crawl through in continued secrecy.

Passing the first obstacle in his plot to recapture the military complex, Elucido focused his thoughts on the Mess Hall. From atop his perch on the hill, he had seen several Nullblights entering the hall. By his best estimation, there were about a dozen enemies awaiting his arrival. Once they noticed his presence, it would be a fight for his life to dispatch the remaining Nullblights from the Shadow Garrison's forces. He would only get one shot at a stealthy attack before his cover was blown. He recalled the swiftness with which the Nullblights moved when he encountered them on Nomen. Their slender build was no less threatening than when he first confronted their savagery. Above all else, however, seeing their massive teeth snarling once again brought him the most fear.

Elucido approached the window of the eatery. He peered through the window on the back wall of the building to gain insight into the danger he was about to fight. The beasts had gathered at the dirty, broken tables. Some standing, others seated, they sloppily devoured the packs of human flesh that had been processed at the slaughterhouse. Their large fangs tore through the packaging efficiently, allowing them to consume the entirety of their meal in only a few mouthfuls of scarcely masticated sustenance. His anger and disgust amplified as he watched them eat, knowing what had transpired during the processing of their meals.

Fueled by his anger, he stormed into the room, blasting the doors open with a large fireball. Before the occupants could react, Elucido followed up with a barrage of fire and ice, freezing some of the Nullblights' feet in place just long enough to ignite their remaining flesh with the power of the Red Elemental. Three beasts were ensnared by their icy shackles, shrieks of agony echoing from their lungs as their skin melted from bone, charring what was left of their corpses in a matter of seconds. The remaining monsters charged at Elucido with a speed that, despite his experience, caught him off guard.

One beast swung its enormous claws in an upward motion that struck Elucido's hip, sending him hurtling in the air toward the center of the room, a deep gash in the flesh of his upper leg. As he began his descent to the floor of the cafeteria, he encased himself in a shield crafted from the Purple Elemental. The sphere of violet light that surrounded him healed the wound inflicted by the beast's claws, and created a barrier that withstood the next several strikes the Nullblights attempted to bludgeon him with.

Elucido slammed his fists into the ground, magnifying the potency of the Purple Elemental. Upon impact, the ground shook with tremendous force, upending tables and sending the Nullblights into an airborne display of slender, flailing limbs. Before they hit the ground, he blasted four of the enemies with a combination of Red and Yellow Elemental powers—a fiery lightning arc that instantly turned their bodies to ash. He stood, faced the remaining Nullblights, and allowed a faint smile to cross his face as he summoned the next Elemental attack.

A bright combination of red and green light swirled outward, radiating from Elucido's position. Hitting the wall with extreme force, the Red and Green Elemental combination consumed the wall in a blaze of caustic magma. The building's structural integrity degraded, dissolving walls and crashing sections of ceiling upon the Nullblights, converting the next batch of foes into lifeless piles of flesh and bone, ironed firmly into the floor.

Two beasts remained—a number the hero of light had no concerns about fighting. Both Nullblights had successfully dodged the collapsing roof, shifting their movement toward Elucido, desperately trying to kill him before he could strike again. Sprightly as they were, the Nullblights had no chance of reaching Elucido before they were met with a red flame so intense it lit the sky like an amber beacon, converting the beasts into a smoldering vapor that smelled of sulfur and charred flesh. The mess hall had been transformed into a pile of burning rubble, with no Nullblights left in sight. What Elucido hadn't fully planned for was the complete loss of the element of surprise he would have as he continued his assault on the dark fortress.

To the west, Elucido saw a thick mass of Fortisblights emerging from the training facility, made aware of his presence by the blazing pillar of flame that now lit the sky. He was not surprised to find these heavy, muscular beasts at this building. It was consistent with their primary method of assault—force above finesse. They had used the training facility to continue their preparation, constantly engaging in mock battles, always ready for a fight.

Before the remaining heavy blundering beasts exited the building, Elucido summoned a massive ice storm from the Blue Elemental Orb. Two Fortisblights were frozen in a block of ice that filled the doorway, trapping several within the structure. The remaining beasts spiraled in all directions, sliding on the thick sheet of ice that now covered the ground beneath their feet. Elucido shifted his focus to the enemies on his left, following the ice attack with a Red Elemental burst. The extreme heat of the blast transformed the sheet of ice into a boiling pool of water, cooking the muscular limbs of his rivals while the heat from the vapor seared the insides of their lungs. Unable to scream—or even breathe—seven Fortisblights were incapacitated, writhing in agony while they slowly suffocated in the searing vapor.

Three opponents remained on the building's exterior. Knowing that the Fortisblights were creatures of force, Elucido suspected the best tactic would be to fight back with greater force—"*Vim Vi Repello*," as the Defenders of Light would say. His mastery of the Elemental Powers allowed him to do just that. As the monsters grunted in unison, beginning their assertive approach, Elucido added the power of the Purple Elemental to that of the Blue Elemental. This resulted in a massive sphere of ice and stone that materialized nearly ten meters above the beasts' heads. Being unsophisticated brutes, his opponents failed to see the hazard that emerged far above them as they charged at Elucido in a strong-willed, energetic assault. Snapping his fingers and lowering his head, the Luxcreare allowed the large frozen boulder to surrender to gravity and fall squarely atop the muscular ruffians, burying them before they knew what had happened.

Elucido approached the training facility, expecting only a few remaining Fortisblights to be trapped behind the two that were still frozen in the doorway in a solid sheet of ice. He smote the ice with a heavy lightning blast from the Yellow Elemental Orb, electrifying the icy foes with enough amperage to not only stop their hearts, but send a small wisp of smoke rising from their lifeless corpses. He then pushed the Purple Elemental's energy into a protective barrier in front of him, anticipating a heavy bombardment upon his entry into the building.

As he crossed the threshold of the doorway, a Fortisblight pounced on his back, having waited patiently above the entryway for his arrival. Elucido was surprised, falling to his knees at the unanticipated weight of the large beast. Two more enemies—the last of the remaining Fortisblights in the room—joined the pileup, attempting to tear the Luxcreare's limbs from his body.

Elucido combined the restorative power of the Purple Elemental with that of the icy Blue Elemental to bolster the strength of the muscles and tendons in his body, preventing his extremities from a gruesome departure from his torso. Now pinned to the ground under the immense weight of the brutish monsters, he struggled to break free. As the beasts pulled against his arms with all of their might, Elucido felt his body weaken. Unable to regain control over his appendages, he had to be creative in how he fought back against his muscular captors.

He tightened his biceps and gripped the forearms of the beasts with all the strength he had left in his hands. From his core grew a bright emerald glow; the powers of the Green Elemental flowed from his chest, through his arms, and into the flesh of the beasts, infecting them with a strong toxic infusion of energy that devoured their flesh. Their grips on Elucido relented as their fingers dissolved before their very eyes. As the infection advanced, their arms deliquesced into a pool of radioactive organic fluid. The beasts lacked the emotional fortitude to handle the pain that followed. They panicked, running through the room, teeth gnashing in futile ineffectiveness. It was easy for Elucido to dispatch the beasts with just his trusty dagger, run smoothly across their throats, ending their existence with a gurgling spray of thick blood, clearly infected with the harsh toxin delivered by the Green Elemental.

Exiting the training facility, Elucido charged the Purple Elemental's powers into a healing shield and continued his unflagging assault on the military complex. He headed toward the barracks. The large building was fitted with hundreds of beds, now dusty and decrepit. He entered the fetid room, his nostrils contracting to spare him as much suffering from the odor as possible. Upon entry, he recognized the movement of the monsters contained within—a swarm of Veloxblights. There were hundreds of the tiny beasts, each with multitudes of small, barbed teeth. It was impossible for Elucido to discern where the floor ended and the legion of Veloxblights began.

It took only a few seconds for the horde to react to his entry. They moved in unison, as fluid as the waves of the ocean, changing directions and accelerating toward his position. Elucido had little time to react. He disposed of the first batch of Veloxblights with a rapidly fired burst of electricity from the Yellow Elemental. The remaining sea of beasts merely shifted their flow around the pile of expired allies, continuing their assault.

As the next round of monsters arrived at his position, they leapt into the air, heading straight for Elucido's face. He threw a wall of flame in front of his position, the Veloxblights swelling and bursting with small popping sounds as they entered the blazing barricade. One beast survived the defensive barrier and latched on to Elucido's leg. Elucido removed the monster with a swift kick, followed by a hard, crushing stomp that flattened its skull with ease.

The remaining mass of varmints arrived at Elucido's position more quickly than he could react. He shifted into a defensive stance, crafting a wall of stone around his feet. He waited for the creatures to congregate in as dense a group as possible before taking his next action. The rock wall shifted under the control of the Purple Elemental, at his behest. It spun clockwise as prongs of earth protruded, scooping the Veloxblights into a singular mass in front of Elucido. As quickly as the rock barrier had been constructed, it was dismantled by a heavy concussive blast, sending small pieces of stone outward in a wide array of shrapnel, embedding itself firmly in the Veloxblights that stood in its destructive path.

Most of the monsters were annihilated by the earthy munition, the remaining handful of beasts breaking the uniformity of their swarming pattern, entering into a chaotic swirling motion, no longer acting as a single hive. It was easy to pick off the remaining Veloxblights with a series of short blasts of lightning, each crackle of energy tossing them into the air, turning them into brightly illuminated fireflies that quickly burned out as the life left their small bodies. As swiftly as the swarm had amassed, Elucido terminated its threat. He took a moment in the death-ridden barracks to encircle himself with the Purple Elemental's healing light, restoring his vigor and imbuing his body with enhanced strength and agility for the next phase of his assault.

Having fully healed his wounds and caught his breath, Elucido advanced to overtake the creatures that occupied the infirmary. There was no movement outside the building. It was as if no one inside had heard the commotion of his destructive rage. This unsettled his nerves, as he did not know what to expect when he breached the wide double doors that had once been used to wheel in injured soldiers during times of war. He tiptoed to the front of the building to have a look inside before barging in to wreak havoc on those within.

As he reached the windows on the face of the building, Elucido observed a strong green glow from within. He was quite familiar with the neon incandescence radiating from the room. Rutilanblights—the once human mutations that he had encountered on the continent of Spiritus—were lying in hospital beds, hooked up to long plastic tubes delivering an intravenous supply of toxic sludge to the wretched abominations. These Rutilanblights differed from the scrawny, malformed creatures he had previously encountered. The thick green ooze had advanced their mutations, creating long-limbed, glowing, muscular beings. If their looks matched their abilities, Elucido feared what he would face upon entry. He had no choice; he could not let his concern for the beasts' power stop him from advancing toward his objective of regaining control over the stronghold. He took a deep breath and stormed the infirmary.

The creatures were startled at the loud crashing noise from the breaching of the doors. Some of them fell from their beds, others snapped into action, pulling the needles from their arms and squaring up for battle. Before Elucido could focus on his first target, one of the humanoid mutants swung a spherule of caustic sludge from its arms, striking Elucido in the shoulder. The pain was immense—the acidic ooze peeling and dissolving the flesh before his eyes. He had to react quickly to heal his wounds before the decay completely severed his arm from his body. Distracted by the effort it took to heal his wound, Elucido was struck with another toxic blast on his right thigh. He could barely keep up with healing one projectile's effects before he was impacted by another. Three, four, five blasts hit him in succession. Elucido needed to take decisive action to stop the barrage before he was overwhelmed.

Shifting the energy of the Purple Elemental, he captured a ball of the toxic fluid within a bright plum-colored casing. The Elemental's power fused with the green sludge as Elucido fired it onto the ground at the feet of the Rutilanblights. The orb struck the floor and initiated its destructive dissolution, opening a gaping hole in the earth that swallowed five enemies into a deep void. This gave him time to craft a unique combination of Elemental Powers. The Red and Purple Elementals summoned a beautiful mauve flame that Elucido cast upon himself. The blaze created a healing flame that hovered atop his skin—not consuming it in fire but applying its healing effect for an extended duration as he continued to fight the monstrous variants.

He shifted his focus to the remaining combatants. "If the toxic radiation strengthens them," he wondered, "perhaps the healing nature of the Purple Elemental can undo the mutation." He sent a shockwave of the strongest purple energy he could summon toward the remaining Rutilanblights. As the wave of energy concussed through them, Elucido could see the green fluid that had been fed into their veins being extracted into the air behind them in a fine mist, almost as if a ghostly green energy was leaving their bodies. In a matter of moments, the mutations began their reversal. He watched in horror as the beasts slowly transformed into atrophied, mangled beings that he barely recognized as human. Without the power of the mutation to give them strength, their bodies collapsed into piles of disfigured, lifeless flesh.

Elucido felt no pride in his victory over the Rutilanblights. They were his kin—possibly his friends—that had been transformed into the cruel abominations that the Shadow Garrison manipulated to its own dark ends. His heart was heavy for them. He wished he could save them from their cruel fate. For now, however, there was nothing else that could be done for them. Elucido said a silent incantation for their souls and headed for the armory.

There was one type of monster noticeably missing from the battle thus far. Elucido believed he knew what would await his arrival at the armory. Based on his experience in past confrontations, he was certain that a legion of Tenebrae had been watching, waiting for their turn to take a shot at the only one who had dared to challenge their existence. Elucido had faced the Tenebrae before, but he feared their numbers would be much larger than any of his previous encounters. His cleverness had allowed him to find victory in previous confrontations, but wit alone would not take out a horde of these beasts. He didn't feel ready to take on the challenge, but he had no choice; *Lux Superesse Est.*

Approaching the structure, Elucido saw two Tenebrae patrolling the perimeter of the building. He drew them away, firing a small Yellow Elemental light in their direction. Their cores split the ray of light in two distinct branches, each Tenebrae then absorbing the energy from the flaxen beams into the center of their torsos. The beasts turned toward the source of the light, eager to devour its broker. Elucido turned away from them, taking cover behind the rubble of an old barricade out of their immediate sight.

Hiding behind the wall, he curled into a tight ball, hunched down. Elucido covered his face and body with his cloak, masking his presence even further. Breathing as slowly as he could force his lungs to expand and contract, he waited in silence. The two beasts approached confidently, ignorant of the destruction that awaited them. Their nescience was the exploit Elucido had anticipated, and precisely what was needed for his victory. Unaware of the Luxcreare's camouflage and the danger their impetuosity created, they rounded the corner, landing almost directly on top of Elucido. He threw his cape to the side and leapt to his feet, thrusting his upturned closed fists into the core of each monster. As his hands entered the hollow bellies of the beasts, a brilliant shining yellow light surged from his knuckles. The Tenebrae's cores absorbed the radiating amber beams for as long as they could, but the intensity of the energy far exceeded what their bodies could handle. Elucido's mastery of the Elemental Powers had surpassed even his own expectations, as the surplus light erupted outward from the beasts' muscular frames, tearing their bodies in a webbed array that allowed the luminosity to escape its fleshy prison. As the

Tenebrae's limp bodies collapsed to the cold dirt below, the golden light faded, and Elucido relaxed his chest, catching his breath.

Seeing the bright beaming light from the execution of their fellow monstrosities, the remaining Tenebrae exited the armory and quickly gathered in a defensive formation facing Elucido. There were thirty in total, standing at the ready, fully aware of the Luxcreare's position. His adrenaline surged, anxiety flowing freely through his veins. He felt unequipped to handle this many of the Shadow Garrison's elite forces at one time. This, he feared, could be the end of his quest.

The Tenebrae began their advancement toward him, marching in time deliberately, and without haste. Elucido squared up to face them, gathering every ounce of courage he had left in his body. The battle began with Elucido sending the first strike—a wide pulse of flames emerging from the Red Elemental he cradled between his palms. He leaned forward, swaying the flamethrower from side to side, slowing the beasts' advance. He could feel the rage swelling within him—each encounter with the king's monstrosities, every act of destruction he observed had fueled the anger he felt in his heart. The powers of darkness had bred the fury that now consumed him. And while he was not proud of the anger he felt, he knew he could leverage it to his advantage in the fight for light. He fired a barrage of fireballs in quick succession at the Tenebrae to slow their movement further, but they advanced, nevertheless.

With the Tenebrae closing nearer to his position, Elucido shifted his focus to the energy of the Blue Elemental. He thought that the slowing effects of the ice may give him the time he would need to inflict some measure of damage on the fortified flesh of the beasts. He spun in a quick circle, Blue Elemental Orbs in his hands, crafting a thick sheet of ice at the feet of his foes. Many of the Tenebrae found their feet firmly locked in place, encased in an icy prison, unable to move. Others struggled to maintain their footing on the slippery surface they now marched upon. Elucido felt the same coldness that persisted in the air in his heart, the struggles of his journey through Terrus amplifying the bitterness in his soul. He had seen firsthand the frigidity of the world brought upon by the darkness. As Terrus became colder, his bitterness had grown. The resentfulness he felt toward the King of Darkness swelled with every passing memory of what the dark ruler had taken from him and his family.

As the elite Shadow Garrison forces struggled to regain their footing, Elucido initiated the next phase of his assault. He sent a surge of energy from his fingertips, facilitated by the Yellow Elemental's powers. Arcs of lightning flowed freely between the bodies of the Tenebrae, drawing them closer to one another almost magnetically, grouping them into a condensed cluster of bodies. Seeing the beasts gathered in a herd was a sharp reminder to Elucido of the loneliness he had experienced in the age of darkness. He missed his friends and family dearly. He even felt a large measure of longing for the company of his furry friend, Amica, who he hoped was thriving on Vita, waiting for a visit from him in the near future. His loneliness grew the more he recognized that the selfishness of the king had forced him—and the world—into isolation. With another surge of electric energy, the Tenebrae were compressed into an even tighter formation.

Transferring his energy to the earth, Elucido summoned the Purple Elemental into a large orb that circled his location, waiting to obey his next command. He opened his palms upward and swung his arms from his bent knees into the sky above, generating a thick wall of rock that surrounded the Tenebrae, trapping them in a prison of stone. He thrust his arms to the ground, drawing large masses of granite from the clouds that descended upon the Tenebrae with great force. Channeling the ever-present hopelessness that had permeated Elucido's soul, he cascaded more large boulders upon the Tenebrae with increasing zeal, feeling the hopelessness fade with each beast that met its death.

With the beasts still trapped behind the wall of stone, Elucido made the final transition from the Purple Elemental to the Green Elemental. He thrust his arms forward in a pulsing motion, alternating left and right, throwing bright green balls of toxic ooze at his enemies. The blasts coated the beasts in caustic fluid. Thick as their skin was, the Tenebrae were not immune to the destructive effects of the emerald acid. Elucido watched the Tenebrae panic, sharply aware of the fear he held in his own heart. Fear drove most of his actions on Spiritus—fear of failure, fear of death, fear of loneliness. He had witnessed so much trauma and everything he once held dear had been ripped from his life. The toxicity of the gospel of darkness was infectious, spreading fear in all humanity. Elucido, strong as he had become, was still subject to its influence. In this moment, perhaps more than ever, fighting the fear had become utterly exhausting. As he manifested the toxicity and fear he felt into the growing power of the Green Elemental, a pool of toxic fluid filled the stone encirclement, creating a poisonous tank the Tenebrae could not escape.

Feeling all the emotions at once—rage, bitterness, loneliness, hopelessness, and fear—Elucido embraced the power of the Elementals and surrendered his emotions to the darkened sky, sending the Elemental Orbs themselves to hover above the battlefield. Standing with no orbs in his raised, open hands, he was stripped down to his raw self. He stood before the enemy not as the Luxcreare, but as Elucido—son, brother, friend, philosopher, human. In this moment, he felt a peace that surpassed any he had yet experienced in his life.

Embracing his vulnerability, Elucido felt his true power unlocking the fullest potential within him, granting him true mastery of each of the Elemental Powers. Standing with arms outstretched, Elucido surrendered unreservedly to the Aether—in that moment, the Elementals responded to his dominion, raining down terror upon the Tenebrae. Each colored orb—red, blue, yellow, purple, and green discharged their energy simultaneously, raining down an apocalyptic fury of Elemental Powers, consuming the Tenebrae and all that remained of Castellum Nox. Bolts of iced lightning pierced the Tenebrae's chests one by one. Toxic green fireballs engulfed them in flames that liquified their flesh as they cried out in agony. A massive stormy tornado formed around them, sending a poisonous green-blue mist through the air, freezing their joints and ending any hope of escape. Boulders formed above them, covered in flames that oscillated between blue, red, yellow, and green. The final barrage of Elemental Powers descended upon the Tenebrae in a brilliant display of color and light, mighty enough for all of Terrus to see. In an instant, what remained of the Tenebrae was little more than large dark marks in the soil and a foggy mist that hung in the air, refracting the residual illumination of the Aether Orbs in a beautiful array covering the full spectrum of colors of the light.

The onslaught of Elemental energy had razed the military complex to the ground, scorching the earth beneath it. Terrus had not seen this much pain and suffering since the Dark Cataclysm. Nothing was left of Castellum Nox—no buildings, no walls, no monsters. It had been erased from Terrus in a matter of moments. Elucido's power felt complete, his mastery of the Elemental Orbs stronger than it had ever been. Standing in the rubble of the demolished fortification, breathing in the fumes of the smoldering earth, Elucido looked to the horizon. There stood the silhouette of an armor-clad man, who was clearly waiting for him to engage.

Chapter 30

The King's Warrior

In the distance, the outline of a man was visible on the horizon. A short mantle flowed from his back in the breeze while the rest of his armored body remained static, waiting for Elucido to make the first move. There was no doubt in his mind—this was Caligo, the King of Darkness' vile henchman. He was responsible for the creation of the Shadow Garrison's armies, as well as the destruction of so many souls in the Great Battle. Elucido held him in fearful admiration. He recognized his incredible abilities and was terrified of him all the more for them.

Kneeling to the ground and tightening the laces on his sandals, Elucido took a moment to gather his thoughts. He reached into his satchel and retrieved his brother's broach, attaching it to the neckline of his cloak. He wished his brother could be here with him, at his side, defending the light once more. He knew that the responsibility Frater once held as a Defender of Light now rested squarely on his shoulders. He would not let his brother down; he had come too far. Slowly standing, he raised his head, locked eyes with his opponent, and confidently paced toward the blackened skyline.

As he approached the Shadow Garrison's penultimate commander, Elucido's heart raced in anxious anticipation of the fight ahead.

"I see you have found my discarded medallion—I no longer have a need for it, or any reminders of my past life for that matter." Caligo spoke in a low, soft voice, far calmer than Elucido now felt as his eyes fixed themselves on Frater's broach, firmly pinned to Elucido's cloak.

"So, you are the one who took it!" Elucido shouted with a quivering voice, affected by his growing nerves.

"Took it? It was given to me—earned by my place in the former Defenders of Light." Caligo's tone became more energetic at the Luxcreare's challenge.

"You served with Frater?" Elucido's brow furrowed, partially in anger, partially consumed with his increasing incertitude.

"How dare you use that name! That name means nothing!" Caligo barked at Elucido.

"That name means everything! Frater was my brother and friend. And you killed him mercilessly. I won't allow you to escape punishment for your actions." Elucido puffed his chest with the promise of vengeance he delivered.

"You don't see it, do you?" Caligo took a step forward, pulling the hood of his mantle back to reveal his scarred face. Elucido's knees buckled as he recognized the eyes of his brother, Frater, gazing upon him.

"It can't be!" Elucido felt a surge of emotions as he realized that his brother had served the King of Darkness for all this time. The feeling of betrayal enveloped him with a heavy weight that caused him to stumble backward. "But you are..."

"Very much alive, dear brother. You only see me now because you have found your true power in the light. But isn't that the beauty of darkness—it conceals that which you don't want discovered."

"It isn't possible! I don't believe it! You were a Defender of Light, sworn to protect Terrus from the darkness!"

"What has the light brought us but pain and misery? You preach a gospel of hope, yet those who lived in the light wanted nothing but their own selfish desires. They consumed the world and sat idly by as others suffered. They deserve death. They are not worthy of the light."

"You can't truly believe that!" Elucido shouted at his brother, trying to find reason in his conversion to the darkness. "We were happy—loved by friends and family, filled with joy."

"Empty promises! We all know that no amount of hope can prevent the suffering and death we all eventually face. We pretend that it all matters, but in the end we all perish, leaving behind only the agony of loss." Caligo's frustration grew as he began pacing back and forth. He had no interest in defending his choices to his brother.

"You have no idea that harm your choices have caused the world. People don't deserve to be manipulated, cast into servitude, or murdered. You have no right to take their livelihood from them."

"Listen to me, Elucido! Your choices up to this point have been made in vain. You cannot win this fight—join me in support of the King of Darkness and obtain a power that surpasses even that of the Elementals. Claim an eternal life free from loss, vacant of all suffering. Look at all that I have achieved in my service of the darkness. This dark world can be yours, too." Caligo clutched the hilt of his blade as he spoke, uncertain what his younger brother's response would be.

"I am the Luxcreare, and I will restore light to the land, with or without you!" Elucido still held to the hope that his brother could be saved; that he may yet choose to join him in the fight against the King of Darkness. "I am the hope of Terrus! Trust in me, and I can help save you from the darkness!"

Caligo responded. "You are but a fraction of what you once were—shattered, reduced to this pathetic creature I stand before today. Regain your power and join me once more, as my brother and as my equal. Together we will reign darkness upon the land and reach our true potential." Caligo countered Elucido's proposal, unaffected by his call for restoration to the light.

Elucido became increasingly frantic, seeing that he had little chance of convincing his brother to abandon the hopelessness and despair that consumed him. He swallowed the lump growing in his throat and prepared himself for battle.

Caligo drew his blade, a glimmer of light reflecting from its surface, shining upon Elucido's face. This engagement would be far different than the days of their youth, using wooden swords to protect the yard from imaginary monsters. The stakes were much higher. This time Elucido was defending the whole of Terrus, and the monster was his own flesh and blood—his brother whom he loved with all his heart. Never had Elucido hoped to be free from the burden of battle so intensely as now. The thought of a duel with Frater shattered his spirit.

"It appears my powers of persuasion are ineffective on you, dear brother. Do what you must." Caligo gave his brother permission to engage him in combat, as if his words would somehow free Elucido from the burden of choosing to fight him.

Caligo had no ability to control the Elemental Powers, but he was incredibly skilled with his blade and shield. Elucido knew he would need to maintain his distance and attempt to defeat his brother in ranged combat. Unfortunately, Caligo's speed and nimble-footedness would make that task difficult. Caligo initiated the charge toward Elucido, drawing his sword as his feet brought him closer to his challenger, who fired a quick blast from the Red Elemental. Caligo deflected the ball of fire with the wide edge of his fast-swinging blade. Two more bursts followed suit, each one deflected into the depths of the darkness.

Caligo responded with his own assault, charging toward Elucido with his sword at the ready. Elucido waited, timing his rolling dodge perfectly, avoiding Caligo's swing and subsequent injury. Caligo turned and took another swing, this time grazing his brother's shoulder.

"First blood is mine." Caligo taunted Elucido, reminding him that Caligo was his superior in battle.

"You underestimate me, brother, as you always have." Elucido feigned a smile, trying to convince his brother—and perhaps himself—of his confidence.

Caligo thrust his sword toward Elucido's gut, hoping to end the engagement with a quick deadly strike. Elucido rotated clockwise while stepping to the side, watching closely as his brother's sword narrowly missed its target. He followed his evasion with a blast from the Blue Elemental, hitting Caligo in the chest with an icy cannonball. Caligo's armor was strong, absorbing the brunt of the projectile's energy, resulting in him taking only a small step backwards.

Caligo swung again, this time rotating in a full circle as his sword approached Elucido's neckline. Elucido ducked just in time, ensuring that his head would remain firmly attached to his shoulders. Caligo struck Elucido's lowered back with the hilt of his blade, stunning him and stealing the breath from his lungs.

"Rise, brother, and face me like a man! You stand no chance against my superior speed and agility. Show me what you've got—I assure you it will never be enough!" Caligo took a step back, allowing Elucido to rise and regain both his breath and his footing.

Elucido responded to Caligo's command with an indomitable will. He summoned the Purple Elemental, creating a spire of earth that rose beneath his brother's feet, sending him hurtling backwards at an incredible rate of speed. Caligo, despite his sudden acceleration, maintained his composure and landed on his feet spryly, unaffected by the rocky catapult.

"Well played, you caught me off guard—something that rarely happens." Caligo, despite his clear desire to destroy the Luxcreare, looked at him with a glimmer of pride.

Elucido fired an intense blast of lightning from the Yellow Elemental, completely encompassing Caligo. The energy made contact with the Shadow Garrison general, but something happened that caught Elucido by surprise. The metal in the armor was not conductive, and simply redirected the electric onslaught into the ground, leaving Caligo unharmed. It appeared Caligo had crafted armor that the Elemental's powers could not penetrate.

As superior as Caligo's battle strategy was, however, Elucido had always had one strong advantage over his brother—his intellect. Caligo was not unintelligent by any measure, but Elucido had spent his entire life developing his powers of reasoning. If Elucido hoped to find and exploit Caligo's weaknesses, he would have to lean on his ability to out-think his brother.

Elucido drew his dagger from its sheath. "Alright then, Frater—or should I say Caligo—it's your turn to show me what you've got."

Caligo laughed. "You think that dagger concerns me? Your weakness has always been in your overestimation of your abilities. Today will be no different. I accept your challenge."

The general charged at Elucido, fully committed to his movement. What he failed to recognize during his sprint was the faint green glow that emanated from Elucido's poniard. As Caligo approached, Elucido stood motionless, feet locked in place. Caligo moved closer, finally reaching striking distance. As he swung his sword, Elucido rolled forward, closing the final distance so rapidly that Caligo's reach overextended, missing his target. Mid-roll, Elucido reached his arm out, his dagger finding the small gap in Caligo's armor between his knee and lower leg. The blade sliced the flesh at Caligo's knee, but did not penetrate deeply.

Caligo flinched and turned to face his brother. "Nicely done. You drew blood. I don't know that you have ever been able to touch me with your blade. I commend you, but that is the last time you will ever inflict pain upon me." Caligo shook his leg as if to simply dust the affliction from his lower extremity.

Confident in the strike's insignificance, Caligo took an offensive stance, preparing for his next advance. He had not noticed, however, the toxin that was transferred from Elucido's blade into his body. The infection started to decay the flesh beneath his armor, catching Caligo by surprise and dropping him to his knees in agonizing pain. Recognizing the speed at which his flesh was dissolving, and the severity of the damage as it spread, he turned to his brother.

"So, this is how it ends. I suppose if it had to be anyone, it should be you." Caligo, still defiant in his tone, knew that his death was inevitable.

Elucido, gutted by the sight of his brother's infectious decay, summoned the power of the Purple Elemental once more. Panic set in as he focused the healing powers on Caligo, pushing every ounce of strength he had left in his body to bolster the Elemental's effect. Elucido could feel his pulse coursing through his neck as he frantically tried to save his brother. The violet light circled Caligo intently, glowing with a pulse that matched Elucido's heartbeat. Intense as the power of the light was, it had no effect on Caligo's dissolution. Elucido continued his attempts to heal his brother, but the darkness had taken hold so strongly that the Purple Elemental was completely ineffective.

Elucido opened his mouth to speak, but he could produce no words, only a faint groaning sob. He couldn't save Frater—he was too far gone, lost to the darkness. His brother, he reminded himself, had truly died in the Great Battle. It was time to let him go. He was no longer the boy playing in the yard with the wooden sword. Elucido wondered if, perhaps, the darkness consumed some to the point at which they were beyond redemption.

Caligo, barely able to move, pulled a light shard from a small compartment in the hilt of his sword and handed it to his younger brother. With the final breath in his lungs, he spoke to Elucido.

"You will find the final shard of the Aether Orb within..." he muttered before expelling his final breath, eyes locked upon his younger brother as he passed into the eternal darkness of death.

"Within what?" Elucido cried out in desperation. Caligo had tried to point him in the direction of the final shard—perhaps a last act of brotherly love, or perhaps an attempt at atonement for his sins. The Palace of Darkness was the only remaining structure Elucido could think of. Caligo must have been directing him toward the King of Darkness' stronghold. His brother, once a pillar of inspiration for Elucido, had offered one last piece of guidance before his death. There was only one thing left for Elucido to do—march upon the dark tower and confront the king.

Chapter 31

Into the Shadow

Rising from his place at his brother's side, Elucido began his steady walk to the base of the tower at the Palace of Darkness. The walk was not far, but the slow replay of Caligo's death over and over again in his head made the traversal feel unbearably long. The King of Darkness had taken his brother from him, converting Frater to the darkness and using him to bolster his dark army as Caligo. Elucido would never forgive the dark ruler for all that he had destroyed in his quest for power. He vowed that the pain and suffering would end here—with either the destruction of the King of Darkness, or the demise of the Luxcreare. Either way, he knew his encounter with the hopeless despair brought on by the absence of the light would soon be over.

The tower at the Palace of Darkness had been the crowning achievement of the Protectors of Light. It had shone as a symbol to all on Umbra of the power the Aether held, and the protection it offered. The space was clad in gold trim, with ornate carvings marking arches, doorways, and windows. Those who had visited were awestruck by its immense beauty. Now, in the Age of Darkness, it was anything but beautiful. As he entered the tower, a voice bellowed from above.

"Frater's undoing was of your making!" The king's voice echoed in the empty foyer.

Elucido jumped, startled by the powerful resonance of the voice. He tread carefully through the halls, recognizing the expansiveness of the decay the darkness had brought with it. The alluring charm of the decorative entryways was in ruin—gold stripped from the walls, ornate carvings in various states of rot. The red velvet drapes were torn, and the marble floors were cracked and filthy. The only reason the building was still standing was that the King of Darkness wanted it to serve as a reminder to all who would challenge him that he was in control of the world and everything humanity once thought to be important.

"You have made your choice, Luxcreare. Now face me and reveal your true nature!" The booming declaration echoed through the tall, open room, originating from high above where Elucido stood.

Elucido noted that the palace was very isolated, void of any other signs of life. It felt eerie how calm and quiet it was following the chaotic battle at Castellum Nox. Here, at the end of it all, only two remained—the Luxcreare, and the one who stamped all light from the land, sending it into unrelenting darkness.

"I am the darkness. I am hopelessness. I am all that remains when the light is extinguished. You cannot possibly hope to defeat me." The taunting became louder as Elucido climbed the tall, spiral staircase that circled the walls of the palace from bottom to top, uninterrupted in its ascent.

"We are inseparable, Elucido—two sides to the same coin. Join with me and we can make the darkness complete, eternal, unrelenting." As the words reached Elucido's ears, chills rolled up his spine, causing a rapid shiver. The thought of him joining with the Dark King offended every fiber of his being. He was fighting to restore the world, not end it.

Elucido rounded the final corner, entering the grand throne room where the King of Darkness stood, his presence commanding. There was a dark aura surrounding him, making it impossible to discern his true identity. He was clearly human—but beyond that, the shroud of darkness removed any chance of recognition.

"My feeble, young friend, you still have much to learn. You believe you have mastered the powers of the Elemental Orbs, yet you have only just begun to understand their abilities. Come, I will show you the true power of darkness!"

The king remained stationary, aside from a silent nod. At the gesture, all five Elemental Orbs spun into action at his behest. Red, blue, yellow, purple, green all swirled in concentric orbits, accelerating and growing in mass with each cycle around his veiled personage. The king had mastered the use of the Elemental Powers, much like his commanding officers, however, he appeared to have mastered all of the Elementals, his tremendous power on full display. His heavy cloak twisted around him in the flowing air as the Elemental Orbs converged into one path, merging into a singular black orb, electrified at its edges with an intense white light. The Black Elemental Orb arrested all of its momentum in an instant, positioning itself directly in front of the king. Bright edge pulsing around the darkened central void, the Black Elemental awaited the command of its controller. With a snap of his fingers, the King of Darkness dispensed the energy of the orb, sending a shockwave through Elucido's body, causing him to collapse into another vision.

Atop a high tower, amidst the chaos of a great battle, a sharp object flew through the air at high velocity, tearing through everything in its path. Though it moved quickly, the trail of light it emitted made it easily identifiable as a piece of one of the great Aether Orbs. It embedded itself in an unlikely place—the chest of a man who, until this point, had never experienced such pain. The man was small in stature, unassuming, and there was an air of familiarity about him. The searing pain brought him to his knees as the shard landed directly in his heart. Taking a heaving breath, his vision faded to darkness.

Elucido felt as if he knew this man. His connection to the mysterious presence was almost intimate. "Who was he?" he wondered. All of his friends were missing or dead as a result of the Dark Cataclysm. He searched his heart to understand better what this precognition could mean. After a few silent moments, it hit him with the force of a rock slide. "Could it be me? Am I the one in the vision?" Elucido feared the worst, thoughts racing through his mind. Had he just seen a vision of his own death? Was the final shard of the Aether Orb the weapon the King of Darkness would use to kill him? Was there any way to stop this from happening? The vision of his own death taxed his emotions. There had to be a way to change the outcome of this omen.

"Still confused?" The king's voice mocked the Luxcreare, as if he had somehow missed something that was right before his eyes. "Let me shed some light on it!" He snapped his fingers once more.

As the next blast of dark energy surged through Elucido's body, his consciousness began to wane. And then, a flash—another vision. Only this vision was different. This not only felt real but shook him to the core in the way only a memory could. It was at this moment he realized these visions were not premonitions of things yet to come. They were, in fact, memories of things that had already come to pass.

In a dimly lit room stood a cloaked figure. Turning toward the side of the room, his face became visible in the mirror firmly mounted on the wall across from him. Elucido stood before his own reflection, engaged in a powerful internal struggle. Locking eyes with his glassy facsimile, he peered into the depths of his own soul. He knew the power the Aether Orbs had to maintain life on Terrus, and yet he felt the darkness growing within his heart. He understood the consequences of the choice to embrace the darkness. Perpetuating an infinite void of nothingness and despair upon the world would plunge his soul into eternal darkness, from which there would be no redemption. But he saw no alternative. His experimentation with dark forces had led him down a path of destruction and inevitable pain that would forever alter the fate of the world. Gaze firmly focused on the man in the mirror, Elucido challenged the part of himself that was fading into the shadows, searching for a way to regain his hold on hope.

"*There is a part of me that still clings to some measure of hope. But at my very core, I can feel the suffering taking hold. The only way to be free from that agony is to embrace the darkness. I can bear the burden of my own hopelessness no longer.*"

Acknowledging the pain he would inflict upon the world, Elucido saw no other way to end his own agonizing sorrow. He had convinced himself that he could also end the suffering of the world by purging from it desire, love, and loss. The darkness was winning the battle within his soul, overtaking him with every passing thought.

He began practicing, developing the ability to control the Elementals in secret. It took him nearly a year of effort before he finally saw the first light of the Elemental Orbs yielding to his control. It started with a small spark—the Red Elemental flashing before him for an instant before dissipating back into the quiet darkness. Devoting every ounce of free time and spare energy to his newfound abilities, Elucido was slowly able to extend the duration and type of Elemental light that he could influence. Over time, his mastery of the Elementals became absolute.

Having developed the ability to shape the Elemental Powers to his will, Elucido began planning his assault on the palaces of light. His conviction held resolute. He was confident that he could use the Elemental abilities to end the world's suffering once and for all. He recognized, however, that his victory was contingent upon building an army of dark beings capable of defeating the Defenders of

Light—an army he would ultimately call the Shadow Garrison. He had faith in his ability to design and create such a force; however, he was equally certain that he did not have the expertise to command them in battle. Calling Frater into his chambers, Elucido described the darkness dwelling within him.

"My dearest Frater, please enter. I have something important to discuss with you. For some time now, I have felt out of place in this world, as if I were living in a dream—or rather—a nightmare from which I cannot escape. It feels so real, as if the pain of the world is emanating from the very core of my being. The darkness engulfs—no, suffocates me, and I feel as if all hope is draining from my fractured heart. I cannot help but wonder if death would feel welcome, a relief from my suffering. And yet, the world suffers all the same. Power, greed, selfishness, and grief have become all-consuming forces on Terrus. My solitary death, while it would end my pain, would leave the world trapped in its vicious cycle of agony. The only salvation from that burden is to free humanity from all desire, hope, love, and light."

"Certainly, you cannot mean that!" Frater had been surprised by his younger brother's revelation. "I, too, feel the burden of hopelessness at times, but never to this point." Frater lowered his posture, leaning in toward his brother, saddened to learn of the darkness he was carrying within. "I am here for you, brother, to help you in any way I can. There is still light in this world, if only you can bring yourself to see it."

"The time for hope has passed. I have spent the last year of my life searching for what hope is left in the world, in my meaningless existence, and that of all humanity. In all scenarios I play out in my mind, the conclusion is the same—humanity will destroy itself. Search your heart, Frater, you know it to be true." Elucido stood from his chair and took a step closer to his brother.

"I have experienced it too, Elucido. The worst in humanity is piercing—a terrifying force that leaves nothing but destruction in its wake. But I have also seen the light—experienced love, hope, and joy. Surely those moments have meaning." Frater's tone shifted, becoming much more somber. His heart was heavy. He could not disagree with his brother that the world had become significantly darker in recent times. He only hoped that Elucido could find some measure of hope to hold on to.

Elucido replied. "And yet, my brother, when the time comes for us all to die, we leave behind a legacy of loss and pain. To remove love, hope, and attachment in this world is to remove the suffering and pain experienced by their loss. There is no other way to extinguish suffering from this world. I believe—I know—that I have the power to end that agony for us all. Humanity's greed and thirst for power can no longer be left to further the oppression and manipulation of others. Join me in my quest to end humanity's suffering. If you wish to unlock your true power, you must embrace the darkness and give in to hopelessness. You will find that once you have made that choice, the world will be entirely ours. No one will question our decisions, our directives, or our control, for they will be unable to find a path toward hope. Our unchallenged power will be inevitable, and we can use that power to cleanse the world of its pain."

Frater was uncertain how to respond to his brother's request. Elucido was the most intelligent man he knew; if his analysis of the world predicted an endless cycle of suffering in all plausible scenarios, perhaps there truly was no other salvation for humanity. At the same time, seeing Elucido's heart wrenching pain destroyed Frater. He couldn't bear to watch Elucido suffer. The hopelessness Elucido felt was shared by his brother at this moment, slowly taking hold of Frater's heart, the ever-growing darkness permeating the depths of his soul.

The brothers traversed the five sky-continents of Terrus, exploring ancient ruins and studying the multitude of beautiful creatures contained within. Caligo's mastery of battle tactics and movement aided in his design of the monsters they would soon create. Watching birds and beasts hunt and flourish despite their natural predators inspired the blueprints of the dark horrors that would consume Terrus' hope. They experimented on the animals of the world by transforming them using the Elemental Powers. Some beasts could not handle the mutations forced upon them and suffered agonizing deaths. Others thrived, growing more powerful with each iteration of their transformation. With a secret army of beasts now at their disposal, waiting to be unleashed, the brothers were ready to carry out their objective.

The campaign against the Defenders of Light was swift and decisive. Caligo unleashed his masterpiece, the Tenebrae, to devour all light within their vicinity. Everywhere they went, hopelessness and terror took hold; nothing could stop them in their relentless pursuit of darkness. The Nullblights followed in the next wave of the assault, shredding any remaining soldiers in the Army of Light. Their victory was unquestioned. Thousands of monsters swarmed the land, crushing all who stood in their way.

As the battle progressed, Caligo entered the inner sanctum at the Palace of Sheut, gaze fixed upon the powerful Aether Orb residing within. His prized Tenebrae followed him into the room, absorbing the endless supply of light that emanated from the Orb. The light swirled in a beautiful pattern around each beast before being consumed in their cores, the hope of Terrus consumed along with it.

From the depths of the darkness, Elucido—the King of Darkness—emerged. He wrapped his arms around the Aether Orb and spoke an incantation.

"Disperge lumen." The Aether Orb cracked, darkness gathering within the seams of the damaged sphere.

"Lux destruere." The darkness pulsed, spreading the seams of the Aether Orb further apart.

"Intrare desperationem." With an incredible concussive force, the Aether Orb shattered, pulses of energy shooting outward toward each of the continents of Terrus.

The burst of energy from the destruction of the Aether Orb at the Palace of Sheut was more than the other Orbs could handle, each one shattering in an instant, covering the world in darkness. Something happened, however, that the king had not expected. As the Aether Orb in the Palace of Sheut was destroyed, it expelled a shard that landed directly into his chest. He felt a pain searing through his body, almost as if his soul was being torn into pieces. It was in that moment that he realized the separation was not benign. The fracture, the division *between good and evil, was as real as the darkness now drawing over the midday sky. A darkness that began to cover the world as if the sky had fallen.*

The power of the Aether Orb's impact with Elucido's heart split his soul into six pieces, each one manifesting itself in human form. Four incarnations came into existence as the Shadow Garrison generals tasked with protecting the towers at the Palaces of Light—Onymos, Dynamis, Sanguios, and Animus—each containing a unique part of Elucido's personality, now shrouded in darkness. The remaining two pieces became Elucido the Luxcreare, and Elucido the King of Darkness. The king reached the height of his power in this moment, existing as the complete absence of hope, love, and light. The Luxcreare came forth, born of the piece of Elucido's soul that still believed that the world could be restored and filled with light once again. Two sides to one coin—the Luxcreare and the King of Darkness—coexisted in the Age of Darkness, each preparing for the inevitable confrontation that would bring them together once again.

Elucido's gut wrenched, heart racing, pulse moving at the speed of light. Had the very enemy, the cloaked being, been a manifestation of the darkness within himself the entire time? He rejected the premise that this was his doing; he had been fighting this evil from the moment he awoke in the darkness. And yet, he could feel the truth in the vision, the certainty of what had already come to pass. Elucido knew that at least a piece of who he was had destroyed the Aether Orbs, plunging Terrus into darkness.

Despite the hollowness he felt in that moment, one thought stood firmly in his mind—he was still the Luxcreare, the one who could restore hope to the world. Perhaps the shard embedded in his chest saved that portion of his soul, giving him a shot at redemption. The split had preserved the good in him, affording him the chance to atone for his sins.

Elucido had a rare opportunity—to make a better choice than the King of Darkness had made on his behalf. However, the only way he could do so would be to defeat the king—a dark, shadow-image of himself. He had to destroy the part of himself that clung to hopelessness and despair once and for all and replace it with light and life. He had failed to overcome the darkness within himself before, but if he could conquer it now, he might be able to save himself, and in doing so, save the world from an eternity of darkness.

Chapter 32

Out of the Darkness

"Do you believe me now, wretched Luxcreare?" The King of Darkness knew that Elucido had seen the truth in his vision and pushed to drive any remaining hope from his heart. "As I stated, you and I are not so different. We were the ones who made the choice to destroy the Aether Orbs and send the world into darkness. All you must do now is accept that choice and end the burden hope has placed upon your heart. Make your submission final—remove the shard of light from within your heart and allow the darkness to join us completely."

Elucido replied, "Hope is very much alive in me. The parts of me that served as your generals are dead now. All that remains of the hopelessness that consumed me lies within you, and I intend to destroy you and restore light to the land. You will not control me any longer!" Elucido acknowledged the part that he played in creating the Shadow Garrison and destruction of the Aether Orb, but he could see now that the King of Darkness was simply a manifestation of his despair. If he could destroy the hopelessness within himself by defeating the king, he would be made whole again, in the fullness of the light, living abundantly in the hope of Terrus's future.

"I have always existed in your heart and will persist until the day you die. There is nothing you can do to expunge me from within!" The king's confidence was unmatched. He paced toward Elucido, holding a compact onyx sphere at his fingertips, ready for action. Elucido, confident as he had been, was unnerved at the power of the Black Elemental, uncertain how to counter its abilities.

As the King of Darkness approached the center of the room, Elucido summoned a purple capsule around his body, preparing his shield for the inevitable battle between hope and despair. As his defensive cover completed its formation, he collected an orb from each of the Elementals in the palm of his hand. He knew it would take the collective power of the Elementals to have any hope of defeating the darkness the king represented.

A blast of energy surged from the Black Elemental the King of Darkness held, striking Elucido's shield. The inky energy diffused across the surface of the shield, disintegrating it into a wisp of powerless air. The Black Elemental, much like the hopelessness the King of Darkness represented, had an incredible ability to consume whatever it touched. Elucido, shocked at the revelation of how powerful the dark orb was, took a defensive position, preparing for the worst.

The king followed his first strike with another quickly fired Black Elemental. Elucido rolled to his side to dodge the blast, only to find that the power of the dark orb homed in on his position, as if the darkness was attracted to him. Nearing the end of his roll, the Elemental's power struck him in the chest. Flashbacks of pain and hopelessness resonated within him, amplifying their intensity as if he was suffering their infliction for the first time. The strike stole the breath from his lungs and drowned his body with debilitating sorrow.

"You cannot fight the darkness, Luxcreare. It is all-consuming. It permeates every corner of this broken world. There is nothing you can do to stop it." The King of Darkness took a brief pause to taunt Elucido, assured of his impending victory.

Elucido stood, drawing the power of the Green Elemental to his fingertips. He summoned a large bubble of acidic sludge above the King of Darkness and commanded it to fall upon his head. The king vanished, transporting himself across the room as the toxic onslaught of emerald ooze fell to the ground, missing its target. Elucido turned and fired a bolt of lightning from the Yellow Elemental at the chest of the dark ruler. As the voltage arced toward him, the king simply pushed an obsidian shield in front of his chest, diverting the electrical powers around him, remaining unscathed. The Black Elemental's powers seemed impervious to Elucido's mastery of the other five Elemental Orbs' powers. Having easily deflected the Yellow Elemental's electric barrage, the King of Darkness lifted his arms high into the air and slammed them to the ground, thrusting another Black Elemental Orb into Elucido's weary torso, dropping him to his knees.

"Give up. Don't try to fight it. The more you struggle against the darkness, the tighter its grip upon you becomes. You have no choice but to surrender to its power. Relinquish now, and we can rule the world together, bending the darkness to our will." The taunts of the dark ruler persisted, his message becoming increasingly overbearing and burdensome.

Pushing through the growing despondency, Elucido fired a blast from each Elemental in succession, trying desperately to catch the king off guard and inflict some measure of damage upon him before he used the Black Elemental again. The king stood firmly in place, unfazed by the barrage of Elemental powers hurled in his direction. He took one step back and wrapped his arms around the incoming Elemental Orbs, absorbing them and their energy into his body. He looked Elucido in the eye, smiled, and discharged another Black Elemental into his chest. This blast was more powerful than the last. Elucido felt every memory of loss, pain and suffering hit him simultaneously—his brother's death at the center of those evocations.

The king spoke sharply. "You see it as clearly as I do, Elucido—the pain, the suffering, the hopelessness brought on by your fellow man's selfishness and greed. You cannot avoid it. Suffering is an inevitable burden placed upon humanity. Let us end humanity's agonizing grief once and for all, together."

Elucido was struck by the pain of Frater's death, and the role he played in his conversion to darkness and subservience to the king's rule. His suffering, magnified by the powers of the Black Elemental, had become unbearably immense. If he was to survive the despair mounting in his heart, he would have to take action now to defeat the king before he used the Black Elemental powers again. Acknowledging the role the Elementals had played in reshaping his identity—both as the Luxcreare and as the King of Darkness—Elucido attempted to transform the suffering and pain he was feeling by converting it back into a power that could be used for good. He stood, straightened the neckline of his cloak, ensured that Frater's broach was firmly attached, and walked toward the dark potentate.

"Though the darkness may strike me, I will rise, time and time again." Elucido took a step forward as he spoke. The king fired a blast from the Black Elemental. Elucido spun counter-clockwise as the orb arrived, reaching his arms out in an ovalene ring, his mastery of the Elemental Powers allowing him to absorb its power as the sphere entered an orbit surrounding his body.

"No measure of suffering can outweigh the love and light I have experienced. Life is beautiful, and humanity can be filled with hope once more. I refuse to surrender to the darkness." Elucido spun one more time, absorbing the next powerful burst of obsidian energy fired by the King of Darkness.

"Your fear drives your hopelessness. But I no longer fear loss. I embrace the memories I have made with those I love. Their loss is not what defines their lives. We honor them by celebrating their accomplishments, their love, their light." Spinning a third time, Elucido gathered the third onyx orb as it catapulted toward him, adding its power to his. He thrust his arms forward, firing the triple-charged Black Elemental Orbs at the King of Darkness. The rotating helix of calamitous energy was more than the king could protect himself from. It struck him in the chest, tossing him to the other end of the palace throne room.

Elucido felt the power of the remaining Elemental Orbs building within him, driving his instinct to prepare his next move. He crafted a large Red Elemental Orb in front of him, motionless but fully charged. In his left hand, he summoned the immense power of the Blue Elemental, while simultaneously calling upon the Yellow Elemental Orb to expand within his right palm. He pressed the two orbs inside the Red Elemental, watching the light oscillate between the trio of colors contained within. The Purple Elemental Orb formed quickly between his now-empty hands, merging into the massive orb of light that was growing in front of him. Finally, with both hands, Elucido surrounded the multi-colored spheroid with the Green Elemental's powers, amalgamating all five Elemental Powers into one globule that transformed, radiating the brightest white light he had ever seen. Before the King of Darkness stood, the prodigious power of the combined Elementals surrounded him, withdrawing all dark energy from his body. An intense white light flashed, then abruptly dissipated. When Elucido's eyes adjusted to the darkness of the room, all that remained where the king once stood was an empty black cloak, resting calmly on the cold palace floor.

Elucido's shoulders dropped as he wept—not tears of sadness, but tears of relief. He was overwhelmed with emotion at the death of the king. He felt the burden of hopelessness lift from within him, replaced with the vision of humanity's restoration. The world had suffered and lost so much, as had he. But despite that suffering, there was hope for a future filled with light, life, and love.

All that was left for him to do was assemble the shards of the Aether Orb found on Umbra and restore light to the continent. He pulled the four shards he had gathered on his journey from his leather satchel and approached the pillar where the unbroken Aether Orb had once stood. The final shard was contained within Elucido's heart, and he knew that withdrawing the shard would be painful; however, he also somehow knew that extracting the shard from his heart would allow him to let go of his past and forgive himself for all that he had allowed the darkness to accomplish through him. The last piece of the Aether Orb had saved him, allowing what hope was left in his soul to persist. And now, that same shard would complete the Aether Orb and restore hope to Terrus. It was time for him to relinquish the shard from within and finish the quest he set out to complete on Nomen months ago. He placed the four shards on the pedestal and recited the incantation.

"*Congrega lucem.*" Elucido surrendered all fear as the Aether Orb took shape.

"*Uniendis lux.*" As the pieces of the orb illuminated, he relinquished the feelings of hopelessness that still existed inside his heart.

"*Lucem propagationem.*" The light pulsed as Elucido released all remaining darkness from within, turning his palms toward the sky, yielding to the illuminating power of the Aether.

While speaking the last words of the incantation, a sharp pain struck Elucido as the final shard of the Aether Orb extracted itself from his chest to join the remaining pieces on the pedestal. As the shard found its place among the other luminescent fragments, he watched the orb take shape. Then, a flash of light filled the room, propagating from the central tower of Umbra to each of the five sky-continents, bringing Terrus back into a state of full illumination.

The conduit that Elucido had used to travel between the continents opened up, revealing the five continents, each thriving under the bright blue sky. Each landmass had been restored to its former magnificence through the restoration of the Aether Orbs and was now on full display for the Luxcreare to see. Nomen, Elucido's homeland, was filled once again with the beauty of dewy green grass, and the sound of young sparrows soaring through the air beneath the luminescence of the Aether. Vita's electrical storms had subsided, leaving behind an abundance of oases, teeming with charming desert life, flourishing like never before. Cor, once subject to the siphoning of life, radiated life-giving energy—creatures large and small thriving under the glittering bright light. Spiritus's toxicity had reversed as the whole of the continent healed. Rivers flowed into grand lakes of crystal-clear water, filled with incredible aquatic animals, while the marshlands had transformed into a lush green forest, occupied by brilliantly colored birds. Even Umbra, the home of the King of Darkness, had been restored. Where there had been destruction, homes were rehabilitated. The people placed in the servitude of the king were healed, scales falling from their eyes, their vision cleared, revealing to them once more the beauty the world held. Humanity was healed and ready to rebuild Terrus into a sanctuary of life.

Elucido's face beamed, his hope fully restored, all residual darkness within him expelled. He knew that his success in reassembling the Aether Orbs on each continent would allow Terrus to thrive once again. The journey of the Luxcreare gave humanity a second chance to experience the beauty of the light, the never-ending joy of love, and the magnificent purpose of a life well lived. Terrus had entered a new Age of Enlightenment. For the first time since the darkness had fallen upon the land, Elucido could see clearly—not just the world itself, but the power that hope possessed. He knew with the greatest assurance that those who believe in the light cannot be overcome by the powers of darkness.

Elucido gathered his belongings, ready to return to his birthplace on Nomen and continue to rebuild his homeland. Eager for the life he would find, he walked briskly across the palace floor to enter the Aether Conduit and expedite his journey home. As he left the throne room through the conduit, a gentle breeze passed through the space, shifting the now deceased King of Darkness' cloak aside. Where the body of the king once lay, there appeared a faint glow—the outline of a dark orb beginning to take shape.

Acknowledgements

While clichés tend to be overused, they also tend to be true. In this case, "no man is an island" couldn't be more relevant to the completion of my first novel, *Shadow of the Cataclysm*. Over the last few years, I have pursued the dream of crafting a book that interested me as a fantasy reader, gamer, and storyteller. None of that pursuit would have been possible without the substantial support of my friends and family. So much more goes into completing such a large project than simply one person's ideas. To my fellow game designer and best bud, Brendon, your encouragement and belief in my abilities has been a constant source of motivation. To my father, Andy, your feedback and input on how to be a better storyteller, along with leading by example (check out A.W. Baldwin's books if you love a good adventure) have been of insurmountable value. To my sister, Sarah, your skills as an editor and author have served as a guiding light on my journey of self-improvement. To my beta readers—Sarajean, Tony, Enrico, Amanda, Anoushka, Brendon, Larry, Sarah, and Andy—your revelations have helped this story soar to new heights, and I am forever grateful for your input. And last, but certainly not least, to my lovely wife Sarajean.

SHADOW OF THE CATACLYSM

Your patience, support, encouragement, and belief in me mean more to me than any story I could ever tell. You are the brightest light in my world, and I am humbled to walk alongside you on our journey. Thank you all.

About the Author

S.D. Baldwin is a game design mathematician, computational scientist, and indie author, writing primarily in the fantasy genre. When not making games and writing, he enjoys spending time with his wife and beagle, traveling, and playing video games. *Shadow of the Cataclysm* is the first of his published novels, and he continues work on new fantasy adventures. His unique style is influenced by some of his favorite authors, video games, and his time spent studying philosophy.

Baldwin earned his Ph.D. in Computational Science and Statistics from the University of South Dakota in 2011, with a focus on optimization of continuously differentiable functions in n-dimensional space using interval analysis. He also holds a Master's degree in Mathematics, and a Bachelor's degree in Mathematics and Computer Science with a minor in Theology and Philosophy. While math was his primary focus, he found the opportunity to study philosophy as often as his schedule would allow. He continues to use his degrees in mathematics as a game design mathematician.

Stay tuned for more information such as author events, awards, and new books!

www.sdbaldwinauthor.com

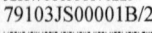